"*I'll* give you mouth-to-mouth."

After he said it, Trey stared at her lips. Energy crackled in the air. Not the kind of energy her exhausted limbs needed.

"I meant," he clarified, "if it should become medically necessary."

Was it her imagination, or was he a little red in the face?

"Thanks, but Daniel's a doctor and better qualified," she said.

His eyebrows drew together, all joking aside. "Don't mess with me, Sadie. If you don't keep away from Daniel, I'll warn him and Meg you're in love with him."

She opened her mouth, but no words came out. Probably because his threat had stopped her heart.

Dear Reader,

Did you ever just *know* you were right…and then discovered you were wrong?

It happens to me often enough that I'm no longer totally shocked by my own fallibility. But Sadie Beecham, heroine of *Her Best Friend's Wedding,* is seldom wrong. So when she falls in love with a guy she's convinced is The One, she must be right…right?

Even if he's in love with her best friend? Yep, Sadie is determined she'll get her man. Too bad Trey Kincaid, brother of the bride, is equally determined she won't!

I do hope you enjoy *Her Best Friend's Wedding.* To let me know what you think, please email abby@abbygaines.com. Or, to read an extra After-the-End scene, visit the For Readers page at www.abbygaines.com.

Sincerely,

Abby Gaines

Her Best Friend's Wedding
Abby Gaines

TORONTO NEW YORK LONDON
AMSTERDAM PARIS SYDNEY HAMBURG
STOCKHOLM ATHENS TOKYO MILAN MADRID
PRAGUE WARSAW BUDAPEST AUCKLAND

Recycling programs
for this product may
not exist in your area.

ISBN-13: 978-0-373-71712-5

HER BEST FRIEND'S WEDDING

Copyright © 2011 by Abby Gaines

All rights reserved. Except for use in any review, the reproduction or utilization of this work in whole or in part in any form by any electronic, mechanical or other means, now known or hereafter invented, including xerography, photocopying and recording, or in any information storage or retrieval system, is forbidden without the written permission of the publisher, Harlequin Enterprises Limited, 225 Duncan Mill Road, Don Mills, Ontario, Canada M3B 3K9.

This is a work of fiction. Names, characters, places and incidents are either the product of the author's imagination or are used fictitiously, and any resemblance to actual persons, living or dead, business establishments, events or locales is entirely coincidental.

This edition published by arrangement with Harlequin Books S.A.

For questions and comments about the quality of this book please contact us at Customer_eCare@Harlequin.ca.

® and TM are trademarks of the publisher. Trademarks indicated with ® are registered in the United States Patent and Trademark Office, the Canadian Trade Marks Office and in other countries.

www.Harlequin.com

Printed in U.S.A.

ABOUT THE AUTHOR

Abby Gaines wrote her first romance novel as a teenager, only to have it promptly rejected. A flirtation with a science fiction novel never really got off the ground, so Abby put aside her writing ambitions as she went to college, then began her working life at IBM. When she and her husband had their first baby, Abby worked from home as a freelance business journalist...and soon after that the urge to write romance resurfaced. It was another five long years before Abby sold her first novel to Harlequin Superromance in 2006.

Abby lives with her husband and children—and a labradoodle and a cat—in a house with enough stairs to keep her semifit and a sun-filled office with a sea view that provides inspiration for the funny, tender romances she loves to write. Visit her at www.abbygaines.com.

Books by Abby Gaines

HARLEQUIN SUPERROMANCE

1397—WHOSE LIE IS IT ANYWAY?
1414—MARRIED BY MISTAKE
1480—THE DIAPER DIARIES
1539—THE GROOM CAME BACK
1585—HER SO-CALLED FIANCÉ*
1597—HER SECRET RIVAL*
1609—HER SURPRISE HERO*

HARLEQUIN NASCAR

BACK ON TRACK
FULLY ENGAGED

*Those Merritt Girls

In memory of
Gerald van Waardenberg
(1962-2010)

A gifted musician
A talented writer
A good friend

Grace under Fire

CHAPTER ONE

"I MIGHT," SADIE BEECHAM said briskly, "bring someone home with me for Nancy's birthday party."

Silence.

Sadie shook the cordless phone. "Mom?"

"Oh, honey." Her mother's voice was a mere breath down the line. "Have you met The One?"

"Mom! I've brought guys home before." Sadie stepped away from the beef bourguignon simmering on the stove for tonight's celebratory dinner and patted her damp forehead with a paper towel. Her bungalow's ancient air-conditioning wasn't up to the challenge of keeping the kitchen cool during the heat of a Memphis summer.

"Not in the last ten years, dear," Mary-Beth Beecham said. "The last one was that boy with the piercing in his lip."

Sadie shuddered. She knew her mother was doing the same. That *was* a long time ago. A brief attempt during her sophomore year at Princeton to prove she could tread the wild side just like any other coed. A theory she'd rapidly disproved.

"Okay, I haven't brought anyone home lately. But you've met guys I've dated. This is no big deal, Mom."

The last thing she needed was her parents acting as

if they were meeting a prospective son-in-law. Even if that's exactly what he was.

Sadie opened the kitchen window in the hope of creating a breeze. On the back porch, her latest batch of plants—camellias and limonium—had died in their pots, despite the expensive soil nutrients she'd fed them. The neighbor's cat must have been doing its business in them again.

"I want to know all about your young man," Mary-Beth demanded.

Sadie turned her back on the limp, browning foliage. "He's a doctor."

A squawk down the phone. "A doctor! He sounds wonderful."

Sadie couldn't help grinning in response to her mom's enthusiasm. "He's very nice," she admitted. *He's perfect.*

The doorbell rang. Phew, saved from descending into girlish chitchat, a skill she'd never mastered. "Mom, I need to go. He's just arrived. Meg gets back tonight, too, so we're all having dinner." Dinner for three—she couldn't wait.

"Okay, dear, you go. Give Meg a hug for me, and tell her not to worry, we have her mom's party well in hand. And call me soon. I can't wait to tell people about this *doctor* of yours," Mary-Beth added archly.

Sadie puffed out an exasperated breath. "Mom, no need to tell the whole world." She was still fending off inquiries from her parents' friends about when she was going to win the Nobel Prize. Mary-Beth had made the exaggerated claim during her last visit, boasting about Sadie's brilliance as a seed biologist.

"Just your father, then," her mom soothed.

"Fine." Behind Sadie, another long trill of the doorbell suggested impatience. Then a thump on the door, and the handle rattling. Seemed Daniel was as eager to see her as she was to see him. Sadie's irritation evaporated. "Coming," she sang.

She set the phone back on its stand and hurried to the door. "Sorry," she called as she unlocked the deadlock. She flung the door wide. "Come in—Meg!"

She just managed not to feel disappointed it was Meg Kincaid, her childhood next-door neighbor, best friend forever and now roommate, on the doorstep, rather than Daniel. "Welcome home! I wasn't expecting you just yet... Why didn't you let yourself in?"

"My key's buried somewhere in there." Meg indicated the trundle suitcase next to her. She hugged Sadie. "The flight landed an hour early. It's so great to be home. Six weeks was way too long...even if it *was* Paris." She stood back as Sadie maneuvered the case over the threshold for her.

Meg slipped out of the high-heeled red pumps that were part of her flight-attendant uniform and flexed her toes on the polished wooden floorboards. "Man, that feels better." She pushed her dark bangs off her face, an endearing, reflexive gesture that never achieved anything—her hair settled right where it had been. She'd flown halfway across the world, yet she looked as fresh and pretty as if she'd stepped out of a *Cosmo* article titled "How to Look Your Best, 24/7."

"I need a drink." She padded down the hallway behind Sadie. "Something smells good."

"I hope so. I followed the recipe exactly, so as long as Martha Stewart knows what she's talking about…" Having missed out on the cooking lessons her mom had given her sister, Sadie wasn't as confident as she'd like to be.

In the kitchen Meg absorbed the sparkling state of Sadie's glass-fronted cupboards and the clear counter. Her sigh was part satisfaction, part envy. "This place is so tidy when I'm not here."

"Boarding-school discipline," Sadie reminded her. "My secret weapon. Besides, it's not as if you're here even when you *are* here," she joked as she pulled a bottle of pinot grigio from the fridge. She didn't know how Meg managed to sleep at all between her party lifestyle and her job. She reached over to the counter, where three glasses were neatly lined up.

"*Three* glasses?" Jet lag or not, Meg didn't miss a thing.

Sadie busied herself pouring even amounts of wine into two of the glasses. "There's someone I want you to meet."

"A man?" Meg's squeal was gratifying. She grabbed the purse she'd slung over the back of a dining chair. "I'd better put my face on and get out of this uniform—we don't want your *boyfriend* thinking your best friend's a slob."

"You've never looked slobbish in your life…and be-sides, he's just a friend." She didn't want Meg getting overexcited the way her mom had.

Meg tilted her head to one side. "Now you've got me interested."

What was that supposed to mean? Sadie had listened to friends revealing their I'm-in-love stories over many a glass of wine, but she realized now she'd failed to observe the nuances. She hoped she wasn't blushing. *Top research scientists don't blush,* she told herself sternly.

Meg took a slug of her wine and set her glass down. "Two minutes." She patted Sadie's arm, then headed to her bedroom. She'd never in her life freshened up in two minutes, so Sadie didn't expect to see her for a while.

She poured some wine for Daniel—pinot grigio was his favorite—and wiped up a few drops that had spilled on the stainless-steel counter. She rinsed out the dishcloth and tucked it in the wire basket in the cupboard beneath the sink.

The doorbell rang. Once. Briefly. That was Daniel—no impatient banging on the door or rattling the handle. A man confident in himself, who liked to do things right. Just like her.

No wonder she'd fallen in love with him so fast.

Sadie forced herself to slow her walk, but she couldn't contain her goofy grin as she opened the door. "Hey."

"Hi, Sadiebug." Daniel had come up with the nickname the first time they'd had lunch together. She loved it.

He stepped inside, his kiss landing at the corner of her mouth. Reminding her of the embrace they'd shared last night. Their first proper kiss, after a delicious dinner at the nearby Two Trees Grill, where they'd talked about their families, their ambitions, their mutual passions—work,

Russian literature, 1980s rock music, running. Admittedly, running was a very *new* passion for Sadie—she'd better warn Meg not to look too surprised.

Afterward, Daniel had brought her home, and here in this very hallway had taken her in his arms. Then… the kiss. Remembering, Sadie felt a warm glow inside.

Daniel had pulled away after a minute or so, looked into her eyes and said, "Hmm."

Which she took to be a male version of *wow.* "Hmm," she'd said happily back.

"How was your day?" Sadie asked as she led the way to the kitchen.

"Full-on. Our free diabetes testing was a crowd puller. The few spare minutes I had were spent preparing for my meeting with the SeedTech panel tomorrow." Daniel ran a medical clinic for low-income families in Memphis's Northside neighborhoods. But his interest in childhood nutrition had brought him to SeedTech, the botanical research firm where Sadie worked. Sick of always being "the ambulance at the bottom of the cliff," he'd joined the panel that reviewed SeedTech's research into medicinal plants, projects that in the long term would benefit poor people everywhere. Sadie had met him a few weeks ago when she presented her project to the panel.

"Mmm, dinner smells superb." Daniel lifted the lid of the casserole dish on the stove and peeked inside. "Not just a pretty face and an impressive brain—she can cook, too."

His grin made her heart flip. She would have loved him if he'd been ugly as sin, but his warm brown eyes and slightly-too-long hair—he worked so hard, he seldom found time to get a cut—were adorable.

He accepted a wineglass from her and clinked it against hers. "Here's to you."

To us. Sadie sipped her wine and smiled.

"Um…hi." Meg spoke from the doorway.

Sadie beamed. "Meg, meet Daniel Wilson. Daniel, this is my best friend Meg Kincaid." She couldn't have said who she was prouder of. *Please let them like each other.*

Daniel drank in Meg's silky dark hair, her long lashes, porcelain-perfect complexion, her sweet smile… His jaw dropped.

Uh, maybe not quite that much.

The natural pink of Meg's cheeks deepened, and her smile turned irresistible.

Too late.

How ironic that the first fault Sadie should find in Daniel was his rapid amnesia about that great kiss they'd shared. From the second he met Meg, his manner toward Sadie had been no more than platonic. *Warmly* platonic, sure… In a matter of days, Daniel and Meg were an item. Every time she saw him with Meg—and since they were at great pains not to exclude her, that was often—her heart cracked a little further. What she felt for him, what she thought they'd both felt, radiated in his face whenever he looked at Meg.

She should refuse their invitations, but she found herself drawn to their relationship like a bug to a Venus flytrap.

"Things still going well with Daniel?" she asked Meg one Saturday afternoon as they wandered through a boutique on Beale Street in search of gifts for Meg's mom's sixtieth birthday. The party was only a week away.

"Wonderful." Meg held up a funky leather belt. "How about this?"

"Not sure if that would actually meet around your mom's middle. So...you've been seeing each other, what, three weeks?" Three weeks, three days and eighteen hours, by Sadie's count.

Overhead, the Muzak played "Hopelessly Devoted to You."

"I know what you're thinking," Meg said.

Sadie's heart thudded. She'd been so careful to hide her feelings. "What?"

"That I always say things are wonderful at this stage. And I'll change my tune soon."

Sadie let out a breath of relief. Meg was infamous for her intense but brief relationships. Sadie couldn't remember the last time one of her boyfriends had survived more than six weeks. If Meg followed her usual pattern, Sadie just had to hold out another two and a half weeks, max.

Feeling guilty for even thinking that way, she held up a silk floral-patterned scarf. "Your mom would like this. It's pricey, though."

"I didn't send anything for Mother's Day, so it needs to be good." Meg took the other end of the scarf and spread the fabric. "Mom loves roses, I'll take it."

As they headed for the line at the cashier, Meg asked,

"How did you know Daniel and I would be right for each other?"

"I didn't." Had Meg ever used the words *right for each other* before? Sadie shivered in the air-conditioned store.

"Then you're a natural-born genius." Meg fluttered her eyelashes at a male clerk, who beckoned them to another cash register without a line. "Of course, we all know that." She dropped the scarf on the counter. "Daniel says you're the smartest woman he's ever met." No envy, just awe of Daniel's every word. "We owe you big-time."

"Don't mention it," Sadie said with wasted irony.

The Muzak segued into "Breaking Up Is Hard to Do." A timely reminder to call her mom, who still thought Sadie was bringing a man to the party. She would phone home tonight and say she'd broken up with her doctor friend.

As if they were on the same wavelength, rather than different emotional planets, Meg said, "Guess what? I invited Daniel home this weekend, and he said yes!"

A knife twisted behind Sadie's ribs as she pinned on her widest smile. "Of course he did."

CHAPTER TWO

SADIE AND DANIEL finished work early on Friday. Meg wasn't flying that day, so by four o'clock the three of them were heading out of the city in Daniel's Toyota Prius—he always tried to minimize his contribution to global warming. Weeks ago, when Sadie had envisaged this journey, she'd pictured her and Daniel up front, Meg in back. Instead, she was the third wheel, trying to be sanguine about the dopey looks being traded in the front seat. Comforting herself with the thought that the natural life of this romance was probably another week and a half at best.

"Are we there yet?" she chirped—in imitation of her nephews and nieces—as they drove down Sanga Road in the heart of Cordova, once a small town but now an outer neighborhood of Memphis. She tried not to think about the disappointment her mom had struggled to hide on the phone at the news Sadie wasn't bringing a date. She just had to get through this without anyone figuring out that Daniel and her "ex-boyfriend" were the same man.

Her strategy was simple: put on her happy face and refuse to answer questions about her love life. If that didn't work, launch into a monologue about apomictic hybrid crops.

Meg directed Daniel to make a left onto Maple, and a moment later they pulled up outside the white-and-blue Victorian at number twenty-four, the Kincaids' house. Sadie's family lived next door at number twenty-six, an almost identical Victorian painted green with a red trim. Both houses' front doors opened, then Mary-Beth Beecham and Nancy Kincaid hastened down to the car, halloing greetings.

"Scared?" Meg asked.

Sadie almost said *terrified,* then realized the question was aimed at Daniel.

"Only because it's so important," he said tenderly.

Fighting an uncharitable gag reflex, Sadie snapped open the car door and clambered out.

"Sadie, honey." No lingering disappointment over the date issue, just the warmest welcome in her mom's hug. "It's so good to have you home."

Pain and loss welled in her throat. "You, too," Sadie choked nonsensically. It had been so hard these past weeks, pretending to be thrilled for Meg, watching Daniel lavish his attention on her best friend in a way Sadie had to admit he'd never done with her. Suddenly she was exhausted. She wanted nothing more than to collapse on her old bed and pull a pillow over her head. But first... "Mom—" she beamed with all the conviction she could fake "—let me introduce you."

Before she could utter the words she'd been steeling herself for, words she hadn't yet quite managed to say in her own head—*This is Daniel, Meg's boyfriend*—a truck pulled up at the curb. A shiny black Ford F-150, which in this former farming hamlet had the desirability factor of a Ferrari in the city.

The man who climbed out was broad shouldered, lean hipped, laconic in jeans and black T-shirt.

"Trey," Meg squealed. As her brother hit the central lock, she ran out onto the road and threw her arms around him.

"Yeah, yeah, Meggie." Trey Kincaid made a half-hearted effort to disengage. Their sibling relationship was a blend of loyalty and sniping in varying proportions. For the past ten years sniping had been dominant, but absence must have temporarily tipped the scales in the other direction.

Meg dragged Trey to the curb—not that she could have budged him an inch if he didn't want to move—chattering all the way.

"Hi, Sadie." Trey's dark gray eyes met hers, then swept her powder-blue T-shirt and darker blue wrap skirt with a familiar, distracted, slightly puzzled scrutiny. As if he wasn't quite sure how she fit in around here but wasn't interested enough to find out. "Won that Nobel Prize yet?"

Reminding herself she was on an I'm-so-happy-being-single kick, she shot him a dazzling smile. "Hello, Trey."

Trey's chin jerked back, and he looked harder at her. "Uh, hi," he said as if he'd forgotten he'd already said that. His gaze flicked over her curves, down her legs, then up again. He looked confused. Then alarmed.

Good grief, he thought her smile was about his supposed gorgeousness. Sadie hadn't attended Andrew

Johnson High, the local school, but she knew from Meg that as quarterback, Trey had always had a bevy of cheerleaders around him—the attention had obviously gone to his head and stayed there.

Still, his arrival had allowed Sadie to recoup her inner calm. She turned back to her mother and felt almost relaxed as she said, "Mom, this is Daniel." She swallowed. "Meg's boyfriend."

Her mother hugged both Daniel and Meg. "Don't you two make the cutest couple?" Her gaze darted in Sadie's direction, the nearest she would get to expressing regret that her daughter's big romance had fallen through.

Meg introduced her brother to her beau. As the two men shook hands, Trey subjected Daniel to a long, hard scrutiny.

"You finally chose one who looks like he can hold down a job." Typical of Trey not to bother to hide his surprise. But then, he'd never possessed the good manners Sadie admired in Daniel. Then, too, Meg had had some "interesting" boyfriends over the years.

"He's a doctor," Meg said proudly. "And a Tigers fan." Trey was a longtime supporter of the Memphis Tigers baseball team.

"Did you see that whitewash against the Braves last week?" Trey asked. He and Daniel spent a minute rehashing the game. As they talked, Daniel laced his fingers through Meg's and smiled down at her.

Sadie looked away, though she'd been forced to observe far worse recently.

"Do you fish?" Trey asked when the baseball conversation petered out.

Daniel's gaze wavered. Sadie couldn't picture him sitting in a boat for hours on the off chance a fish might come along. "Happy to give it a try," he said.

"June's not the best time," Trey said, "but maybe I can take you out fishing someday soon. I know a good spot."

The day took on a surreal hue. As far as Sadie knew, Trey had never put himself out for one of Meg's admirers. Now he was offering to share his fishing spot on the lake, a local legend whose exact location was known only to him.

Meg kissed Trey's cheek. "I figured you guys would love each other."

"How could I not love anyone related to you?" Daniel grinned. "Trey, I hope you'll take that in the spirit it's intended."

Trey chuckled.

Ha, ha, ha, Sadie thought sourly.

Polite as always, Daniel turned to include Sadie's mom in the conversation. "I've heard so much about you and your family, too, Mrs. Beecham. I feel as if I know you already."

Sadie tensed.

"Call me Mary-Beth," Sadie's mother said. "Though why Meg should tell you about my family, I can't think."

"I meant from Sadie," Daniel explained. "She's the one who got me and Meg together."

He slung an arm across Sadie's shoulders and kissed her hair somewhere above her right ear. One of those gestures she'd interpreted—*mis*interpreted—to mean she was special to him. Even now she couldn't help melting against him just the tiniest bit, and imagining for a nanosecond that this had all worked out differently, that she and Daniel—

She realized Trey's gaze had narrowed on her. That while everyone else listened to Meg rattling on about Sadie's incredible intuition, introducing her and Daniel, he had been observing her.

"Feeling the heat, Sadie?" Trey asked. "You're wilting."

At barely five o'clock the temperature was nowhere near the mid-nineties that had dominated the afternoon. She straightened away from Daniel. "I'm fine, but thanks for your concern," she said crisply.

"This is wonderful having you all here together," Mary-Beth said. "Tomorrow's barbecue will be just like old times."

Not quite. In the old days, Meg's father, Brian, had presided over the grill alongside Sadie's dad, and her oldest brother, Logan, regularly defended his record for consuming the most burgers in one night. But Brian and Logan Kincaid had died in a fishing accident when Sadie and Meg were high-school seniors.

Trey had given up his college football scholarship to take his father's place running Kincaid Nurseries, the family garden center. Turned out he was a natural businessman, just as he was a football player—over the years he'd added more garden centers in surrounding neighborhoods.

"Let's get you all settled in," Nancy said to Meg and Daniel. "Trey's staying for dinner tonight, so we'll have some time to get to know each other ahead of our busy weekend."

Sadie watched Daniel and Meg walk up the path through Nancy's spectacular front garden. Her own parents' garden was equally impressive—Sadie's mom and dad had taken turns presiding over the Cordova Garden Club, and Kincaid Nurseries was the club's number-one sponsor. As next-door neighbors, the two families were a match made in heaven.

Sadie turned away before she could watch Meg and Daniel walk into the house. Shutting her out.

One weekend. I can survive one weekend.

THERE WASN'T QUITE a full complement of Beechams around the seventies glass-topped table in Sadie's parents' dining room that night. Sadie's older brother Jesse, his wife, Diane, and eight-year-old twins, Hannah and Holly, came to dinner, along with her sister, Merrilee, three years younger than Sadie, and her husband, Ben, and infant son, Matthew.

But Sadie's younger brother, Brett, and his wife, Louisa, had stayed away. Two of their three preschoolers were recovering from chicken pox and today was officially the last day of their contagion. They'd be at tomorrow night's barbecue. Kyle, her oldest and only unattached sibling, had breezed in, claiming he had to rush off to see his latest girlfriend, but he was still sprawled in his seat opposite Sadie. Her brothers and sister had all remained in Cordova.

"It's like Grand Central Station around here," Gerry Beecham, Sadie's dad, said. "Wives, husbands, kids…

and to think you and I worried we might have an empty nest, Mary-Beth."

Mary-Beth blew him a kiss from the far end of the table.

"It's a shame we don't have you here more often, Sadie, love," Gerry continued.

Sadie's bungalow in uptown Memphis was just over half an hour away. Her parents acted as if she lived on the other side of the country.

"Sadie was never going to stay a Cordova girl," her mother said fondly.

You made sure of that. Sadie quashed a flare of resentment. Sending her to a boarding school for gifted children at age ten, after her elementary-school principal had her IQ tested, had *not* been an act of rejection. Her parents had been proud but overwhelmed by the prospect of "raising a genius to fulfill her potential," as the principal put it. They'd sent her away for her own good.

She speared three beans with her fork. "I really don't live that far away," she muttered, knowing she was wasting her time.

Going to college at Princeton had widened the distance between her and her family, and now it seemed her default setting was "away." Even when she was right here.

She tried to concentrate on the conversations rippling around her—the dramas of the PTA, a new cupcake recipe, a camping trip to the Smokies planned for later in the summer. But her family always considered her "above" such mundane topics, so no one asked her opinion or shared their cupcake tips. Not that she would have known what to do with them.

Sadie's mind wandered next door. She wondered how Daniel was getting along with Nancy. Fabulously, of course. He was the kind of guy every mother dreamed her daughter would bring home.

"Sadie?" Her father said.

She jolted back to the present, and realized everyone was looking at her. "Sorry, I was daydreaming." She thought back. Hadn't Merrillee been complaining about her cupcakes not rising?

"Did you wait too long before putting them in the oven?" she asked her sister. "If the baking powder released its carbon dioxide gas too soon—" She broke off. "Hey, I wonder what percentage of global warming is caused by bakers forgetting to put their cakes in the oven." She chuckled...and realized everyone else was staring at her, baffled.

Okay, maybe it wasn't hilarious. But Daniel would have got it. Would have laughed.

Sadie blinked, hard.

"I was asking when we'll get to see that garden of yours, love," her father said.

"Uh...it's not quite there yet." Sadie didn't like to admit to the atrocious state of her garden—the love of everything botanical was one thing she shared with her parents, who between them had four green thumbs and sixteen green fingers. All of her siblings had inherited both the talent and the enthusiasm.

Shame the gene pool hadn't had one green digit to spare for Sadie. When she'd bought the bungalow two years ago, she'd had visions of creating a lush, peaceful, enticing landscape.

Her failure was a constant frustration, all the more aggravating because it didn't make sense. As a seed biologist, she knew the theory of plants inside and out. She had the passion, too—a beautiful garden could bring tears to her eyes, and she loved getting her hands dirty. But her attempts to actually grow anything seemed doomed to failure.

"I haven't had much time for gardening, I've been so busy at work." She switched to a topic she could tackle with a hundred percent confidence, before the questions got too probing. "We're looking at developing new strains of wheat with a higher protein content."

She started on a layman's description of the project. Five minutes later she was pleasantly surprised to realize she still had her family's attention. Usually eyes were starting to glaze over by now. "Anyway—" she gave a little laugh, unnerved by their rapt expressions "—I'm loving it."

"It sounds great," Merrillee said encouragingly.

"Right over my head, sis." Jesse swished his hand above his spiky haircut to demonstrate. "I wish I had your brains."

"Your life sounds super fulfilling, Sadie." Diane, Jesse's wife, smiled kindly.

"Uh…thanks." How odd. That sounded like the sort of comment you made when you were— Wait a minute!

The reason everyone was listening with such interest to wheat-protein statistics wasn't that they'd developed a sudden interest in crop biology. Sadie would bet a million bucks that her mom had told them she had a boyfriend, and then told them they'd broken up.

They felt sorry for her!

Her cheeks grew hot. "I'm really, really happy with the way things are right now," she said emphatically. It would have been true, too, if she hadn't made the mistake of falling in love with Daniel.

"Of course you are, dear," her mom said. A chorus of overearnest agreement ran around the table.

"It's just, balance is important," Kyle said. "I'm not saying you need to get married—" his shudder made everyone laugh "—but there's more to life than work."

Her oldest brother was a firefighter, as well as a serial dater. Sadie's other siblings also had careers they loved. Jesse had a graphic-design business, Brett was a town planner, Merrillee had trained as a nurse. All smart, busy people. But somehow more...multidimensional than Sadie. They'd managed to stay connected to one another.

Sadie drew in a deep breath, inhaling the scent of summer shrubs wafting through the open window. It didn't matter that she wasn't connected. It didn't matter that her lack of a boyfriend emphasized the differences between her and her family. If they truly understood how important her work was—not just to her, but to the planet...

One look at their concerned faces said she'd be wasting her breath. That was what she loved about Daniel—he did understand. She sneaked a glance at the gold carriage clock on the sideboard, the one First Cordova Bank had presented to her father after forty years' service. It was stuck on three-thirty—surely it must be ten o'clock by now. She made a show of yawning and stretching. "I'm beat. I think I'll go to bed."

Merrillee looked at her watch. "At ten past eight?"

"Can't handle the pace, city girl?" Jesse teased.

Rats.

She resisted the urge to point out that, since annexation, Cordova was part of the city. "I've been putting in some long hours at the lab." She excused herself as she pushed her chair back. "By the way, Merrillee, you have baby spit on your shoulder."

Okay, so that was petty.

"Would you like some cod-liver oil to help you sleep, honey?" her mom asked. Mary-Beth believed cod-liver oil solved every conceivable problem. Sadie had once tried to explain that despite its high levels of omega-3 fatty acids, it wasn't a cure-all, and in fact its high vitamin A content made it nutritionally risky, but her mom didn't want to know.

Sadie turned down the offer, along with the predictable next offer—a cup of hot cocoa—and hurried upstairs. As she left the room, Merrillee was dabbing with her napkin at the ever-present stain on her shoulder.

Safe in her old bedroom with the door closed, Sadie donned her pajamas—red tank and plaid cotton pants—in case anyone wanted proof she was tired.

Her bedroom window looked onto Meg's. As kids, they'd held up signs to each other, illuminated by flashlight when necessary. After Sadie left for boarding school, their nighttime communications were limited to vacation periods, but they'd continued nonetheless.

When Sadie and Meg graduated to cell phones, they'd sat in the chair they each had by the window, feet propped on the sill, so they could see each other as they whispered conversations after lights-out.

They'd been closer than sisters.

Now Meg's curtains were closed. Surely she and Daniel hadn't gone upstairs already? And surely Nancy wouldn't put them in the same room? Sadie's stomach twisted.

She hadn't asked Meg if she and Daniel were sleeping together yet. Meg's job often took her away overnight, so Sadie was unsure if her friend's absences were due to that, or to staying at Daniel's. Normally they talked about everything—at least, Meg shared all the details of her more exciting life. This time, Sadie hadn't asked and Meg hadn't told.

Trey's truck was still parked out front. Behind it was a faded red Buick LeSabre.

Did Trey have a girlfriend over? The only person Sadie knew who'd driven a LeSabre that color was the minister at Cordova Colonial Presbyterian. His daughter had been in Meg's class.

She couldn't imagine Trey dating the minister's daughter. And it probably wasn't the same Buick.

But what if it was? And what if the reason Nancy had invited the minister over was that Meg and Daniel—

"Shut up," Sadie ordered herself. "Meg's never dated anyone longer than six weeks. This won't be any different."

She plunked herself into the chair and opened the novel she'd started reading last night—Dostoevsky's

Crime and Punishment. She'd read it years ago, but she and Daniel had been debating Dostoevsky's views on the evils of rationalism, and she wanted to refresh her memory.

She couldn't settle.... After three pages she closed the book and fished her old bird-watching binoculars out of the depths of the closet. But she was at the wrong angle for next door's dining-room window.

"Blast," she muttered.

She had to know who was visiting.

Back to the closet, this time for the gray hooded jacket with the broken zipper she'd left behind on her last trip home. She pulled it on over her pajamas. If she got caught leaving the house by the back door she'd say she was stepping out to smell the flowers.

They would buy that.

As it turned out, her family was having a riotous good time discussing the twins' eccentric social-studies teacher and Brett's son's grass allergy—Gerry didn't believe in it, but he wouldn't dare say that tomorrow night when Brett was here. No one noticed Sadie sneaking out.

Meg's dad had built the backyard gate between the two houses so the two girls could visit without having to go near the road. It hadn't been used in a while, judging by the creak of the hinges.

The Kincaids' dining room was the downstairs front room on this side. Sadie skulked past the kitchen and bathroom...then started to worry that shortsighted Mr. Fargo across the street might phone the cops. She stopped acting suspiciously and walked boldly up to Nancy's prize gardenia bush. She would snap off one of the white blossoms and use it as her excuse for loitering.

She chose a bloom and twisted. Nothing happened.

Sadie jiggled the stalk from side to side. Still nothing.

"Come off, you stupid damn flower."

This plant had stems of steel.

Next time she came spying, she'd bring pruning shears.

At last the blossom broke off, losing a few petals as it came free. Sadie took a deep, relieved sniff of its heavy perfume. Armed with her alibi, she headed for the front corner of the house.

Like her mother's, Nancy's dining-room window was covered by a semisheer curtain. Sadie heard Nancy's voice through the smaller, open window at the top. It sounded like... Had she just said *church?*

With a swift glance across the road to check that there was no sign of Mr. Fargo, Sadie crouched beneath the window. She dropped the gardenia and gripped the ledge. Slowly she raised her head.

Four pairs of feet rested beneath Nancy's reproduction Louis XVI dining table. Through the mesh of the curtain Sadie distinguished Meg's sandals and Daniel's loafers—hooray, they weren't in bed together. She risked rising a bit higher. Nancy's black pumps and a pair of sneakers. Male or female?

"What the hell are you doing?" said a deep voice from behind her.

CHAPTER THREE

INSTINCT MADE SADIE duck down, then, as she came up again, she banged her head on the window ledge.

"Ow!"

"What's going on?" Trey's hand closed around her arm. He dragged her aside, mercifully out of view of the window.

Sadie rubbed hard at her head. "That hurt."

"Why are you spying?"

She tugged herself free so she could chafe her arm where he'd gripped her. "Where did you come from?" she countered.

"I live here."

"No, you don't." Sadie knew he had a house on the other side of Cordova. Five whole minutes away.

He sighed. "You're still a know-it-all. Okay, my mother lives here and she considers it my home, even if I don't." He hooked his thumbs in his jeans and stared her down. "What are you doing?" he asked again.

Devoid of a rational answer, Sadie played for time. "You still didn't tell me where you came from."

"I was on the porch. I heard someone cussing out the plants."

The flower she'd had so much trouble detaching. She bent and snatched it up. "I was in my room and I smelled this amazing scent, so I came down to pick a gardenia."

He glanced at her parents' house. "You did well smelling those with your bedroom window closed."

"How do you know my window's closed?"

He rolled his eyes. "Then after you got your flower..." he prompted.

"*Then,* Miss Marple, I heard an unfamiliar voice, so I thought I'd see who your mom had visiting."

"Uh-huh." His gaze flicked over her pj top, which unfortunately had shrunk in the wash. It was too tight across the front and the gap between top and pants bared an inch or so of midriff. "Hmm," he said.

As if she hadn't heard enough of *hmm.* Which she now understood didn't mean *wow.*

"I'm going home," she said crossly. "Good night."

The gleam in his eyes reminded her of the few times he'd paid her enough attention to bait her back in their teens. Mostly they'd ignored each other—the jock and the science geek had nothing in common.

She took a step away, then turned. "So who *is* visiting your mom?"

"None of your business. Though you'd be *very* interested," he taunted.

It really was the minister, here to talk about weddings.

"Sadie? You okay? You've gone white."

"Huh?" She blinked.

Trey cursed. He grabbed her hand and led her around the front of the house, where he pushed her down onto the porch swing. "I always thought it was a good thing your parents sent you to genius school—it stopped you turning out like Meg's scatterbrained friends," he said. "But you grew up a hell of a weird woman."

Just what Sadie needed—another reminder she didn't fit in. And she didn't believe that backhanded compliment, since he'd dated several of Meg's "scatterbrained" friends.

"Just tell me who's visiting your mom." Her voice wobbled. *I'm losing my grip.* She grasped the edge of the swing seat as if it was an extension of her sanity.

"I would have thought you'd recognize that LeSabre."

She held her breath, waiting for the ax to fall.

His knee nudged the swing, setting it rocking. "The minister's car, remember?"

"The *minister* is visiting your mom?" It came out high-pitched.

"Not him, his wife." He left the railing to sit next to her, disrupting the swing's motion.

Sadie planted her feet on the porch, stilling the swing. "The minister's wife is visiting with your mom."

"That's what I said." He rubbed his chin. "For a girl who got the highest SATs I know of and won a full scholarship to Princeton from the Outstanding Tennesseans Foundation, you're kinda slow."

"I just took a blow to the head." She scowled and rubbed the sore spot where she'd collided with the window.

He grinned, and it made him look like the quarterback again.

"So why is the minister's wife here?" she asked.

"Mom's paying her to do the flowers for the lunch on Sunday. There's a list of jobs a mile long for the likes of you and me, so Mom thought she'd need the help."

Nancy had been an active member of the community her whole life, and her sixtieth birthday was a two-day event—the Saturday-night barbecue for "family," which included the Beechams, and a lunch for her wide circle of friends, as well as family, on Sunday.

Two events where Sadie would have to watch Meg and Daniel canoodling, and fool everyone into believing she didn't care. "It's great we can all celebrate Nancy's birthday with her," she said, reminding herself of the one positive in all of this.

Trey sobered. He scuffed the porch with his shoe. "Yeah."

Five years ago his mother had suffered a stroke. Fairly severe, but she'd recovered faster than the doctors expected, with only a barely discernible limp and a slight slowness of speech to show for it.

Sadie cleared her throat. "What do you think of Daniel?"

"Nice guy, far as I could tell."

"He's not Meg's usual type, though, is he?" She twisted to face Trey. He was sitting closer than she realized, and she ended up looking right at his lips. Which made her think about Daniel and that kiss…

He grimaced. "Sadie, I think I know the real reason you were skulking around tonight."

She pressed her hand to her mouth, but not fast enough to prevent a mortified cry escaping.

"I have to tell you—" he drew back and the swing creaked "—there's no point."

She closed her eyes. *Please, make him stop.*

"I know you got dumped recently…."

Her eyes flew open. Her mom had told the *whole world* about her supposed breakup?

"But—" Trey spread his hands in a gesture of regret "—I'm not interested."

It took a second for his words to pierce her humiliation. "You think I was spying on *you?* That I like you?"

She couldn't decide if she was relieved he hadn't guessed the truth or outraged at his inflated opinion of his own charms.

He shrugged. "I find it hard to believe this trespassing incident is about your curiosity over who visits my mom. I figure you're looking for a distraction from your broken heart."

"Did my mother really say I got dumped?" she demanded.

He winced. "Uh, I heard it from Mom. Maybe she just said it was a breakup. The point is, Sadie, even if you weren't my sister's best friend, practically family, I'd never date—"

"—a geek like me," she finished. It wasn't just her own family who insisted on making her feel like an outsider. She stood up. "You've been in Cordova too long, Trey. Out in the big wide world, people don't get hung up on labels that—"

"Whoa." His eyes glinted as he looked up at her. "I was going to say I'd never date someone on the rebound."

"Oh. Right." Time to put an end to this discussion

before she laid out all her insecurities for his scrutiny. Sadie took a step backward, and her ankle bumped the iron swing stand, hard.

"Ouch!" She reached down to rub her ankle, exposing more of her midriff to Trey. Which he would probably interpret as an attempt at seduction. "You don't have to worry about my interest in you," she said. "Like the male worker ant, it doesn't exist."

"What?" He stood, and as she was barefoot, he had more inches on her than she remembered.

"All worker ants are female," she explained.

"Is this your convoluted way of saying you weren't spying on me?"

"Exactly," she said, relieved.

His brow relaxed and he chuckled. "You might need to simplify things if you want to be understood by the folks around here, Ms. Sadie." His deep voice lengthened to a country drawl.

She rolled her eyes. "This discussion is unproductive—"

"Like the male worker ant," he suggested helpfully.

"—so I'm leaving." She hobbled across the porch on her sore foot. "Good night, Trey."

He dropped back onto the swing. "I don't know about good," he reflected, "but you sure made it more interesting."

"Glad one of us enjoyed it," Sadie muttered.

IT HAD BEEN A sweltering day, and now with Gerry Beecham's famous gin-and-juniper-marinated pork chops sizzling on the grill alongside a mustard-coated beef fillet and a ton of hot dogs for the kids, Saturday night in the Beechams' backyard was hot as fire.

Trey flipped the hot dogs Gerry had asked him to keep an eye on; only Gerry himself felt qualified to prod the chops or the fillet. Everyone had worked hard today—dividing along strict gender lines into cooks and cleaners, or handymen—to get ready for tomorrow's lunch. Now they were enjoying a well-earned evening of relaxation.

Trey rubbed the back of his neck. The heat was bringing him out in hives. Or maybe it wasn't the heat, maybe it was all this togetherness. He was trying to spend less time with his family, not more. He was happy to celebrate his mom's birthday, but this kind of gathering—full of married couples talking about their kids and their camping vacations and their SUVs—was the worst.

His gaze tracked his mom, talking to her cousin and Mary-Beth, then his flighty sister, standing next to sturdy Dr. Daniel. In Meg's case, a dose of suburbia would be a good thing. An excellent thing.

Trey didn't need to look farther to know exactly where Sadie was, which he found slightly disconcerting. She was his kid sister's sensible best friend, part of the wallpaper of his life—and like wallpaper, he generally didn't notice her.

But this weekend…something was off about Sadie. She wasn't herself. Different enough that he couldn't ignore her. Which was how he knew she'd spent the past fifteen minutes jiggling her baby nephew on one hip while explaining plant reproduction to a bunch of kids, using Mary-Beth's prize-winning Golden Spangles camellia for demonstration.

"And when the bee carries the pollen from one plant to another," she concluded triumphantly as Trey listened, "that's when you get pretty flowers."

One of her nieces, about five years old—he couldn't remember her name—put up her hand.

"Do you have a question about vegetative reproduction, Caitlyn?" Sadie asked, pleased. "I admit, I did skip a few steps, honey."

"What kind of flowers do princesses like best?" Caitlyn asked.

Sadie blinked. "Princesses…uh, princesses aren't my area of expertise, honey."

Trey felt his shoulders relax. That was more like the Sadie he knew. She'd never been one of the girlie-girls, which was doubtless why that radiant smile she'd bestowed on him when she arrived yesterday had spooked him. The Sadie he knew was down-to-earth, calm, aloof. Wallpaper.

Meg called to her. As Sadie handed the baby to Merrilee and went to join his sister and Daniel, Trey was too aware of her figure in her white capris and yellow tank.

It felt as if someone had redecorated.

He flipped a hot dog and it burst out of its skin, startling him. Trey took a step back from the spitting fat. So Sadie Beecham had grown some curves that he'd only just got around to noticing. Big deal. Trey was over Cordova women, just as he was over everything else about his life here.

"Trey?" Meg called. "Can you come here?"

"Kyle, how about I leave these hot dogs with you?" Trey asked Sadie's brother. After a ceremonial fist bump and handover of the tongs—barbecues were a major ritual around here—he took his beer and joined the others.

"Save me from these two, please." Meg waved at Daniel and Sadie. "They're trying to baffle me with science and it's depressingly easy."

Daniel ran a finger across her shoulder. "Sweetheart, we're just warming up." He winked at Sadie.

Meg groaned.

"We're talking about whether Sadie's work with new wheat strains for the developing world could help diabetes-prone kids here in the U.S.A.," Daniel explained to Trey.

"I've heard wheat can cause diabetes in some people," Trey said. He'd read something about it in *New Scientist.*

Sadie squinted at him, as if she'd had no idea he spoke Science. "That's type 1 diabetes," she said dismissively. She turned to Daniel. "In theory, if you raised the protein level, thus lowering the glycemic index, wheat-based foods would pose a lower risk to type 2 diabetes patients."

"Which would make life much easier for low-income families who can't afford a low-wheat diet," Daniel said.

He and Sadie grinned at each other.

Then Sadie reached behind her to lift her hair off her neck, a cooling-down gesture that lifted her breasts.

Daniel lowered his gaze to her cleavage. And left it there a second longer than reflex dictated.

What the—? Trey accepted the other man's dropped gaze was an instinctive response to Sadie's movement, but the guy shouldn't linger, not when he was dating Trey's sister.

Trey stepped in front of Sadie to block Daniel's view.

"Can't we talk about books?" Meg asked. "English was my best subject. I wiped science from my brain after I dropped it in tenth grade." She held up a hand. "When I say books, I don't mean that Russian stuff you two read."

"I'm enjoying that book of yours," Daniel told Meg. "*The Politics of Poverty*. Brilliant."

"Hey, that's mine." Sadie edged around Trey to get back in the conversation. "I lent it to Meg."

"Oops." Meg faked a guilty look, and Daniel laughed.

"You should read it. You'd enjoy it, Meg." Unconsciously Sadie fingered a lock of her hair. It had been mousy-brown when she was younger, Trey remembered. Today it had gleaming gold highlights.

As if he was mirroring her, Daniel stroked Meg's dark hair.

Immediately Sadie's hand dropped to her stomach, as if she felt nauseated. Her eyes on Daniel were wide and unhappy.

Trey's sister-protection sensors went on high alert. He tried to shut them off—Meg's expectation that other people would fix her problems irritated him like nothing else—but old habits died hard.

Sadie likes Daniel. That was why she'd been sneaking around his mom's place last night.

It couldn't be true...could it?

As Meg leaned into Daniel and they began a murmured conversation of what sounded like mutual, breathless compliments, Sadie blinked suspiciously fast.

Dammit!

Trey leaned into her. "Get a grip," he muttered.

She started, which at least pulled her attention off the doc. "Excuse me?"

His hand closed around her elbow; he turned her so she couldn't see Meg. "Quit looking as if you're about to commit suttee on the grill because my sister's boyfriend touched her."

She tugged, but he didn't release her. "That's ridiculous," she hissed.

"Exactly. You're making a fool of yourself."

"What are you two whispering about?" Meg asked.

They froze. Sadie turned beet-red to the roots of her hair.

"Sadie's telling me about her exciting life as a future Nobel laureate," Trey said. Meg's gaze traveled to the hold he had on her friend's elbow, so he let go. "You must have some interesting colleagues at that lab of yours, Sadie."

"Uh..." she said.

"Intelligent guys on a decent income," he clarified. "Have you dated anyone there?" *As in, go find your own man. Leave Meg's alone.*

"You're being weird, Trey," Meg said.

"Are those your criteria, Sadie?" Daniel teased. "I didn't know you were looking."

Sadie's brother Jesse approached, bearing a bowl of chips. "No ordinary guy will do for Sadie," he said, butting in to the conversation. "He'll need to be a genius, the noble do-gooder type, willing to treat her with the awe she's used to."

Sadie took a couple of chips with one hand and punched Jesse's shoulder with the other. "Shut up."

"Those are some high standards, Sadiebug." Daniel took a handful of chips but his gaze remained on Sadie. His expression held fondness and...was that regret? And what was with the *Sadiebug?*

"She deserves the best," Meg said loyally. "Whereas I definitely don't need a genius—my guy has to be dumb enough to love me despite my flaws." She grinned. "A platinum AmEx would come in handy, too."

Daniel laughed. "Sorry, sweetheart, I may be the boss at the clinic, but I'll never earn millions. The best you can hope for is that I'll be able to support you in the manner to which you're accustomed."

Support Meg? That sounded serious.

Meg and Daniel were too busy gazing into each other's eyes to notice the strangled sound from Sadie. As Trey watched, her face turned red.

To think he'd grown up next door to her and had never known she was a psycho.

Grasping her arm again, he swung her away from the group. "Breathe," he ordered in her ear.

Sadie stared at him, mouth open, eyes glazing over.

"If you don't breathe, I'll sit you down and shove your head between your knees until everyone knows what a nutcase you are."

She dragged in a great gulp of air, wheezing like an asthmatic.

"Now out," Trey ordered.

She let the air out again.

"Am I going to have to instruct you through every breath for the entire weekend?" he demanded.

"I— No." She coughed.

"Are you okay, Sadie?" Meg asked.

They'd attracted the attention of the entire company. Sadie closed her eyes, as if people wouldn't be able to see her if she couldn't see them. It was an oddly defenseless reaction.

"She was choking on a chip," Trey explained, bailing her out. "All clear now, Sadie?"

"Absolutely." She smiled shakily.

"Better add 'able to perform the Heimlich maneuver' to the checklist for your perfect man," Jesse said. "Too bad your doctor boyfriend dumped you."

Trey felt a twinge of sympathy for her.

"What doctor boyfriend?" Meg and Daniel asked simultaneously.

"I have no idea what he means," Sadie said.

She'd had a major breakup, and she hadn't told her best friend?

Her mom overheard. "Honey, I'm sorry. When you mentioned you were bringing a boy home—" Mary-Beth made her sound sixteen again, and Sadie was clearly unthrilled "—I told a couple of people."

Trey figured everyone here had heard that at last Sadie had a boyfriend who might stick. The surrounding faces were studies in loving pity. All except—

"What boyfriend?" Meg asked again. "How come I never heard about him?"

Uh-oh. Suddenly Trey figured it out.

Meg turned to Daniel. "Did you know—" She stopped, then whirled back to Sadie, her eyes wide. "Tell me it wasn't—" Just in time, she clamped her mouth shut.

Jesse, who'd always been quick-witted, picked up on the unspoken question. Unfortunately, he'd also always been a loudmouth. "No way, Sadie," he hooted. "Was *Daniel* your boyfriend?"

CHAPTER FOUR

NOW WOULD BE A GOOD TIME for the world to end, Sadie decided. *One minute ago would have been even better.*

Her mother made a protective, worried sound, like a lioness about to maul Meg, or Daniel, or both. Jesse let out a low whistle. Brothers. Who needed them?

Sadie did the only thing she could—she laughed.

It came out squeaky.

"Of course Daniel wasn't my boyfriend," she said. Shrilly.

Varying degrees of mortification and sympathy showed on everyone's faces. No one believed her. Behind her, a hot dog spat on the grill; the smell of charring beef made Sadie feel sick. She couldn't bear it if Daniel realized how she felt about him.

She had to do something.

Her brain, the one that commanded a hefty six-figure salary, sputtered and died.

Her mother wrapped an arm around her, a loving tentacle. Any moment now Mom would drag her into the kitchen for a dose of cod-liver oil and a cup of hot cocoa.

"Mom." She pulled away, and this time the laugh was better—more incredulous, less hysterical. "I told you, it wasn't Daniel."

"Then who was it?" Jesse, the idiot who'd dropped her in this mess.

"It was Wesley," Trey announced.

Every head in the place swiveled to him.

"Wesley?" Meg darted a confused look at Sadie.

"She met him before she even knew Daniel," Trey explained.

"Why didn't I know about him?" Meg said skeptically.

Sadie found her voice. "I met, uh, Wesley—" and didn't he sound like a hottie, with a name like that? "—when you were in Paris, covering for the European staff on strike. We weren't together long, just a few weeks. We broke up right before I met Daniel. Which—" she widened her mouth into a smile "—was why it was so great to meet a guy who was just a friend."

She prayed her mom wouldn't add up the timing of her phone call and correct her.

"Wouldn't that have been a coincidence, both of you dating doctors?" Mary-Beth said.

Bad timing, Mom. The suspicion that had been lifting settled back onto the faces around Sadie.

"He's a vet," Trey said firmly. "Dr. Wesley Burns, veterinarian."

What the heck?

"How do you know all this, Trey?" Meg asked.

"Sadie told me about him last night," Trey said. "She came over and we sat on the porch awhile."

The interest in everyone's eyes was better than pity. And at least Trey hadn't mentioned she was in her pajamas or stealing flowers or peering in the window. *Ugh, I really was a mess.*

"She thought I might know Wes," he elaborated. "That we might have been in the same dorm at Duke."

"But they weren't," Sadie said quickly.

"No," Trey agreed. "But Wes and I worked in the same bar on Friday nights."

A headache drilled into Sadie's temples. She would kill Trey. Just as soon as this barbecue was over and their families had accepted the fabrication about Dr. Wesley Burns, she would kill Trey and take great pleasure in doing so.

Trey grinned at her. He'd always been too damn cocky. How was it that he was one step ahead of everyone, including her?

But his stupid story was her only hope.

"So…what's Wes like?" Sadie's mom asked wistfully, entranced by the thought of the veterinarian son-in-law she'd almost had.

Meg was still looking suspicious.

"Great guy," Trey said. "You'd love him."

Sadie choked on her wine, and Trey patted her back solicitously. Time to steer this fantasy in a direction more flattering to herself.

"Unfortunately," Sadie said, "Wes is a traditionalist—he envisaged me staying at home having babies. But of course, my work is too important to me. I couldn't contemplate giving it up, so I had to break up with him."

Uh-oh, Trey had a dangerous gleam in his eyes. She should have remembered that the few times he'd engaged enough to tease her when they were kids, he'd effortlessly come out on top.

"Wes would make a great dad, judging by his talent with animals," he said. "Dogs, cats, rabbits…and does he have a way with hamsters."

Sadie almost growled. Not only had he given her a boyfriend with the uninspiring name of Wes, a vet when she would have preferred a cardiologist, but now he was consigning Wes to the bottom rung of the pet ladder.

"But his main client is the Memphis Zoo," she said.

"You mean he works on lions and stuff?" The breathless inquiry came from one of the twins. Sadie was too flustered to identify which one.

"Lions, tigers, elephants," she confirmed.

"Which is his favorite?" the other twin asked.

"The, uh, leopard." She realized the girls wanted more. "Because it's so noble and intelligent and sensitive. Just like Wes himself."

A snort from Trey.

"Oh, honey, he sounds incredible." Yikes, Sadie's mom was just about in tears at the thought of the man her daughter had loved and lost.

"Mom, I'm over it, really," she assured her. "Wes was a great guy—he fit the dream, you know. But it wouldn't have worked."

"I heard he was never the same after that camel bit him," Trey said.

Sadie began to mentally run through ways of killing him. She discarded them all on the grounds they wouldn't inflict sufficient pain.

"I wish you'd told me," Meg said, hurt. "I would have been there for you."

"I know, sweetie, but by the time you arrived back stateside, I'd been having fun hanging out with Daniel, and my number-one focus was introducing you two to each other." Not quite true, but at least she was talking about real people.

"You're something else, Sadie," Daniel said admiringly.

"She sure is," Trey agreed.

That *something else* was likely a poached egg—Sadie felt as if she didn't have a bone left in her body. "Dad, I'm starving. Is dinner ready?"

"Coming right up." Her father brandished his tongs. "Don't worry, honey, my pork chops will take your mind off that leopard-loving loser."

Trey let out a burst of laughter that lit up his face and reminded Sadie he really was a great-looking guy. Shame about the personality.

"What I don't understand..." Jesse began.

"If you all don't mind, I'd rather not talk about Wes," she announced bravely.

Jesse's wife, Diane, smacked him upside the head for his insensitivity, which gave Sadie some satisfaction, while the rest of her family agreed immediately to a ban on talking about Wes. At least in front of her. Sadie had no doubt that after she returned to Memphis their sympathetic discussions of her failed love life would be a bonding experience.

Meg hugged her, and Daniel planted one of those

kisses on Sadie's hair. Much to Trey's irritation, Sadie noted with satisfaction.

Still, his nutty story had taken the heat off her. As people headed toward the food, she murmured a grudging "Thanks. Sort of."

"Don't mention it," he said with unaccustomed grace. Then, "Now, how about you do me a favor?"

She gritted her teeth. "I already did. I let you live."

Humor flashed in his eyes, then disappeared. "Stay away from my sister's boyfriend."

Typical. For as long as Sadie could remember, Trey had moaned about Meg's inability to "stand on her own two feet." But he could never resist butting in when he thought his sister needed help.

As if Meg needed protection from her best friend!

Before she could tell Trey to mind his own business, her father handed her a plate piled with food. Then Daniel arrived back with his meal. "This looks great." He sounded his normal self, not as if he believed she was secretly in love with him.

"Dad's the best barbecue chef, so long as you don't count the calories." Sadie struck a casual, friendly tone, aware of Trey's close scrutiny. Did he expect her to *obey* him?

"Want to go for a run in the morning?" she asked Daniel. "That way I get two helpings of dessert. You should come too, Meg." Smart strategy, she congratulated herself. By acting natural and casual with Daniel, she would deflect any lingering suspicion of past feelings for him. Trey's sharp, disapproving intake of breath was icing on the cake.

"You guys go for it," Meg said. She hated running, and when she wasn't flying liked to sleep in until nine. "I'll catch up on some z's."

"So, 7:00 a.m.?" Sadie asked Daniel. "That'll give us time for a decent run before the day gets busy."

Daniel picked up a piece of garlic bread. "You're on."

Sadie smiled at him. And ignored Trey's thunderous expression.

SADIE STEPPED OUT ONTO her parents' porch at six fifty-five on Sunday morning and took a deep breath of fresh air scented with grass, her mom's lemon trees and Nancy's gardenias. In the jacaranda tree that grew on the Kincaid side of the fence but spread most of its shade over the Beechams' yard, a mockingbird had burst out with its early-morning song. As she laced up her running shoes, it moved from a series of whistles to smoochy, kissing sounds.

Sadie stood on one leg to begin her quad stretches. Or what she hoped were quad stretches. When she'd fallen in love with Daniel practically at first sight and he'd asked if she ran, she'd said yes. Which was the right thing to do because he'd asked her to go running with him, and hadn't minded that she was a beginner. And that was the start of their...friendship.

"This'll be good for you," she reminded her reluctant left quad. Her stomach growled, but she'd learned the hard way that if she ate now she wouldn't be able to run more than a hundred yards without developing a stitch.

As the Kincaids' front door opened she hopped a little,

pulling her left foot closer to her butt to lengthen the stretch.

Trey stepped onto the next-door porch.

Wearing shorts and a T-shirt. And running shoes.

He waved. "Morning."

Sadie's foot thudded to the floorboards. "What are you doing here?"

"I stayed the night—didn't want to drive after all that drinking."

As she recalled, he'd had maybe two beers over four hours. Nowhere near the limit. Not that she'd been watching.

He strolled down the steps to the sidewalk. "Thought I'd join you on your run." He patted his flat stomach. "Anything to counter the effects of age."

She didn't give him the satisfaction of admiring his physique. "I guess it's a free country—I can't stop you running with us." She jogged to the sidewalk, trying to look fit.

"Us?" His forehead creased. "Did I forget to say Daniel's not coming?"

"Excuse me?"

"I told him I'd turn a blind eye if he wanted to sneak coffee into Meg's room," he said smugly.

Sadie banished the image from her mind.

"But Daniel was worried about you having no one to run with," Trey continued, "so I offered to stand in."

She clenched her fists at her sides. "I don't want to run with you." She might as well go back to bed with a bowl of granola.

"Like you said, you need to work off last night's

calories," he said. She sucked in her stomach out of reflex, and glared when he chuckled. "Don't you think it'll look suspicious if you cancel out because Daniel's not coming?" he continued.

"I'll be canceling because I don't want to run with you." But he had a point, dammit.

And he knew it. "Where are we going?" he asked.

Sadie looked past him. "*I'm* heading down Arlington and around the reserve."

"Works for me," he said. "Maybe we should come back along the Parkway."

That would add another twenty minutes; she'd be unlikely to survive. "I don't have time. Mom has me down to peel about a thousand potatoes for the potato salad." She clasped her hands behind her head and twisted from side to side.

"Okay, Arlington is fine by me. It overlooks the lagoon and I like a nice view when I run." His gaze took in her curves, accentuated by the exercise.

"Don't you have stretches to do?" she snapped.

"I'm stretching my imagination." He lingered on her legs.

"Aren't you afraid I'll take your suggestive remarks too seriously? I seem to recall you warning me off you."

"I'm not worried after last night," he said. "It's obvious I'm not the one you're interested in."

Her face on fire, she bent to adjust her shoelace. Then without another word, she started running. A purely symbolic gesture, since Trey caught her up in a few easy strides.

Her burst of speed lasted all of a hundred yards.

"Something wrong?" he asked when she slowed.

"You go on ahead. I'm taking it easy today."

He matched her pace. "I can do easy." As they passed a wrought-iron fence, he pointed at the lawn beyond. "One of my teams laid that a few weeks ago."

"Very nice," she panted insincerely.

"Not the best time for sowing grass, but the Colberts were adamant they want the best lawn on the street for the Fourth. Of course, so were the McIntoshes down the way. Who am I to deny anyone the lawn of their dreams?"

"You're…a prince," she managed to say.

He turned around and jogged backward while he surveyed her. "Pooped already?"

She shook her head.

He shrugged and turned the right way around. "I'd better call Mrs. Colbert this morning, tell her to get some water on that grass," he mused, his tone as even and unhurried as if he was standing still.

"Why are you being so chatty?" Sadie snatched a breath before she continued. "You haven't said this much to me ever."

"I'm lulling you into a false sense of security before I start grilling you about Daniel."

She grunted and put on a spurt of speed.

Trey waited until Sadie slowed down again—about half a minute—before he launched into the conversation he really wanted to have.

"So, you were dating the doctor."

She stared straight ahead, mouth grim, cheeks flushed

pink with exertion. They'd been running—if you could call it that—for about three minutes.

She shook her head, then nodded, then shook it again. "I *thought* we were dating," she said. "Turns out we were just seeing each other."

He scratched his head. "I've never understood how women can get that so wrong."

She glared at him.

"Did you sleep with him?" Trey asked.

Sadie stopped running. "As if I would sleep with someone I wasn't even dating."

"You wouldn't be the first to make that mistake."

Her chest heaved. He couldn't tell if it was emotion or exhaustion. Either way, it drew his attention to her figure, which, he admitted to himself for the tenth time since she'd arrived on Friday, was sensational from top to toe.

"You still like him," Trey said, "even though he's dating Meg." He almost wished Daniel was here now, to see Sadie bright red, dripping perspiration.

"Of course I like him," she said. "He's intelligent, funny, charming, sensitive—"

He stuck a hand over her mouth, and whatever accolade she intended next came out a muffled "umph."

"You like him too much," he said calmly.

He felt a puff of breath against his palm. He dropped his hand.

"Meg's with Daniel right now. I accept that," she said.

"So you don't plan to come between them?"

"Of course not."

But he'd seen a flash of guilt in her eyes. "What are you planning?"

"Nothing."

"Tell me," he demanded.

"Stop ordering me around. I'm not your sister."

"Tell me, *please*," he said. "Put my mind at rest, so I don't have to warn Meg to be on her guard."

She paled, which at least reduced the redness of her face. Then she said, "If anyone's going to get hurt, it's Daniel. And you know it."

"Meg seems as serious as he does."

She blew out a breath that would have lifted her bangs if they hadn't been plastered to her forehead. "History suggests that in a couple of weeks, Meg will have moved on."

"Ah, I get it." He adopted a high voice, in imitation of her. "I know you're upset, Daniel, but I'm here for you." Caught up in his role-playing, he grabbed her hand and looked deeply, soulfully, into her eyes. She had nice fingers, even when they were sweaty. Nice eyes, too. The light hue reminded him of blue delphiniums.

She wrested her hand away. "Don't be such a jerk."

"Daniel dumps you for Meg, and you'll take him back when she's done with him. Don't you think that's kind of pathetic?" he asked.

She stiffened. "Scarlett O'Hara spent her whole life pursuing a man who'd chosen someone else, and she's one of the strongest women in literature."

He snorted. "As in, she's not real. And if you're suggesting your crush on Daniel compares with some

Southern belle fighting to save her ancestral home from marauders…"

"Now *you're* being pathetic." Sadie poked his chest, which was just about the most annoying thing she could have done. "Look, Trey, you might think it's pathetic to want Daniel after Meg breaks up with him, but I'm not used to being handed whatever I want. I don't get to go through life flirting and smiling and having people favor me for my good looks."

"Meg is your *friend*," he reminded her, even though she'd neatly summed up some of the most irritating things about his sister.

"And I adore her. As does everyone else. With the possible exception of you."

Damn, how had Sadie picked up on that, when he'd barely seen her in years? "Don't try and deflect attention from your scheming," he said.

"Meg gets an easy ride in lots of ways, but she's had tough times, too, so I'd never begrudge her." She was talking about his dad and Logan, Trey realized. "But if I have a goal, I expect to struggle to achieve it. I'm willing to put the work in. To go after what I want single-mindedly." She paused. "Aggressively."

"You're too late. Daniel chose Meg."

Sadie toed a crack in the sidewalk with her sneaker. "Of course Daniel is attracted to Meg. I've never met a man who wasn't. But I deal in facts and logic, and the fact is, he and Meg have nothing in common."

"Opposites attract," he retorted. "Which makes them the ideal couple." He didn't exactly believe that, but even when Sadie had been a teenager, there'd been no room for pussyfooting. You had to come down hard with your opinion and stick to it through whatever obscure logic that brain of hers devised.

"I think he's confused," she said thoughtfully, as if Daniel was a seed under a microscope. "He's at an age where it's natural to think about a long-term relationship. But a part of him is rebelling against commitment. Subconsciously he's choosing someone unsuitable, guaranteed not to work out."

This wasn't logic—this was denial on a global scale.

"Sadie, I don't think Daniel is rebelling against commitment."

Something flashed across her face. Fear? "I believe most men do at some stage," she said with a hint of uncertainty. "Look at you, a classic example. Over thirty, by most women's standards a hot guy—" the crinkle in her forehead made it plain she found *most women's* taste questionable "—and still playing the field like super jock, according to your sister."

"I'm not *afraid* of commitment. I have way too much commitment in my life. And Daniel's not afraid, either." Aware of his muscles cooling off and starting to stiffen, Trey began jogging.

Sadie trotted at his side. "Trey, it doesn't matter which of them realizes first how unsuited they are, I'm certain this thing will end soon." Conviction grew in her voice. "It would be pointless for me to hold it against Daniel forever that he'd once liked Meg."

The sentiment went against Trey's deepest belief: being second choice was no choice at all.

"*I* believe he and Meg are serious," he said.

They ran in silence for a minute or two. As they turned the corner onto Arlington, they passed the Jones place. Where once there had been two tons of dirt and a tangle of scrub, there was now a flowing garden that invited people to linger among its colors and scents. It was one of Kincaid Nurseries' biggest success stories, but it had almost been a disaster. After demanding several redesigns, Mrs. Jones had fired Kincaid's because the company's landscape designer "didn't get it." When Trey visited her to discuss the problem, it turned out he and Mrs. Jones were on the same horticultural wavelength. Although he wasn't a landscape designer—most of his time was spent on the management side of the business rather than on the plants—they'd reworked the design together. The client had been delighted with the result.

Sadie stopped running. She steadied herself with a hand to the trunk of a maple tree; Trey could see a tremor in her calf muscles.

"Meg loves parties and travel. Daniel is sensible and responsible and settled," she said when she'd caught her breath.

For someone who was convinced she was right, she was working awfully hard to prove her point.

"They have less in common than—than you and I do," she continued.

"If you really want a boyfriend, wouldn't it be simpler if you found someone else?" he asked. "Come on, Sadie, there must be other—"

"I don't just *like* Daniel," she blurted. "I *love* him."

CHAPTER FIVE

SADIE CRINGED. Trey was staring at her as if she'd lost her mind.

Then one side of his mouth rose and he said, "I love Daniel, too."

She stumbled on her shoelace and would have sprawled headlong if Trey hadn't caught her.

"*What* did you say?" she demanded.

"Seems you and I have more in common than you thought."

"What did you *mean?*" Because clearly he'd intended to put her off balance.

"Daniel is exactly what my sister needs," he said. "What's not to love?"

She wiped her forehead with the back of her hand. "I've had enough of your inane views. You can run a different way home." She stepped off the curb.

Trey caught her hand. "I'm not done talking to you yet."

"Too bad, because I'm done with you." Her whole arm tingled. The overexertion was probably giving her a heart attack.

He tugged her backward, forcing her to step up onto the curb or trip over. "Come in here." He indicated a white wooden gate set into a high fence.

Sadie shivered as perspiration cooled on her skin. "Quit ordering me around and quit dragging me."

"Fine." He folded his arms as if he might otherwise give in to his caveman instincts. "Please come into this garden with me, Sadie," he said with excessive politeness.

"Why should I?"

"I don't like arguing in the street. Mrs. Jones said I can show her garden to prospective clients anytime."

"I'm not a client."

"It's a great garden," Trey coaxed. "You'll love it."

He'd hit her soft spot. She might not be any good at growing plants, but she adored a beautiful garden.

And just maybe she was curious about why he thought Daniel and Meg would last.

Sadie stuck her chin in the air and preceded him through the gate. Then stopped.

"Oh, wow." She gazed around the garden, scarcely hearing the clang of the gate closing behind her. A canopy of Japanese dappled willows. Crape myrtles. A redbud tree arcing over a pond filled with water lilies. It looked like a Monet painting, only better—impressionist art was too vague for her taste. "Trey, it's gorgeous. Kincaid Nurseries designed this?"

"The concept was mine," he said. "Our landscape architects refined it."

"I didn't know you were a designer."

"I'm not," he said. "How come you're in love with Daniel? I thought your work overrode the urge to settle down like the rest of your siblings."

Now that she'd stopped moving, every muscle in her

body screamed. She sank onto the grass, ignoring the vestiges of dew. "You're right that I'm not hanging out for the PTA meetings and the cupcake recipes," she said. "But love isn't something you plan. When you find someone special, you have to go for it." She trailed her fingers through the pond water to find the waxy leaves of a water lily. "What if Daniel is the only man for me? My whole future could be at stake."

"Sounds like your biological clock ticking," he said, unimpressed. "You're what, thirty?"

"Twenty-nine," she said. "Same as Meg. And that stupid term was probably invented by some man afraid of commitment. Women are born with a fixed number of oocytes—egg cells to you—that decrease over forty years or so of fertility, starting around the age of twelve. Every woman's biological clock is ticking, regardless of age."

Trey wasn't so easily distracted.

"Leave Meg and Daniel alone," he said abruptly, sitting beside her.

She fingered the water lily. "I'm not doing anything wrong."

"And stop mauling that lily."

She bristled at the command, but stilled her fingers out of respect for the flower.

"It wouldn't hurt to take a good look around before you decide Daniel is your fate, would it?" he asked. "There must be thousands of eligible males in Cordova alone, and you probably know half of them. Who did you date in high school?"

Sadie would have liked to reel off a list of teenage

suitors, but the guys at her "genius school" were late starters, and back here in Cordova her flat chest and general shyness had meant most of Meg's attempts to introduce her to local boys hadn't worked out. "I dated Kevin McDonald at the end of senior year. The guy my parents bribed to take me to the Millennial Centennial dance after you turned me down."

The turn of the millennium had also marked one hundred years of Cordova being called Cordova, after a succession of other names hadn't stuck. The dance had crowned a week of Fourth of July celebrations and had been the biggest event in a generation.

Trey winced. "You're not still steamed over that, are you? You only asked me to the dance because you were desperate."

"You knew that?" she said, disconcerted.

He rolled his eyes. "You thought I'd believe my sister's best friend, who clearly thought all football players were morons, had suddenly developed a crush on me?"

"I did think you were moron enough for that," she admitted.

He laughed, his ego undented. "It wasn't my fault your parents reacted by phoning all over town to find you a date. But back to the current desperate state of your love life—" He paused. "Hey, do you sense a recurring theme here?"

"Two repetitions are insufficient to form a pattern," she said stiffly.

He grinned. "Here's a thought. Kevin McDonald will be at Mom's lunch today, and he's divorced. A definite contender."

"I can tell from that gleam in your eyes there's something wrong with him."

"Let's just say that if you liked Kevin back then, there's a whole lot more of him to like now."

Trey could afford to scoff at someone else's spreading bulk—he was still in great shape. Muscle corded his forearms, and his legs were lean and strong. Unlike her, he hadn't broken a sweat on their run. Sadie peeled her tank away from her damp skin to admit some air. When she caught Trey watching, she dropped the fabric.

"Maybe Lexie Peterson has spread, too," she suggested. Lexie had been one of Meg's friends, a cheerleader, the perfect girlfriend for the quarterback. These days, she had her own party-planning business in Memphis.

"Lexie's still hot, she emailed me photos recently."

"Ew."

"Swimsuit shots," he said.

"I expect it's her uniform for those pool parties she organizes," Sadie said kindly. "Poor girl probably catches endless chills."

He laughed. "I used to think you were boring, Sadie Beecham. Being thwarted in love suits you."

Tears leaped to her eyes before she could banish them.

"Way to ruin a moment," he said, disgusted. "Forget the doctor, cupcake."

The *cupcake* jolted both of them. She stared.

"Figure of speech," he explained.

"I knew that," she said.

Trey stood. "Are we agreed you'll stay away from

Daniel?" He stuck out a hand; when she took it, he pulled her to her feet.

"Meg and Daniel are my friends, so I will continue to spend time with them," Sadie said. "And I'll be there for both of them when this thing ends."

Trey growled.

Sadie brushed her hands against her shorts as she started back toward the road.

"I'll be watching you at lunch today," he said. "If you do anything to hurt Meg..."

"I wouldn't!"

"Then why are you wearing sexy clothes?"

She glanced down at her tank, darkened by a damp patch between her breasts.

"At the barbecue last night," he clarified. "You didn't used to wear stuff like that."

"You didn't used to look. Those clothes weren't new."

"And when you arrived yesterday you gave me that flirty smile."

"That *fake* smile," she corrected. "I was putting on a cheerful face for my family."

"You can trot out all the excuses you want," he said. "I don't believe you." With his hand he applied pressure to the small of her back. "Come on, you've had a rest—time to run some more."

She started to move. Her lungs protested immediately, her breath rasping.

Trey looked down at her in disgust. "I'd better get you home before you collapse."

"If I do, Daniel can give me mouth-to-mouth," she said, unable to stop herself from goading him.

"*I'll* give you mouth-to-mouth," he retorted.

His gaze alighted on her lips. Energy crackled in the air. Not the kind of energy her exhausted limbs needed.

"I meant if it should become medically necessary," Trey said lightly.

Was it her imagination, or was he a little red in the face?

"Thanks, but Daniel's better qualified," she said.

His eyebrows drew together, all lightness gone. "Don't mess with me, Sadie. If you don't keep away from Daniel, I'll warn him and Meg you're in love with him."

She opened her mouth, but no words came out. Probably because his threat had stopped her heart.

Before she could recover, he was gone, running effortlessly away from her.

TREY HAD JUST GOT off the phone from an orchid breeder in Florida on Monday morning—he was negotiating an exclusive agreement to sell the guy's award-winning new orchid in Tennessee—when Daniel arrived in his office doorway.

"Dan, come in." Trey went to shake his hand.

"Thanks." The doctor took one of the vinyl seats that dated back to Trey's dad. "Actually, I prefer to be called Daniel."

"Sure." Trey perched on the edge of his dad's desk, a rough-hewn pine top mounted on two trestles. "Hope you don't mind me asking you here, but I wanted to talk."

"Would this be about my intentions toward your sister?"

"You guessed it." Trey liked the fact that he didn't shy away from a potentially awkward subject.

"Better make it fast, then," Daniel said. "Meg and Sadie are browsing in the store."

Trey frowned at the mention of Sadie. She'd annoyed him from start to finish of their so-called run—apart from when she'd made him laugh—yet the lingering image he'd been left with, and been unable to expunge, was of her lips, thanks to her provocative comment about mouth-to-mouth.

A totally unjustified preoccupation, given she'd looked like a sweaty tomato.

She'd ignored him all the way through lunch yesterday, but he'd noticed she kept her distance from Daniel. Score one to Trey.

Of course, after they all went back to the city tonight, he'd have no idea what she was up to.

"So you and Sadie are pretty good friends?" Trey asked. The other reason he wanted to talk to Daniel—to be sure the guy wasn't about to two-time Meg.

"I met her in a presentation at SeedTech," Daniel said. "Then again in a couple of follow-up meetings and phone calls. The two of us clicked, so we started lunching together a couple of times a week, and doing stuff after work."

"Can be hard for a man and a woman to draw the line at friendship," Trey said.

Daniel's eyes slid briefly away. "I'm not saying I didn't consider something more. Sadie and I have a lot in common, and my parents love her. I always thought I'd end up with someone like her."

He'd introduced her to his parents? No wonder Sadie had thought she was on target for a big romance. Trey felt a surge of annoyance toward Daniel.

"She's a lot of fun, too." Daniel's smile held fond reminiscence.

"She's hysterical," Trey said blandly. Actually, Sadie *was* kind of fun. In an odd, unpredictable way.

"Then I met Meg," Daniel said. "We didn't have anything obvious in common—she's not what my parents expected—but you know. *Kapow.*"

"Right." Trey had no idea what *kapow* meant when it came to women. In football, sure. In a stunning garden. But when it came to women, he'd never been hit by whatever was lighting up Daniel's face now.

Sadie should be worried.

"It's a relief to find Meg has such a great family," Daniel said. "Though I have to say I was intimidated about meeting you." He spoke with the ease of a guy who wasn't truly intimidated. "Meg talks about you as if you're Superman."

He must have caught Meg on a good day, or at least one when they hadn't talked in a while.

Daniel grinned. "I knew you couldn't be all that, but I wasn't sure I'd measure up to your standards."

Trey was reminded of the conversation at the barbecue about Sadie's "standards." Presumably Daniel met them all.

"Just don't hurt my sister," Trey said. "That's the standard."

"I won't." Daniel's eyes turned serious. "If Meg will have me, I intend to stick around."

"Uh, great." Annoyed that his first thought was concern for Sadie, Trey took a screwdriver out of the penholder on his desk and flipped it between his fingers. "But there's something I should warn you about."

Daniel clasped his hands behind his head. "You mean, Meg doesn't have a great track record with relationships?"

"Did Sadie tell you that?" Trey demanded.

Daniel gave him a quizzical look. "Meg did. She warned me not to fall for her. Of course, by then it was too late."

Trey tapped the palm of his hand with the screwdriver. "I've never heard of Meg warning guys off before. Usually the first they know of it is when she hands their skewered hearts back to them."

Daniel flinched.

"I'm thinking it's a good sign," Trey assured him.

Through the office window he caught sight of Meg and Sadie. He waved at his sister.

Meg came in, but Sadie loitered outside. Good.

"Mom wanted me to talk to you before you head back to town," he said.

Trey would have been happy to let Meg discover his news in her own time—he would've been interested to know how long it took her to notice that the business that had kept a roof over her head and put her through college had changed.

Meg plopped down in the seat next to Daniel's. "Shoot."

"I hired a guy to manage the stores in the New Year. A chief operating officer. I've been training him, and now he's up to speed."

Meg was nodding, uninterested.

"So I'm leaving," Trey said.

"Whoa...what?"

"I'm leaving Kincaid Nurseries." Just saying it made him feel lighter.

Meg jumped to her feet. "Sadie, get in here," she called.

"We don't need her," Trey said.

"It'll save me repeating it in five minutes' time." A classic example of Meg-style reasoning. Heaven forbid she should have to exert herself to pass on some news.

As Sadie entered the office, Trey observed her truly excellent legs in her denim shorts. Not relevant.

When she lined up next to Meg, he noticed the two women were the same height, but differently proportioned. Sadie's legs were longer. Definitely not relevant.

"Trey's leaving," Meg announced.

"Goodbye," Sadie said coolly.

Trey bit down on a smile.

"I'm serious." Meg thumped back into her chair. "He's leaving the business."

"I'm leaving Memphis, too," Trey said.

Meg's eyes widened. "You can't leave town! What will Mom say?"

"Mom's known about this for months," he said. "I have another week's worth of handover to do with Eugene, the new guy. Then I'm out of here."

"But you love this place," Meg said.

"I'm sure it suited you to think so."

His sister slid him the sneaky one-fingered salute she'd perfected, the one their mother never spotted but Trey always did. Neither Daniel nor Sadie saw it; they both looked indignant on Meg's behalf, so he hurried on. "But the truth is, I ended up running the business because there was no one else to clean up the mess when Dad and Logan died. I was the last choice, not the best choice."

"Where will you go?" Meg asked.

He lifted one shoulder. "I have leads on a couple of opportunities."

"What about your house?"

"I'll rent it out." It was only ever a place to stay, not somewhere he was attached to.

Meg was breathing hard. "What if Mom gets sick again?"

"You'll be half an hour away." That concern had weighed on him, too, but in the end he'd concluded his mom's next stroke might be years off. It might never happen. He couldn't hang around "just in case." "Of course, I'll come back if I'm needed, but you can handle any minor medical issues."

"You can't leave me to deal with stuff like that." Her voice rose. "How can you be so irresponsible!"

Daniel put a hand on her knee. "Sweetheart…"

"As if you would know a responsibility if it bit you on the butt," Trey retorted.

Sadie stood. "Daniel, do you want to help me choose some plants while these guys talk?"

Trey couldn't believe her nerve, taking advantage of him and Meg being caught up in an argument to get Daniel to herself.

Daniel glanced anxiously at Meg. "Maybe in a minute."

"Please?" Sadie coaxed.

The way she was smiling at him lit up her whole face.

"*I'll* choose some plants for you later," Trey said. "Stay right here."

She mouthed something at him that he didn't get, but sat down again.

"Why are you doing this to me?" Meg asked.

Trey groaned. Oddly, Sadie did, too, almost under her breath.

"You can't have just decided this out of the blue," Meg continued. Her eyes widened. "Is it about a woman? Did someone break your heart and now you're leaving to—?"

"There's no one left to break my heart," Trey interrupted. "All the fun girls left town. Only the un-fun ones are left." He directed a look at Sadie.

"Lexie's still around," Meg objected. "I see her all the time. Trey, maybe you should give her another try."

Trey had dated Sexy Lexie, as the guys used to call her, soon after he dropped out of college. "This isn't about me dating. It's about your need to grow—"

"Wasn't Lexie voted in high school most likely to die of overtanning?" Sadie asked quickly.

Not only was her question rude to Lexie, it was extraneous to his argument with his sister. But just like that, the tension evaporated and Trey found himself fighting a laugh.

Meg eyed her friend in surprise, but took the question seriously. "Lexie was Most Likely to Get Offered—and Accept—a *Playboy* Contract."

Trey wasn't surprised she remembered. His sister had loved every minute of high school, and had been a member of the prom court every year. But she'd had friends across the spectrum, and her popularity had never gone to her head. Those years were the last time Trey had truly liked her.

Her gaze softened, the hurt accusation leaving her eyes. "Trey, do you remember what you were voted most likely to do?"

"No," he lied.

"To play in the Super Bowl," she said sympathetically.

He shrugged. "Getting a football scholarship to Duke was a long way off that ambition. Who's to say I'd ever have got there?"

"I think you would." Great, now she'd turned supportive. She didn't realize her loyalty only made him more keenly aware of what he'd missed out on.

"You were voted most likely to marry a doctor," he said, to move things along.

Meg had declared in her junior year that she wanted to be a nurse so she could date hot doctors. She'd given up on the nurse ambition after Dad and Logan died, saying the job was ghoulish, but the doctor thing had stuck.

As Trey expected, that got Daniel's interest. "Were you, now?" he murmured.

Meg chortled. "Maybe."

Sadie scowled at Trey. Did he have to push Daniel at Meg like a Victorian father with twelve daughters to marry off? The way he was acting, you'd think Sadie was planning to seduce Daniel among the philodendrons.

All she'd wanted was to remove him from an argument destined to show Meg in the worst possible light.

"What were you voted most likely to do, Sadiebug?" Daniel asked.

"Actually—" she found herself smiling at the thought of how much Trey would hate this "—I was voted most likely to marry a doctor, too."

Trey's head jerked around. "You were not."

"Uh-huh." She smiled serenely.

Meg jumped in. "Sadie was really voted most likely to win a Nobel Prize, but the idiot doing the layout accidentally pasted the wrong caption beneath her photo. The typo wasn't noticed until after the yearbooks were printed." She winked at Sadie. "But maybe you should aim for a doctor rather than Nobel glory, anyway." She slid her hand down Daniel's thigh to his knee. "Doctors make the best kissers."

Sadie couldn't help it—she glanced guiltily at Daniel. And caught him doing the same to her.

Meg, gazing into her boyfriend's eyes, saw that look. She whipped her hand away. "Daniel?" Her voice was high. "Did you—did you kiss Sadie?"

CHAPTER SIX

TREY STRAIGHTENED. How had he done that? Without appearing to move, he became taller, fiercer.

Daniel was sweating bullets.

Sadie rubbed her palms against her shorts. "Uh, Meg, you know how I was on the rebound from Wesley, before you even met Daniel." Her voice caught, and she hoped it sounded like heartbreak over Wesley Burns, veterinarian to the animal stars.

Meg looked suspicious. Trey, of course, knew there was no Wesley. He was staring at Sadie as if she'd just laid one on Daniel, right there in front of his sister.

"Sadie and I did kiss," Daniel said. "Just once. But it was…" He gave Sadie a wry smile.

Amazing. "Terrible," Sadie said. *The best kiss of my life.* "Awful."

"I wouldn't say *awful.*" Daniel clutched his chest, mock-wounded. "But there was no spark."

The worst thing was, Sadie could see he meant it. About *that* kiss!

"Zilch," she chirped. "Nada." A warning look from Trey said she risked protesting too much.

Meg managed a cautious smile. "And this was before you and I met?" she confirmed with Daniel.

"Of course." He touched her cheek. "Once I met you…"

"Meg, why don't you and Daniel grab a coffee from the in-store café," Trey said. "Tell Pammy I said it's on the house. I'll help Sadie decide on some new plants."

The relief on Daniel's face added to Sadie's mortification. She held her breath until they'd left the office.

A rush of pain came with the exhalation. Her ribs throbbed as she stared after Daniel and Meg. It should be her holding his hand, sharing his coffee, having his babies…

"Sadie?" Trey touched her shoulder from behind, oddly gentle. "Thanks for that."

She blinked hard. "I didn't do it for you."

"I know." A pause. "You okay?"

"There *were* sparks, dammit." She hadn't intended to say that. Her shoulders shook.

"I'm sure there were." Trey's pitying tone was enough to dry her eyes.

She turned around, squinted at him. "You don't believe me."

"I don't see any chemistry between you and the doctor," he admitted.

"It was the best kiss," she said. "Major combustion."

"Sure it was," he soothed.

She swiped at a stray tear on her cheek. "I know what I'm talking about," she said scathingly. "I have kissed other men."

"Maybe you've been kissing the wrong ones."

Compared to Daniel, her previous relationships *had* been the wrong ones. And now the right man didn't want her. Sadie swayed. Trey took a step closer and cupped her elbows in his hands.

"What am I going to do with you?" he murmured.

Something about his tone, a huskiness...

"Not what you're thinking," Sadie said sharply.

It was totally illogical to assume Trey Kincaid wanted to kiss her. But his gray eyes were intense, focused on her lips, as they'd been yesterday morning.

To have a man look at her as if her mouth intrigued him, when Daniel had just made it painfully clear he was indifferent... She stiffened her backbone. "You like *fun* women, remember?"

"True," he said lightly. "But you're showing definite promise."

Her smile was unwilling. He wasn't Daniel—she didn't want him.

"I'm the geek next door," Sadie reminded him. "A know-it-all. And weird, to boot." None of the insults he'd lobbed her way this weekend had hurt the way Daniel's *no spark* comment had.

He furrowed his brow. "I should run screaming from the room." But his thumbs caressed the points of her elbows with short, firm strokes.

"Great idea." It came out in a harried breath. Sadie nodded toward the door and said more crisply, "Don't let me hold you up."

"This is *my* office." His hands moved to her shoulders in a slow glide that produced goose bumps all the way up her arms.

"Your air-conditioning is too low," she said. "The

ideal indoor ambient temperature without exposure to direct sunlight or drafts is sixty-eight degrees."

His mouth, much closer to hers than it should be, quirked. "I'll take it under advisement." Humor had softened the planes of his cheeks.

"I need to leave," Sadie said quickly.

And didn't move.

Trey's lips met hers.

Firmer than Daniel's was her first thought. Her lips moved and she kissed him back, just to verify her initial judgment. He nipped her bottom lip, startling her into parting her lips, and began an exploration of her mouth. Thought sizzled to nothing, like water on a hot stone, as his urgency drove hers, building a heat that cauterized her wounds.

This shouldn't be happening.

Sadie wrenched her mouth away. "Trey, stop!"

He obeyed instantly, leaping back from her as if she'd just announced she'd been exposed to anthrax. He bumped against a framed landscape diagram on the wall, tilting it on a crazy angle.

"Hell," he said.

Not the reaction she most liked to hear after a kiss. *Hell* had to be even worse than *hmm*. What was wrong with her, that men deemed kissing her either a nonevent or a mistake?

But he was right. This time it *was* a mistake. Her mistake.

"I'm sorry." She dropped her gaze so she couldn't see his dark hair, mussed in a way it hadn't been a minute ago. She didn't remember doing that.

"*You're* sorry?" He straightened the picture frame. "*I* kissed *you*."

"Yes, but I shouldn't have…" She closed her eyes. "I used you."

Stark silence.

"To compare the spark factor?" Anger was threaded beneath the words.

"No!" She couldn't even remember why. The whole episode was a blur of heat. "To—maybe to forget my troubles." And now she felt as if she'd cheated on Daniel. Which was stupid, stupid, stupid.

Trey shoved his hands into his pockets. "Troubles you've brought on yourself. Let it go, Sadie."

"Daniel *gets* me," she said. "He understands my work, he loves that I love it, just like he loves his job."

"Meg loves her job, too."

She ignored him. "He cares about giving back, he's close to his family. When I'm with him I'm totally at ease. We *fit*. I can't let go of something I think is meant to be."

To her surprise, she'd silenced him. He ran a hand over his hair to smooth it.

"So, once again, I'm sorry." Sadie touched her lips, oversensitized by his kiss. "For using you like that."

He scratched the back of his neck. "Forget it, Sadie. I already have."

BY MONDAY EVENING Sadie figured it was safe to say she'd survived. Trey hadn't enlightened Meg or Daniel about the late, unlamented Wes Burns, and her family had made no further reference to him. If they were worried about her single state, at least they knew it was by choice—she was the one who'd ended things with Wes.

Good grief, Wes isn't real! She picked up her pace as she carried her bag downstairs in preparation for the return to the city.

"You want some help with that bag, honey?" Her father emerged from the kitchen.

"It's fine, Dad." *I am woman. I am strong.* She huffed a little as she heaved the bag to the front door, which her dad opened.

Outside, the scene was a mirror of their arrival. Both families on the sidewalk, hugs all around. Daniel's arm around Meg, Trey standing to one side, thankfully not looking at Sadie. Because he might have forgotten about that kiss, but she was still plagued with guilt.

"It's been wonderful meeting you." Nancy squeezed Daniel's hands. "You seem like one of the family already."

Sadie cringed at Nancy's lack of subtlety, even as her mind rejected the prospect of Daniel ever being a part of Meg's family.

Too bad her mind had no say over the matter.

Because Daniel threaded his fingers through Meg's, beamed down at her and said, "Shall we tell them, sweetheart?"

No no no no no. The next seconds moved in slow motion, the universe disobeying all commands shouted in Sadie's head to cease and desist.

"Let's!" Meg said excitedly.

Her mother's countenance lit in anticipation, and slow smiles of delight broke on Sadie's parents' faces.

"That walk Meg and I took to the lagoon last night, under that full moon..." Daniel was clearly enjoying his elaborate scene setting; Sadie wanted to slap him.

"Daniel proposed and I said yes!" Meg squealed.

Daniel's protestations that they'd wanted to buy the ring before sharing the news were lost in a sea of congratulations.

I've lost him.

Sadie's chest felt hollow, as if someone had cut out her heart and forgotten to replace it. The buzz of conversation receded against the rushing in her ears.

She realized Trey had crossed the space between them and was now right beside her.

"You okay?" he murmured.

Without looking at him, she nodded, the barest movement of her chin that allowed her neck and shoulders to remain rigid. If she sagged even an inch, she might collapse.

He touched her arm, warning her it was her turn to hug Daniel (gingerly) and Meg (enthusiastically).

"Wonderful news," she lied. "I'm so excited."

"Me, too!" Meg gave Trey a smacking kiss on the cheek. "You finally got what you wanted, bro. I'm about to grow up once and for all."

"I'll believe it when I see it," Trey said.

"You won't have long to wait." Daniel shook Trey's hand. "We plan to marry in September."

"Three months to plan a wedding!" Nancy said in delighted horror.

Too soon! Too late! Ninety-some days of hell to endure.

"We've already made some decisions, Mom," Meg assured her. "Like, where we'll get married."

"We met with Reverend Charles at Cordova Colonial Presbyterian at lunchtime today," Daniel said.

"And we've chosen our maid of honor," Meg added slyly.

No no no no no.

You'd think Sadie would have realized by now that chanting in her head wasn't an effective tactic.

All eyes turned toward her.

"Fantastic!" she said with Oscar-winning enthusiasm.

CHAPTER SEVEN

SADIE DROVE HOME from work on Friday night with her hands clenched tightly around the steering wheel of her new Lexus compact. Like Daniel's car, it was a hybrid, though she considered hers an edgier choice.

She didn't want to think about Daniel.

Normally she'd retreat into thoughts of work, but work wasn't going well, either. She'd told her family she was excited by the wheat-protein project, but truth was, it had ceased to excite her months ago. What kept her awake at night was another scientific possibility. Wheat related, but far more experimental. Outlandish.

Sadie wasn't an outlandish person.

She'd mentioned her theory to her boss, asked for permission to investigate further. He'd turned her down flat—he was accountable to commercial partners who wouldn't invest in a project so far off the radar.

She could quit, find another lab that might let her conduct her research. But she loved SeedTech—it was like family.

She needed to talk through her options with someone who had her best interests at heart. Her parents would insist they qualified, but they wouldn't see any upside to professional risk. Meg claimed any discussion of Sadie's work gave her a headache. Daniel...well, he wasn't an appropriate confidant right now.

Sadie thumped the steering wheel. She shouldn't have argued with her boss today. She'd made him look stupid in front of his superior, the kind of thing people didn't forgive, guaranteeing that she'd struggle to get clearance for her new project even if her boss loved it. It was a crappy end to the worst week of her life.

"Get over it," she told herself out loud.

As if telling herself so would fix a broken heart. Her mom's cod-liver oil would have more chance.

"Enough," she scolded herself. She hated wallowers—if you had a problem, you should fix it.

She either had to accept she'd lost Daniel, or she had to do something about it. To show him and Meg they were making a big mistake.

That's what I'll do. I'll show them. I'll start tonight.

She swung into her driveway, careful as always to avoid a sidelong glimpse of her garden...and stamped on the brake.

Her crappy week had just got crappier.

A black truck filled her usual parking space. Trey's truck.

Sadie pressed the heel of her hand to the horn and blasted.

The door of the truck opened with deliberate slowness, and Trey climbed out. His worn jeans fit snugly and his light cotton plaid shirt, open at the neck, set off his tanned skin.

She buzzed her window down, stuck out her head. "You're blocking my driveway."

"Your deductive skills are amazing," he said. "That free Ivy League education was worth every penny."

"*Why* are you blocking my driveway?"

"Meg invited me to dinner. I hear Daniel's cooking."

"I wouldn't know," Sadie said stiffly. "They've been staying at Daniel's since we got back from Cordova." She grabbed her purse and laptop bag and got out of the car. "You came all the way into town just to see your sister?"

"It's not a long way," he pointed out. "But it so happens I had a meeting at the airport with an old friend who was passing through—a possible job opportunity."

"In garden design?" she asked, interested despite herself.

"No, not in garden design," he said, annoyed. "Why would you think that?"

"Because you designed that amazing landscape for Mrs. Jones, why else?" She locked the car using the beeper. "So did you get the job?"

"How was your day in genius land?" he asked.

"I'd tell you, but you wouldn't understand." Hmm, he didn't want to answer her question about the job. He must have missed out… She wondered what it was. If he was disappointed. Maybe he'd realize leaving his business and family was a dumb—

"Something else I don't understand." Trey's face and voice were hard. "What happened here?" The sweep of his hand encompassed her garden.

"What do you mean?" Sadie asked defensively.

He gazed around. "Words fail me."

"I'm hoping," she muttered.

"Your parents claim you have a 'wonderful, English-style cottage garden.'"

Which was the kind of neat, prissy, buttoned-down garden Trey would expect her to have. Not this bunch of bedraggled rhododendron bushes, a wizened rose or two, some dried-to-a-crisp box hedging and assorted shrubs too awful to mention.

"What did you use?" he asked. "Napalm?"

"No, but thanks for the idea." Her look said *he* would be the victim of any napalm she got her hands on.

"I take it your parents haven't seen this place?" The house itself looked nice enough—a Craftsman-style bungalow, with a deep porch framed by traditional heavy tapered brick pillars. But if her parents had seen the yard, they wouldn't be bragging about her gardening prowess.

"They visited a year ago, when I moved in." She kicked the tire of his truck. "Trey, please don't tell them what a disaster this place is."

"They could stop by anytime," he reminded her. "Maybe you should warn them."

She pffed. "My family think I live at the other end of the earth. No one's ever 'popped in.' I told Mom and Dad I'd invite them back when the garden's done."

Trey shook his head, mystified by her logic. "If you ask, they'll probably help you."

"No!" She paled. "This is a big deal to me. Don't tell them, please."

Trey thought fleetingly of all the years he'd been able to ignore Sadie.

He'd phoned his sister today partly to check up on Meg…but mostly because he couldn't stop thinking about Sadie's stoic, devastated face as she'd pretended to embrace her role as maid of honor.

Meg's dinner invitation had been the perfect opportunity to determine the lay of the land. He hadn't expected *the land* to be scorched earth.

"Why?" he asked. "Why is this so important?"

She set her laptop bag and purse at her feet. Heavily, as if their weight was too much. "Everyone in my family is mad about gardens."

"They're some of my best customers," he agreed. Her siblings all had accounts at Kincaid's, as did her parents.

"I love gardens, too," she said, "at least as much as they do. But I can't grow anything. I should be able to, and believe me, I've tried. But—" her hand swept toward the desolation of her front yard "—this is my dirty little secret."

She sounded so serious, he was tempted to laugh. "Sadie, you're not doing drugs or selling yourself on the streets. Making a mess of a garden isn't the worst thing you could do."

She plucked a leaf her rhododendron bush couldn't afford to lose. As she rolled it between her fingers, Trey recalled making "cigarettes" out of rolled-up leaves when they were kids. He'd have been about six, which made Meg and Sadie, his fellow "smokers," four. They'd sat around his mom's birdbath, puffing away in imitation of his dad, who'd kept up his roll-your-own habit until he died.

"When I was in college," Sadie said, "I did a couple of genetics classes. We carried out DNA tests on our hair, compared the results with a classmate's and came up with a statistical likelihood of being related to each other."

"Like a one in two billion chance," he suggested. The kind of numbers bandied around by defense lawyers in criminal trials on TV.

"Yeah." She opened her fingers, watched the leaf flutter to the ground. "Only, I didn't do my comparison with another student. I came home for a weekend and bagged a few hairs from Mom's hairbrush."

"Going after extra credit?" Trey asked.

She looked directly at him. "I thought I was adopted."

It took a moment for her words to sink in. Even then, they didn't make sense. "What?"

"I'm so different from the rest of my family," she said. "Every year that goes by, we seem to have less in common. I figured there had to be a scientific reason."

"There is," he said. "You have an extraordinary IQ, which led you to a different education, different kind of career…"

"That's sociological, not scientific."

He studied her face. "You have your mom's chin—" slightly pointy "—and your dad's eyes." Though he'd never thought of Gerry Beecham's eyes as delphinium-blue. "I assume the DNA test proved you were one hundred percent Beecham."

"Unless there was some literally freakishly coincidental commonality in our genetic profiles…"

"There wasn't," he said firmly.

"No." She sighed. "My folks say the same thing about the chin and the eyes. I always thought they were making it up. Just to be nice, to make me feel less of an outsider."

"You don't think I'm making it up?"

She slid him a glance. "You're not that nice."

Trey found himself smiling. "So, cupcake, if my inferior brain is following your logic correctly, you don't want your family to know you're a loser in the garden—" she scowled, and his smile widened "—because it'll rob you of the last link you imagine you have with them."

She nodded.

"You'll still have the chin," he comforted her.

"Gee, thanks."

He chucked her under said chin. "Come on, Sadie, be logical. You don't have to be the same as your family to feel a part of them." He didn't like the thought of her feeling so separate that she doubted her own genes.

"There has to be *some* commonality," she argued. "I'm determined to make this garden work on my own."

Trey clamped his mouth shut so he wouldn't be tempted to dispense advice. He wasn't the guy to advise about family relations, and it wasn't his problem if Sadie was the world's worst gardener. He was getting out of the garden business.

"I'm hungry." He bent to pick up her bags. "Let's go inside—I figure the house can't be as bad as the garden."

MEG HEARD SADIE's key in the front door, then her brother's voice.

She slid off the kitchen counter, where she'd perched to watch Daniel chopping green peppers. "Trey's here. And Sadie."

"Great." Daniel didn't look up from his task. He had no idea how important her brother's visit was to her. Meg didn't like that she hadn't discussed it with him, but a guy like Daniel, dedicated to doing the right thing, wouldn't understand.

She hurried out to the living room—the front door opened directly into the high-ceilinged space.

"Hey, guys," Meg said.

She waited until Trey had set Sadie's bags down, then went to hug him. After a moment of surprise, he returned the embrace. She could practically read his thoughts. *Didn't we just do this last weekend?*

Yes, but she wanted to remind him of the family ties that bound them. Inextricably.

"I'll go get changed," Sadie said.

Good—Meg needed time alone with Trey. But first... "I'll get the wine," she said. Her plan was to relax him with alcohol.

When she returned from the kitchen, a bottle of wine in one hand, four glasses threaded through the fingers of the other, he was still on his feet, examining the room. Cream-colored walls, polished oak floors with a charcoal rug in the trendy new shag, a large fireplace at the far end. The space was cheerful, with its red sofas. Homey. Meg would miss it.

It was a small price to pay for a new home with Daniel.

Joy bubbled up inside her at the prospect. "Did you have a good day?" she asked Trey as she handed him the bottle and the corkscrew.

He sliced through the foil cap in one clean movement and pulled it off. "It was fine." He began to twist the corkscrew into the cork. "I never realized Sadie has zero gardening talent. The garden was a shock."

Meg grimaced. "I know. She hates to talk about it. You won't mention it to her parents, will you?"

Deftly he pulled the cork from the bottle. "When did I ever snitch on either of you?"

"True," she agreed, pleased he'd come up with a positive memory.

"Has Sadie seriously tried to grow anything out there?" He handed her the wine.

"Everything," Meg said. "She even tried cactuses, which she hates, a couple of months back. The store promised they were indestructible—she was hopping mad when they wouldn't refund her money." She poured the wine and handed him a glass.

Trey frowned into his drink. "Customers who neglect their plants then try to blame their demise on the retailer are my least favorite people."

"Sadie doesn't neglect them," Meg assured him.

At that moment Sadie returned, wearing skinny jeans and a crossover T-shirt. Meg noticed how Trey's gaze lingered on her. She'd caught her brother staring at Sadie several times last weekend. Was it possible…? No, she couldn't think of two people less suited to each other than Trey and Sadie.

"I'll see if Daniel needs help in the kitchen," Sadie said.

"Great, thanks." Meg wanted privacy for her talk with Trey.

Her brother watched Sadie go. "Why don't we join them?"

Meg staged a yawn. "I worked a full 777 from Buenos Aires today. My feet are killing me." She sank onto the couch and propped her feet on the coffee table.

"Kitchen," Trey said, and walked away. Leaving Meg with no choice but to follow.

To her irritation, Trey insisted on hanging around while Sadie and Daniel finished preparing the meal. Sadie wasn't any more of a cook than Meg, but she willingly undertook what Daniel called the sous-chef tasks.

Twenty minutes later dinner was served—baked ham, coleslaw and buttered new potatoes.

"This coleslaw has just the right amount of crunch," Meg said appreciatively. "You two make a great culinary team."

Sadie's cheeks turned pink as she darted a glance at Trey.

Sadie liked Trey! Meg had to struggle not to laugh.

"How are the wedding plans going?" Trey barked.

Meg raised her eyebrows, but resisted teasing him. She needed his goodwill. "Easy peasy," she said. "It's mostly done."

"Not mostly, sweetheart." Daniel spooned cranberry relish onto his plate. "Your mom has a list a mile long."

Meg gave him an indulgent look—they all knew Nancy would do the work, not her. "There are a few things still left to organize," she admitted. "We have a dress fitting next week, remember, Sadie?" To Trey, she explained, "I didn't have enough time to get a custom-made dress, but I found the perfect one and it only needs a little altering. And they have a really nice selection of bridesmaids' dresses. Reasonably priced," she added, since the family business was doubtless paying for the wedding.

"I'll be there," Sadie said brightly. "Just don't put me in pastel pink."

"I'm thinking turquoise for you," Meg said. "What do you all think of that?"

Sadie nodded.

"I have no idea," Daniel said. "But you'll look beautiful whatever you wear, Sadiebug."

Meg loved his chivalry.

"How many bridesmaids are there?" Trey said tightly.

"Just Sadie and Lexie," she said.

"My mom wants to come along to the fitting," Daniel said. "She thought it's a good chance to get to know you better."

"Wonderful," Meg lied. Which she excused on the basis that Daniel was telling a white lie, too. His mother, Angela, had made it clear Meg wasn't the kind of girl she wanted for Daniel. Meg had no doubt her attending the fitting was Daniel's idea.

"Trey, we wanted to ask you to give Meg away at the wedding," Daniel said.

"I'd be delighted," Trey said. "I don't suppose they'll let me physically wash my hands of you during the service?" he joked to Meg.

Ha, ha. "I'll ask the minister," she said sweetly. "We have an appointment for premarital counseling tomorrow."

"Right after our appointment at the jeweler—we're choosing an engagement ring." Daniel reached across the table for Meg's hand. He caressed her bare ring finger. As always, his touch made her tingle from head to toe.

"So soon?" Sadie blurted.

Meg stared at her.

"I mean, don't you want to think about the ring for a while?" Sadie asked.

"If we wait much longer we won't have one before the wedding," Meg said. "We've looked at a lot online. I think we have a good idea what we want."

Daniel tugged her hand to his lips and kissed it.

"Who's your date for the wedding, Sadie?" Trey asked, his voice sharp.

Meg smirked.

"I'm not seeing anyone." Sadie fidgeted with her knife.

"Still pining for Wes?" Trey asked coolly.

Sadie's eyes narrowed, but she didn't reply.

Once again Meg felt a twinge of hurt that Sadie hadn't told her about her romance with Wes. But maybe Meg had been so caught up in her excitement about Daniel she hadn't paid as much attention to Sadie's life as she should. Maybe a little fling with Trey would help Sadie get over Wes.

"Sadie, how about we set you up with that friend of Daniel's I mentioned?" she suggested, hoping to spur Trey into action.

Manipulating Trey had never worked.

"Great idea, Sadie," he said. "Get back on the horse."

Meg gave him a warning frown. If he was interested in Sadie, he needed to do better than that. As if he'd ever take advice from her.

Sadie forked a mouthful of coleslaw. "You're right," she said after she swallowed. "I should date someone new. Trouble is, I'm not great with first dates." She set down her fork. "Meg, maybe you and Daniel could double-date with me and Daniel's friend, just to get us started."

"Great idea, Sadiebug." Daniel raised his glass to her. "One double date, coming up."

"That'd be so cool," Meg said. "If you hit it off with him we can all hang out together."

Trey looked distinctly annoyed, but Meg couldn't swear he was jealous.

"Where do you two plan to live after the wedding?" he asked.

She should be used to his abrupt changes of subject; he'd had no patience with her since Dad and Logan died.

"My place is big enough for now," Daniel said. "Until we have kids." His tender smile was balm on the sting of Trey's brusqueness.

"Kids will be a few years away." Meg had seen a flare

of surprise on Sadie's face. "We need to get to know each other first."

"Which could take a while, given you're away so much," Sadie said. "You're barely here."

She really must be feeling neglected.

"My absence keeps the place tidy, at least," Meg quipped. Daniel was as tidy as Sadie. Hopefully he'd be equally flexible about clearing up after her when the mess got too much for him.

"True," Sadie said. "Though I admit it can get lonely here on my own—you think you're living with someone, but half the time you're not."

Trey let out a hiss.

Daniel looked disconcerted. "We're thinking Meg will switch to ground staff sooner rather than later, aren't we, darling?"

"Sooner *or* later," Meg amended.

"But you love to fly," Sadie said.

She was right—Meg couldn't imagine not being able to take off every week. She sipped her wine. "I guess everyone needs to compromise sometime…which is what I want to talk to you about, Trey."

The lead-in was far from ideal, but at this stage of the night she couldn't see a chance to talk to him alone.

"What's that?" He was giving Sadie the evil eye for some unknown reason, and he didn't look at Meg.

"This plan of yours to skip town—you need to change it."

Meg found herself with the undivided attention of everyone at the table.

"Excuse me?" Trey said.

She didn't allow his glacial expression to put her off. This had been possibly the happiest week of her life, hands down the happiest week of the past eleven years, and if she could just convince Trey to stick around, it would be perfect.

"Trey, I get that you want a new job, no problem," Meg said urgently. "But Mom needs you here. She might say she's okay, but who knows when the next stroke will hit?" She grabbed his arm, which unfortunately caused his wine to slop over the edge of his glass.

"Hey!" He used his napkin to mop the puddle on the table. "Of course I'll come back if I'm needed."

"But…" She cast an agonized look at Daniel. Couldn't her idiot brother make the effort to figure out what she was trying to say? "If Mom had to go into the hospital…"

"You'll be fine," he said.

Meg had the impression he was enjoying her discomfort. Jerk!

"Sweetheart, are you okay?" Daniel asked.

She pressed her fingers to her temples. "Trey, I'm the first to admit you've had to bear the brunt of the responsibility in our family. But if you're leaving just so you can punish me—"

"Don't be stupid," he said, his face flushed. "I've worked my tail off at a job I don't particularly like to secure my family's future. The years after Dad died went into keeping the business going, then sending you to college, then building the firm into something that can provide for Mom in the long term and cover any emergencies. I've done my time. Now I'm finished."

"But where will you go?" Meg knotted her fingers in her lap.

He sat back, challenging her with his gaze. "It's as easy as ABC," he said. "Anywhere But Cordova."

Damn. She'd handled this wrong. She was casting around for another argument when Sadie spoke up.

"Trey, Meg won't cope if your Mom gets sick."

"Sadie!" Meg said, mortified. It was the point she was trying to make, but not so blatantly. Not in front of Daniel.

To her surprise, Trey looked just as appalled.

"That's it!" he barked at Sadie. "Out in the kitchen."

Sadie looked down her nose at him.

"Now," he growled. "Or I'll tell—"

She jumped to her feet and stalked from the room.

Tell *what?* Meg wondered.

Trey folded his napkin with deliberate movements that suggested a man summoning restraint. Then he stacked their empty plates with the same controlled force and carried them to the kitchen.

The heated exchange and his methodical clearing away had combined to kill the conversation about Meg's ability to support her mom through an illness.

"What was that about?" Daniel asked, looking after Trey.

"I think—" relief lightened Meg's voice "—they like each other."

CHAPTER EIGHT

"YOU'RE TRYING TO break Meg and Daniel up," Trey accused Sadie as soon as the kitchen door closed behind him.

She didn't pretend ignorance. "I'm pointing out some of the factors they may not have considered in their rush to get engaged. Such as, Meg enjoys her job far too much to be grounded."

He put the plates on the counter and opened the dishwasher. "More grounded is exactly what she needs."

"Daniel told me he hates living alone—which is what he'll be doing when Meg's flying." She stacked the plates in the machine.

Trey clattered silverware into the cutlery basket, then looked around for more dishes. The counter was clear. The pans had been washed and put away.

"Daniel hates mess." Sadie followed his gaze, read his mind. "I love Meg, but she's a slob."

"He loves her, too," Trey pointed out.

Sadie flinched. "I've had years to adapt and I'm not planning to live with her forever. Daniel doesn't know her. Someone needs to point out the facts. To both of them."

Trey tipped the remainder of his wine down the sink and put his glass in the dishwasher. "All I see is you desperately scrabbling for reasons why Meg shouldn't marry the man *you* want."

Sadie poured powder into the dispenser. "I just don't think two people so totally unsuited should rush into marriage."

"Next you'll say you're just being a good friend," he mocked.

She closed the dishwasher door so fast, she almost took his hand off. "I *am* a good friend. I've always been the one to point out dangers to Meg."

That was true. It was thanks to Sadie that Meg hadn't driven home from a party one summer with a senior who'd been drinking. Two other girls had been injured in the ensuing crash. And Sadie's predictions of stained teeth had led Meg to abandon a brief flirtation with smoking, after Trey's and his mom's lung-cancer warnings had achieved nothing.

"This is nothing like telling Meg not to smoke when she was a kid," he said. "She and Daniel are adults—they can make their own decisions."

"Their own mistakes," she corrected him.

Here on her own territory she was more collected than she'd been at her parents' place. So confident she was almost starting to sound reasonable.

"You have way too big a conflict of interest to get involved," he said.

"Think of it as a science experiment. I have a hypothesis—Meg and Daniel are making a mistake—that I'll test by asking questions. If they're right for each other, my questions won't make any difference. And if they're wrong, they'll appreciate—"

"And if they're wrong for each other," he interrupted, "you'd take Daniel after he's been with Meg?"

She paused, her finger on the dishwasher's start button. "He's had a few weeks with her. Intense weeks, yes. But in the big picture, the rest of his life, that's nothing."

Trey put his finger over hers and pressed to turn the dishwasher on. Hard.

"Ow." She pulled away.

"I can't decide if I admire your single-mindedness or if I feel sorry for you."

She drew in a breath. "Just as well your opinion doesn't matter to me. And that you have no say over my life."

He loomed over her. "Where my sister's concerned..."

"Stop," she ordered. "I don't know why you're so determined to interfere, when you don't have the first clue about Meg. You don't even know she hates to be around sick people." Her voice was furious, but low enough to be covered by the noise of water spraying in the dishwasher.

Trey snorted. "*That's* your excuse for trying to make her look unsympathetic in front of Daniel? You were covering for her squeamishness?"

"That's not exactly it," she hedged. "But when she hears about people being ill or having an accident, she always goes into denial about how sick they are. I remember one time my doctor thought I might have meningitis, and Meg flat out refused to discuss it. She insisted it was flu and I didn't need to go to the hospital."

"What was it?" he asked, alarmed at the thought of Sadie—of anyone—having meningitis.

"Flu," she admitted.

"Dammit, Sadie!" Relief roughened his voice. "All you've proved is that Meg has good instincts. The reason she doesn't want to stick around if Mom's sick isn't squeamishness. She said herself she's never had to take responsibility, which I admit is partly my fault. And she doesn't want to start now—but that's too damned bad."

Sadie stared.

"What?" he asked.

"*That's* why you're convincing yourself Daniel and Meg are right for each other. You want Meg to grow up, and you'll marry her off to the wrong man, then leave town to make it happen."

"I'm not marrying her off, and my leaving town has nothing to do with her." He leaned against the counter. "But you're damn right it's time she grew up. So don't tell me I shouldn't leave because she has a hang-up about illness."

"There are lots of good reasons you shouldn't leave," she snapped.

He groaned. "Please don't enlighten me."

"Your mom thinks the sun rises and sets on you, Meg loves you even though you're mean to her, you're part of a family business that links you with your father and your brother forever. You have no idea—" she poked him in the chest "—how lucky you are."

He grabbed her wrist and tugged, jerking her close to him. "Don't. Do. That."

His knuckles grazed the soft curve of her breasts; she tensed. Trey didn't back away.

"It's eleven years since Dad and Logan died," he said evenly. "Aside from that first year and a bit at college, I haven't done any of the things I planned. I've been living my father's life, my brother's life...anyone's but mine."

"It's too late to resume your football career."

"I know that." He eyed her with hostility.

"So...what? Your leaving is about sowing your wild oats?"

"Do you really think I'm that one-dimensional?" he asked.

"Aren't you?" She dropped her gaze to where his knuckles still touched her breast.

He let out a huff of laughter. "Touché." And didn't move.

She smiled. And didn't move.

"Mind you," he mused, "I can't promise there won't be any wild oats sown."

"Does your mother know about this?"

His shout of laughter must have been audible in the dining room. "The fact that my mother, along with everyone else around here, knows too much about my life is the whole point."

"So you plan to go wild."

"I plan to find a job I really love," he said. "But if I meet a few nice women along the way..."

"*Nice* being a euphemism for slutty," she guessed. Humor made her eyes a brighter, forget-me-not blue.

"You have a way with words," he deadpanned.

His hand still snug against her chest, he felt the quiver

of her laugh. Sensation shot through him, conjuring up the memory of that kiss in his office, a memory he'd thought he'd firmly expunged. Now he remembered the heat of her mouth, the imprint of her body against his...

Trey relinquished his grip, stepped away.

With the fingers of her other hand, Sadie circled her wrist where he'd held her. "Trey, be careful," she said, serious again. "What if you go away, and when you want to come back, it's too late?"

"You mean Mom's health?"

"I mean what if you grow apart? You have something really special with your mom. It would be sad to lose it."

As far as Trey knew, he had the same ups and downs with his mom as anyone else did with theirs. Probably a few more downs.

Sadie was biting on that lush bottom lip of hers. *I've definitely been here too long if I'm thinking of Sadie-next-door as lush.*

"You told me I've been in Cordova too long," he reminded her. "That night you were looking in Mom's windows."

She colored. "I didn't mean you should leave. I'm worried for you."

Trey blinked, oddly touched. "Do you think you're putting your own feelings onto my situation?" he asked. "Just because you grew apart from your family doesn't mean I will. Not least because Mom won't have other kids to cozy up to, especially once Meg's married."

The mention of Meg's impending marriage put an immediate distance between them.

Sadie grabbed the kettle and began to fill it from the faucet.

Trey ran a hand through his hair. "I don't know how we got so far off topic."

"We were talking about you wanting Meg to marry Daniel because it suits your plans."

Trey sighed. "We're not going to agree on that, but can we at least agree that due to your conflict of interest, you should refrain from pointing out what you consider their insurmountable differences?"

"I didn't say they were insurmountable," she prevaricated.

"Their noninsurmountable differences, then."

She turned off the faucet. "Okay."

"Okay?" he said suspiciously. "Why do I get the feeling that was too easy?"

She set the kettle on the stove. "I'll agree not to point out Meg's and Daniel's noninsurmountable differences, but in exchange I want Wes Burns dead and buried."

"Poor Wes," Trey said.

"I mean it, Trey. No more mention of him, and no threatening to tell Meg or Daniel the truth about him."

"Okay." This still felt too easy. "So we're agreed," he clarified, "that Wes Burns's name will never cross my lips again. And you won't say anything else about Meg being afraid of sick people or traveling too much, or about Daniel getting lonely."

"That's right," she said patiently.

So why did he have the feeling he was missing something?

"Sadie," he warned, not sure exactly what he was warning her against.

She sighed theatrically. "Tell you what, as a sign of good faith, I also promise not to spill coffee over the wedding dress, lace the cake with rat poison or kidnap the best man." She sauntered to the door, stuck her head out. "Do you guys want coffee?" she called.

"You're scary," Trey said from behind her. Despite her promise, he made a mental note to keep an eye on the wedding dress, the cake and the best man.

He still felt as if he was missing something. He kept thinking about it while he and Sadie made coffee, assembled mugs, milk, sugar, spoons. At some stage he realized he was having a good time.

Doing battle with Sadie, guessing what she'd do next, trying to outwit her, was the most fun he'd had since… since he'd helped Mrs. Jones with her garden design.

Go figure.

CHAPTER NINE

"AND THAT'S IT. Profit up twenty-five percent on the same quarter last year, on revenue that's up eighteen." Trey closed the red budget folder that had been around since his father's time and slid it across the boardroom table to his mom. The numbers were all on the computer, but Nancy preferred paper.

She patted his hand. "This calls for cake."

The "boardroom" was his mom's kitchen, and the table was part of the scarred oak dining set where Trey had taken for granted countless meals when his family had been intact. His mother helped out packing orders at the main branch of Kincaid Nurseries one day a week, but she liked to discuss the financial side here at home.

"I made red velvet," Nancy said over her shoulder as she opened the refrigerator.

"Sounds great, Mom." Red velvet cake was Meg's favorite. His, too.

A minute later he was facing a large slab of cake and a cup of steaming coffee, two things whose contribution to his well-being were disproportionate to their value.

Out of courtesy, he used the fork his mom had supplied. "This is sensational," he said around a mouthful of cream-cheese frosting and moist cake. "What's the occasion?"

His mom shrugged. "Do we need one? How about another quarter of great results in the business?"

How about the last quarterly report he would deliver?

"I'll drink to that." Trey raised his mug in a toast, then drank his coffee.

Nothing to keep him here now. He could leave tomorrow. If he was so inclined.

Nancy glanced at the clock on the stove. "I'm heading to the city soon. I need to be on the road by five past."

She sipped her coffee, and silence fell. Trey noticed a downturn in her mouth.

"Everything okay?" he asked. "Meg and Daniel still engaged?"

She paled. "Why? Do you know something I don't?"

"Of course not," he said quickly. "How are the wedding plans?"

"Fine, apart from the fact I seem to be doing all the work." Which might explain the dark circles under her eyes.

"You should insist Meg helps you." As if that would ever happen.

"She's never here, thanks to that job of hers. Besides, a girl only gets married once," Nancy said, letting Meg off the hook for the millionth time.

"Or twice," Trey said. "Or three—"

His mom swatted his shoulder. "Cynic. I believe this will be my daughter's one and only wedding, so I'm more than happy to do the work."

"She doesn't know Daniel very well." It irked Trey to

voice Sadie's doubts. But it didn't hurt to sound out an objective observer.

"I'd only known your dad two weeks when he told me we'd get married one day." His mom's smile turned dreamy.

Trey could have kicked himself. They'd been having a perfectly good conversation about the present, and somehow he'd triggered a return to his mother's glorious past. Mind you, just about everything did that.

"Meg emailed some photos," Nancy said. "I printed them off." She went to the telephone and retrieved several sheets of paper from the tray on the shelf beneath it. "Take a look."

The first photo was a close-up of Meg's hand sporting a large diamond on her ring finger. The next few were taken in a setting he recognized—Sadie's living room.

Pictures of Meg and Daniel, as he expected. But his snap-happy sister had also taken shots of Sadie with Daniel, laughing and kidding around. The last photo showed all three of them at Cordova Colonial Presbyterian, where the wedding would take place. Daniel had an arm around each woman.

Daniel's nuts about Meg, Trey assured himself. Yeah, but this whole relationship was so sudden, how deeply rooted could his feelings be? And Meg...she was cute, she was fun, but she had the stickability of a Post-it note.

Could they withstand the tensions inevitable in any relationship?

"Sadie thinks Meg and Daniel have nothing in common," he told Nancy.

The corollary—Sadie and Daniel had a lot in common. Sadie's stupid crush actually made sense.

Even if she *had* responded to Trey's kiss in a way no woman in love with another guy should.

Dammit, he wasn't going to think about that.

"I'm not so sure Meg and Daniel are that different," Nancy demurred.

"Daniel's responsible," Trey continued. "And steady and thoughtful."

His mom eyed him reproachfully. "You think your sister could hold down her job if she wasn't those things?"

"I guess," he muttered, foregoing a more definite answer, since he'd often wondered precisely that. Heaven help Meg's passengers if she should ever have to evacuate the plane in an emergency. She was too used to being the one rescued.

"It's true Daniel could lighten up a little," Nancy said. "But Meg will see to that."

As Trey saw it, his sister needed less frivolity, not Daniel more.

"In many ways Daniel reminds me of Logan," his mom said.

Trey managed not to roll his eyes. Maybe one day they might get through a conversation without his mom touting his brother as the paragon of every virtue.

"Logan was levelheaded like that," Nancy continued. "He had that courteous charm about him, too."

Unlike Trey, who could be churlish and frequently was. He grunted churlishly.

"Logan was passionate about his work, the same way

Daniel is," she said. "That's very attractive in a man—it's part of why I fell for your father." His parents had still been in high school when they met—Nancy's parents had hired Brian Kincaid to work in their garden after school.

Easy for his mom to talk about a passion for one's work. Of course Dad and Logan had been passionate... they'd *chosen* their profession. Trey had been railroaded into it at a time when running a garden center was bottom of his list of One Thousand Things to Do Before I Die. It hadn't risen much higher in the intervening years.

He pushed his chair back. "Thanks for the cake, Mom. I gotta go."

Nancy looked at him in a way that suggested he'd disappointed her yet again, merely by not being his brother. Well, he never would be Logan, and he was used to being second best. Hell, he'd made a career of it.

"So now that you have me worried, you're going to leave?" she asked.

"Uh..."

"You're right, your sister can be flighty." Nancy set down her fork. "Daniel's a wonderful man and I believe he loves her deeply. I'd hate the wedding to be derailed by Meg's emotional flip-flopping."

Had his mom just admitted Meg was a spoiled brat?

Trey leaned his chair back on two legs. "I'll do everything I can to help keep things on an even keel." Including managing the maid of honor.

"How will you do that if you're not here?" Nancy asked.

"I'm doing it already. And after I leave I'll stay in

touch via email and cell phone." If only to make sure Sadie wasn't reneging on their deal.

Nancy pushed her plate away. "Trey, I want you to stick around until Meg gets married."

Trey's chair crashed down on all four legs. "Mom, no, I have plans." And the wedding was two months away.

"Your plans aren't fixed in stone yet, are they? I haven't heard anything about a job."

That's because he wanted everything signed and sealed before he revealed his plans.

"That's not the point," he said. "I promise I'll be back for the wedding, and in the meantime I'll give you and Meg my full moral support."

"I've never understood why you have to leave in the first place," his mom said fiercely. "You want a break from the garden centers, fine. You certainly deserve one. But why not stick around Memphis?"

"Apart from that one year in college, I've never lived anywhere else. I've barely had time to vacation out of state."

"Memphis is good enough for the rest of us." His mom knuckled her forehead. "I didn't mean to sound like that. It's just…I'll miss you."

"You'll have a new son-in-law to get to know. Dan strikes me as a guy who'll become part of the family fast."

"Daniel," his mom corrected.

See, the doctor already had her taking his side. Ugh, that was childish. "Going away will give me some perspective," Trey said. He didn't add that sticking around was making him bitter.

"You're the last person I thought would need to go find himself," his mom said.

How could she say that? He'd been living by everyone else's expectations for so long he had no idea what he expected of himself.

"So will you stay?" she asked. "Help make sure this wedding happens? Please, Trey."

Stay was the last thing he wanted to do. But maybe... to set his mom's mind at rest.

Besides, he really did want Meg to settle down, though he knew that wasn't noble or bighearted.

"Yeah," he said. "I'll stay."

His mom's delighted hug made him feel a tiny bit better about the decision.

"Okay, now I need to go," Nancy said. "I'm taking Meg's wedding shoes to the dressmaker for the fitting."

"Didn't she try the shoes on when she bought them?"

"She needs to try them with the dress, silly. To get the length right."

Wedding dress.

"Is this the fitting the bridesmaids are going to?" he asked.

"Of course. You're not still interested in that trashy Lexie, are you?" His mom shot him a disapproving look.

Sadie would be at the fitting. Sadie, the maid of honor who'd promised to stop planting doubts in the mind of the bride.

Did he trust her?

Hell, no.

If he was going to stick around to fight Meg's battles, he might as well cover all the bases. And have some fun in the process.

"Where are those shoes?" Trey asked his mom.

SADIE PULLED UP OUTSIDE Bride Beautiful just as Lexie Peterson was entering the store. From behind, she looked no different than she had ten years ago—long blond hair, long slender legs.

Sadie wondered if Lexie was still the same on the inside: too cool for her own good, looking down on anyone less glamorous.

It was lucky the two of them had attended different schools, so their dislike of each other had never been too blatant. During summer vacations they'd put up with each other for Meg's sake. They'd dropped the pretense right after graduation—Sadie hadn't seen Lexie since, though she'd answered the phone to her a few times. And quickly passed the phone to Meg, who flitted with ease between Sadie's small, quieter crowd and Lexie's party crowd.

Sadie pulled her key from the ignition. What did it matter if Lexie had changed or not? She could tolerate the woman, so long as Meg was there as a buffer.

Sadie's cell phone buzzed. Meg.

"Let me guess, you're late," Sadie said. Would she have to make small talk with Lexie, or could she hide out here in the car?

"Worse," Meg said. "Three of my colleagues were involved in a shuttle crash on the way to the airport. Only moderate injuries, but I've been called up for a flight to Tucson."

Sadie quashed her instant relief—it was clearly inappropriate to celebrate a traffic accident. "Of course you need to go," she said. "I'll tell the store we're postponing the fitting."

"Don't do that," Meg said swiftly. "We're already running out of time to get my dress altered. Irena is worried about the length—can you try it on for me?"

"Try on your wedding dress?" Sadie squawked.

"Uh-huh." The blare of a car horn came down the line, followed by a curse from Meg.

"Don't crash," Sadie said. "Meg, isn't it bad luck to have someone else wear your wedding dress?"

"It's worse luck to be injured in a shuttle crash," Meg retorted. "Come on, Sadie, I'm flying every other day this week. Mom's on her way to the store with my shoes right now—she'll be there by quarter to. Try on the dress with the shoes and that's one less thing for me to worry about."

Heaven forbid that Meg should actually have to worry about something, Sadie thought acerbically. Ugh, she was starting to sound like Trey. "Your feet are bigger than mine," she said.

"It's the length of the dress that matters and we're the same height."

"But—" Sadie pulled herself up. If anyone should take on this task, it should be the maid of honor.

"Of course I'll do it," she said. Another blast of a horn came through the phone. "You watch the road. I'm hanging up now."

"One more thing," Meg said quickly. "Don't forget, the dragon will be there, too. I mean, Daniel's mom."

"You call her the dragon?"

"She doesn't like me," Meg said. "Can you say nice things about me? Tell her I'm perfect for Daniel?"

"Uh..." Sadie said.

"Thanks!" Meg hung up.

Sadie's thumb was slippery on the phone's End button. Which was ridiculous. Trying on a wedding dress was no big deal. And she could tell Daniel's mother that Meg was perfect for him. It wasn't as if she'd never lied before.

Anyway, Meg was likely imagining her future mother-in-law's dislike. It was probably tradition.

Sadie pushed herself out of the car on leaden feet.

Irena herself opened the door of the appointment-only boutique and was dismayed to hear the bride couldn't make it. She treated the shuttle crash as if it were a personal inconvenience and only grudgingly accepted Sadie's offer to try on the dress for length.

"We're the same height, but if you'd rather wait until Meg can be here, that's fine," Sadie said hopefully.

"No. You will do it." Irena's Russian accent made it sound like an order, with disobedience punishable by firing squad. "Come, other bridesmaid is here already."

When they reached the fitting-room area, it turned out Daniel's mom was already there, too.

"Angela, so nice to see you." Sadie went to shake Angela Wilson's hand, but the older woman kissed her cheek.

"Sadie, dear, what a pleasure." Angela was just as charming as Sadie remembered.

"Hi, Lexie," Sadie said.

"Sadie! I haven't seen you in forever!" Unexpectedly, Lexie hugged her. On instinct, Sadie pulled away, then got a grip on herself in time to pat Lexie on the back and kiss the air in the vicinity of her cheek.

"You look great." Lexie's smile was wide and white.

"Thanks." Sadie tensed as she waited for the kicker. *You look great...for a geek. You look great...beige is really your color—giggle.* Maybe wearing her beige suit today hadn't been a good idea, even if it was Donna Karan.

Lexie was still looking her up and down. Sadie's palms were damp—crazy that someone she hadn't seen in years could make her feel such an outcast.

"Did you always have such amazing legs?" Lexie asked.

"Uh..." Sadie stepped back and almost stumbled—on her amazing legs—into a rack of bridal veils.

"This is so bad," Lexie chirped. "The smartest girl in town ends up with the best legs. How fair is that?"

Sadie was aware of Daniel's mother listening in, her expression carefully neutral.

"It's, uh, my legs are pretty average." She smoothed down her above-the-knee beige skirt. Her legs were in fact pretty good. But having Lexie say so was weirding her out. Maybe it was the setup for an elaborate joke.

Irena pulled aside a heavy taffeta curtain into a shared changing room. She and her staff had hung several choices of bridesmaid dresses—different styles and colors—in the changing room.

"Turquoise for you." Irena gave Sadie a little push toward the turquoise corner. "And yellow for the blonde."

"Goodness." Daniel's mom eyed the array. "Meg has colorful taste, doesn't she?"

Meg did have colorful taste...but Angela's comment didn't sound like a compliment.

"Meg has gorgeous taste," Lexie insisted, and Sadie felt guilty she hadn't been quicker with her own rebuttal.

"*Fabulous* taste," she agreed, not exactly to outdo Lexie, but to emphasize that Angela couldn't criticize the bride and get away with it.

Still, if the tension between Meg and Angela was based on personal style, Sadie didn't think it was too big a deal.

"Get started, ladies," Irena ordered. "I will return in five minutes." She didn't physically set a stopwatch, but Sadie had the impression the timing would be exact.

The flurried removal of clothing ended the conversation. Sadie had never been the sort to try on a dozen different outfits if there was one she liked; she concentrated on getting into the turquoise dress that most appealed to her without snagging the gauzy overskirt. She reached behind her to zip up just as Irena came back.

The Russian woman clapped her hands twice. "Let me see you, ladies."

Sadie and Lexie turned on command. Sadie felt as if she should salute, as a member of the Bridesmaids' Battalion.

"Oh, my gosh!" Lexie slapped a hand to her forehead. "Sadie Beecham, you grew great boobs, too. I can't believe it. Last time I saw you, you had nothing! What are you—34C?"

"Er, yes." Sadie cringed at the thought of Angela listening to all this. Daniel's mother was a psychologist— she was probably drawing all kinds of conclusions about both Sadie and Lexie.

"Same as me." Lexie winked, welcoming Sadie into the 34C Sisterhood. "This is so cool, seeing you again."

"Cool," Sadie echoed. She wasn't sure she'd ever used that word in her teens, let alone recently. Had Lexie forgotten the years of judging her and finding her *not* cool enough to be part of the gang? Did that mean Sadie should forget them, too?

Sadie was pleased with her own dress, but Lexie looked truly gorgeous with her blond hair tumbling about her shoulders, and her flawless skin set off by the deep yellow.

"Keep still," Irena admonished her, "while I make some tucks. We want your beautiful figure to shine."

Disobeying orders, Lexie gave a little shimmy and winked at Sadie in the mirror. "So, Meg tells me you're single, Sadie? You broke up with someone recently? A vet?"

"Yes." Sadie cursed Trey and his imagination. "But I'm fine about it."

"Plenty more fish in the sea, right?" Lexie's chuckle verged on bawdy. "Have you met Daniel's groomsmen?"

"Not yet." Sadie sensed Angela Wilson stiffening in horror. "But I'm not really looking for someone." *Anyone other than the groom.*

"That's when you find the best guys," Lexie said wisely. "When you're not looking. Smart girl." She fidgeted, earning a tut from Irena. "I can't wait to see Trey. It must be three years since we last got together."

What exactly did *got together* mean? Sadie wondered. "I wouldn't say Trey's a good relationship bet," she heard herself say discouragingly. Why not put the kibosh on a flirtation between Trey and Lexie, since he was so determined to stop Sadie getting her man.

"Oh, I know." Lexie laughed. "But he's so hot, it's always worth a try."

Behind Lexie, Angela's eyes met Sadie's. The older woman shuddered. Presumably she didn't think much of Meg's taste in friends, either. That might make the wedding less pleasant, but it didn't matter in the long run.

"Just don't let Meg arrange your date with Trey," Sadie advised Lexie.

Lexie clapped a hand to her mouth. "Oh, my gosh, you remember that. The Millennial Centennial dance."

"I believe the incident merits a whole chapter in the history of Cordova."

Lexie stared, then snickered. "You're a hoot. When did you get so funny?"

This was surreal. Sadie felt as if she was in a coming-of-age movie, where any moment now Lexie would tearfully confess that all through high school she'd envied

Sadie. For her brain. And because Meg liked Sadie better.

"You were so boring back in the day," Lexie said.

Or not.

"And, frankly, snooty," Lexie added. "But Meg always said you're not like that deep down and I should give you a chance."

Sadie realized her mouth was hanging open. She swallowed. "That's good advice."

Irena finished with Lexie's dress and moved on to Sadie. *The woman must see and hear just about everything in her line of work,* Sadie thought.

"What do you plan to wear to the wedding, Angela?" she asked Daniel's mother.

"I haven't thought about it." Mrs. Wilson's tone said *I don't really care.*

Come on, everyone liked Meg. *Loved* her.

Sadie darted a glance at Lexie to see if she thought there was anything odd about the woman. Lexie's eyes were narrowed.

"I think it's great the way Meg makes Daniel so happy," Sadie said. Theoretically, she did think that. She just couldn't stomach it in practice.

"They're the perfect couple," Lexie added.

She and Lexie were on the same side. Who'd have thought?

"Absolutely." Angela tried to sound enthusiastic, but Sadie took it with a grain of salt.

Daniel was an only child, very close to his parents. If his mom didn't like Meg, it could make their married life difficult.

"Are you and Dr. Wilson looking forward to the wedding?" she asked. Confusingly, everyone in Daniel's family was called Dr. Wilson. His dad was a neurologist.

"Of course," Angela said. "We're both very pleased for Daniel. Though the suddenness of the engagement didn't do much for my heart." She tapped her chest lightly to indicate she was joking.

Not funny.

"You." Irena tugged Sadie's skirt. "You're the one trying on the bride's dress?"

"That's me," Sadie admitted reluctantly

"What a shame," Angela said, "that Meg didn't turn up."

Didn't turn up? "You mean," Sadie said, "how awful for those cabin crew injured in a smash."

"Of course." Angela glanced at her watch. "Sadie, dear, you must excuse me—I have a patient at one-thirty. It's been a delight to see you." After she left, Sadie let out a long breath of relief.

Lexie's sigh echoed her. "What a witch. And that's being polite for Meg's sake."

"I'm not sure you need to be," Sadie said. "I hope Daniel's dad is nicer to Meg." But as she remembered him, Daniel's father was the male equivalent of his mother personality-wise.

"I can't believe Meg's getting married." Still in her bridesmaid dress, Lexie twirled in front of the mirror and gave her reflection a satisfied smile. "She parties harder than I do."

Sadie wasn't sure about that. "Marriage will be a big adjustment," she agreed.

"Is she pregnant?" Lexie asked.

"No!" Sadie's stomach clenched. "I don't think—she would have told me."

"Just checking," Lexie said. "This whole thing seems so rushed."

"You told Daniel's mom they're the perfect couple."

"I just wanted to rile the old biddy." Lexie frowned, but smoothed her forehead as soon as she saw the lines it produced. "I've only met Daniel a couple of times. Super-nice guy, but…"

"Not right for Meg?" Sadie held her breath.

"Yeah. He's too serious, or something. I think he'll put pressure on her to be more like his family. And then she wouldn't be Meg."

At last! Someone else who recognized Meg and Daniel's romance for the unmitigated disaster it had the potential to be.

"Did you tell her that?" Sadie asked.

Lexie leaned into the mirror to examine her eyes. "It's not easy—as a bridesmaid you're supposed to share the love."

"I've said a few things, but didn't get far," Sadie said. "It might help if you talked to Meg. Tell her your concerns, check she's thought this through."

She'd promised Trey she wouldn't raise doubts in Meg's mind. She hadn't promised she wouldn't ask someone else to. Ha!

"I guess you're right." Lexie rubbed at a little patch

of fog her breath had made on the mirror glass. "How about we all have a girls' night out and I'll do it then?"

"Or a girls' night in." Sadie stepped out of her maid-of-honor dress, and Irena lifted the wedding dress down from its high hook.

"You must be very careful," the seamstress warned, as if Sadie would plant a galumphing foot through the net petticoats.

Nancy hadn't arrived with the shoes yet, but judging by the dozens of pearl buttons, it would take a few minutes to get the dress done up.

Sadie stood still, shivering when Irena's cold fingers brushed her back as she managed the buttons into submission. At last the Russian woman stepped back.

"Dress is good," she said.

Right on cue, out in the store, the old-fashioned bell dinged. Nancy with the shoes. Irena's assistant went to the door.

Sadie turned to look in the mirror.

The dress was gorgeous. The boned bodice and cap sleeves blended sophistication and innocence. The heavy satin gleamed expensively. Meg would look incredible. Daniel would be blown away by his bride.

Sadie's chest constricted. She rubbed in the region of her heart with her fist.

Irena stuck her head out through the curtain. "Ah, you have the shoes, excellent."

She whisked the curtain aside, leaving Sadie in full view of...Trey?

"What are *you* doing here?" Sadie asked.

For a moment he froze, his eyes locked with hers

in the mirror. Then he strode forward, jeans and boots ultramasculine among the bridal fripperies, his shoulders taking up more space than they had a right to. The white satin stiletto shoes in his right hand did nothing to diminish his virility.

"Mmm, this is a nice surprise," Lexie purred.

Nice? That wasn't how Sadie would describe the look on his face. Ominous, maybe.

"Why are you wearing my sister's wedding dress?" he demanded.

CHAPTER TEN

OH. THAT.

"If you're indulging some kind of fantasy…" Trey growled.

"Of course not!" Sadie avoided Lexie's avid curiosity as she explained Meg's absence. He barely listened, scanning the changing area as she spoke.

"Where's the coffee?" he interrupted her.

"Someone got out of bed on the wrong side this morning," Lexie said happily. "Irena, do you do coffee?"

Trey's eyebrows drew together. "I meant Sadie's coffee." He turned to Irena. "Did she bring coffee in here?"

Irena spread her hands in blank surprise.

"Trey, are you okay?" Sadie asked. "Oh!" Her blood ran hot in her veins. "You thought… That was a *joke!*"

"What did he think?" Lexie demanded.

That I would spill coffee on my best friend's wedding dress. He was sick!

"Meg *asked* me to try on the dress," Sadie said. "She insisted."

"It's true," Lexie assured him, though she had only Sadie's word for that. "Trey, I have no idea what this is about, but I think you ought to apologize for yelling at Sadie."

Sadie smiled her gratitude.

For one moment she thought Trey would refuse Lexie's suggestion. Then he relaxed.

"Sorry," he said. Then he actually smiled at her.

Presumably for Lexie's benefit.

"Apology accepted." Sadie hoped her excessively gracious tone would annoy him.

But he was busy scanning her figure, starting at the hem pooled on the floor, rising over her hips and waist. When he reached the swell of her breasts over the top of the too-tight bodice—Sadie was curvier than Meg—he stopped.

The sudden heat in his gaze disconcerted her. She almost rubbed her palms down the satin skirt, but a squeak of alarm from Irena arrested her hands short of contact with the fabric.

"You put shoes on now." Irena pushed Sadie toward a velvet upholstered chair.

"Is there something going on between you two?" Lexie asked.

"Trey thinks I might damage Meg's dress in an attempt to stop the wedding," Sadie said as she sat down.

His startled gaze flew to her.

Irena made a half lunge toward Sadie, but stopped herself.

"Lexie feels the same way I do about Meg marrying Daniel," Sadie told Trey smugly. "She thinks they're wrong for each other."

"Totally wrong," Lexie agreed. "But I'd never have thought of wrecking the dress. That's evil."

"I'm not going to wreck the dress." Sadie took one

of the shoes from Trey. And discovered that the boned bodice and full skirt of Meg's wedding dress didn't allow her to lean forward enough to put the shoe on.

"She's talked you into this, hasn't she?" Trey asked Lexie.

"Really, Trey, Sadie may be smart, but I'm quite capable of independent thought."

Sadie sat back and lifted the yards of satin to reveal her feet. "You'll need to put the shoes on for me." She smirked up at him.

Trey sighed as he knelt in front of Sadie, who was exceptionally glad she'd had a pedicure before Nancy's party.

"Give me your foot," he said.

Sadie arched her right foot toward him. He hesitated for one second, then he grasped her ankle with one hand, and with the other slid the shoe on.

The oddest sensation skittered through Sadie. She'd heard the foot was an erogenous zone, but had dismissed it as wishful thinking on the basis of her own limited experience.

But this... The pressure of Trey's thumb on her ankle bone, the warmth of his palm cupping her heel, the slide of satin and leather over her toes...

He dropped her foot; totally relaxed, it thudded to the floor. "Other one," he ordered, his tone impersonal.

"Trey, Sadie and I are going out clubbing with Meg soon," Lexie said. "You should come with us."

"Clubbing?" Sadie said, dismayed. "I thought maybe a bottle of wine at my place. You know, so we can have that *conversation*..." She gave Lexie a meaningful look.

"Meg needs a last wild night as a single gal," Lexie insisted. "As well as her bachelorette party," she said quickly. "No doubt you have something outrageous planned for that."

"Umm," Sadie said, aware of Trey fitting the other shoe to her foot, but determined not to watch this time. "Okay, I guess we can go clubbing. But it's a girls' night. He can't come." She jerked a thumb at Trey.

He got up—he must have finished with the shoe.

Sadie stood, too. Irena pushed Trey aside so she could view the dress. "Nearly perfect," she declared, and crouched at the hem with her box of pins.

"What do you think of the dress, Trey?" Lexie asked. While he was busy with the shoes, she'd done a rapid change into skintight jeans and a low-cut top. She winked at Sadie.

Trey cleared his throat. "Uh, nice." He looked conflicted. The way his eyes roamed her, it was evident he appreciated Sadie's figure. The frown furrowing his forehead suggested he didn't like the thought of her in his sister's wedding dress.

"Okay, I finished," the dressmaker said. "You take dress off now."

Trey folded his arms. "You heard the lady."

Sadie gave him a pointed look. "Trey, could you leave? If I promise not to damage the dress while I step out of it?" She turned to the Russian woman. "Irena, you don't happen to have a cup of bleach lying around, do you?"

"Very funny," he said.

Sadie was smiling as he left.

ON FRIDAY NIGHT, Sadie went out on the double date Meg and Daniel had set up with Daniel's friend Pete.

Her plan was to be sparkling company so that Pete would rave about her to Daniel afterward, and Daniel would be reminded of the great times they'd had together before he met Meg. Just in case he was looking for... alternatives.

It was a far from noble tactic, but she was getting desperate. Lexie hadn't committed to a date for her talk with Meg, and with every day that passed the wedding was getting closer. Besides, Sadie hadn't promised Trey she wouldn't make Daniel jealous.

There was nothing specifically wrong with the date, a dinner at an Italian bistro. Pete was a nice enough guy and he seemed to like Sadie. She was pretty sure he'd tell Daniel that afterward. And Daniel did get a bit squinty-eyed when Pete held her hand across the table. When he asked to take a look at Pete's cuff links, she had the strong impression it was to get Pete's hand away from hers.

She should have been ecstatic. She was. Except...Meg was quiet because she and Daniel had argued about the wedding. Daniel's mother wanted another bridesmaid in the lineup, a cousin of Daniel's. Meg didn't.

Sadie was feeling the strain of the fine line she was walking. The idea was for Daniel to want her *after* he broke up with Meg. And for the breakup to be a source of relief to Meg, once she realized how wrong the relationship was. Sadie didn't want Meg unhappy.

In an attempt to stay lively through her gloomy thoughts, she drank more red wine in one night than she'd normally consume in a week. Pete drove her home, but she declined his self-invitation to come in for coffee and wove her way dizzily to bed.

He was probably regretting driving her home, she thought. It had been unnecessary, since Daniel and Meg had come back here, too.

Daniel was staying over most nights now. Sadie had taken to sleeping with earplugs, just in case. Tonight she stuffed them into her ears with fumbling fingers, pulled off her clothes, found what might have been pajamas, lay on her bed and begged the room to stop spinning.

She woke at six with a dust-dry throat and a headache that felt like a hundred tiny splinters in her right temple. She fumbled for the glass of water she'd conscientiously left on her nightstand, only to knock it to the floor. Rats.

Sadie rolled out of bed, took a moment to steady herself, then shuffled to the kitchen.

A cold pot of coffee sat on the counter—she'd left when Meg and Daniel were making it, and making out, last night. She poured a mug of the brew and zapped it in the microwave. While she waited, she chugged a glass of water.

The microwave beeped. A slosh of cream and two sugars in the coffee and she was good to go. Squinting through her lashes—she hadn't been brave enough to attempt a full eye-open yet—she began the shuffle back to her room.

In the hallway she heard a noise. A muffled male voice from Meg's bedroom. *Daniel.* A giggle, followed by a squeal. *Meg.*

The water she'd drunk too fast surged back up her throat. Sadie swallowed, then clamped a hand over her mouth.

So they'd got over last night's argument, then.

And whatever twinge Daniel had felt over Pete holding Sadie's hand hadn't lasted more than five minutes.

All that soul-searching, feeling guilty, for nothing.

Another giggle drifted down the hall.

Outside, she ordered herself, and turned around as fast as her headache would permit.

She stepped out the front door, closing it quietly behind her. She took a sip of coffee. "Mmm," she said, as if all was well with the world, and the man she loved wasn't in bed—

Not thinking about that. Sadie closed her eyes. Unwelcome images crowded in, so she opened them again. And did a double take.

Huh? How had those plants got on her porch? Pots of something she was too fuzzy to identify were lined up in front of the low wall. Blocking her view of the yard. She rubbed her eyes, wondering if the foliage was a hangover-induced hallucination.

Nope, still there. Sadie scuffed across the porch, feeling about sixty-five years old, to touch a waxy green leaf. Definitely real. Beautiful. An exotic shrub. South American. If her head would stop pounding, she'd remember the name.

"Grista—Griso..." she muttered.

"Griselinia." Trey's head popped up from behind the shrub.

"Aah!" Her mug fell to the porch, spilling its contents

over her bare feet. "Dammit!" She hopped around, even though the coffee hadn't been more than warm, because it gave her a good excuse to allow tears to well up and she felt so damn ill and so damn furious with Daniel and Meg...

"Hell, Sadie, are you okay?" Trey took the steps up onto the porch in a couple of strides. "Sorry, I didn't mean to—" He cursed. "You're crying. You're burned."

He made for the front door.

"No!" Sadie's cry halted him.

"We need a first-aid kit," he said.

"I'm fine—just need some cold water from the hose." She pointed to the faucet at the far end of the porch.

By the time he'd pulled the hose over the railing and turned on the water to a gentle flow, she'd dried her eyes. Trey directed the hose at her feet.

"Yow, that's cold." Sadie hopped again.

Trey muttered something that might have been *I can't win,* but he kept watering her toes.

"Enough," she said after a few more seconds. The icy water had been bracing enough to make her pull herself together.

"You're sure? You're not going to cry again?" Trey twisted the hose nozzle and the water stopped.

She glared. "I needed that coffee."

"Clearly," he said. "I'll get you another one, Ms. Cranky." He headed for the front door.

"Don't go in there," she said.

He paused. Then his expression cooled. "You have a guest. Meg said you were going out on a date last night."

Sadie shook her head. "I sent my date home. Daniel's in there."

Thunder overtook Trey's face.

"With Meg, you idiot," Sadie snapped.

"Right." He smacked his forehead, which saved her doing it for him. "And they're…" He raised his eyebrows.

She nodded. "I could hear…so I came outside."

He gave her a searching look. She blanked her face in response, and when he shrugged, she figured she'd done a good job.

"Doesn't bother me," he said, "so long as I don't have to watch." He put one hand on the door handle. Then released it. Came back to Sadie.

Sadie tilted her head in inquiry.

"Yeah, okay, it does bother me." He leaned against one of the painted brick pillars. "So what do we do now?"

"I'll wait, and you can go home," she said. "What are you doing here, anyway? Why is my porch a dumping ground for dying *Griselinia?*"

"Those shrubs are one hundred percent healthy, and they'd better stay that way," he said. "I figured you'd need something nice to look out on while I work on your garden."

"While you *what?*" She winced.

"Are you suffering?" he asked with interest.

She shook her head, then put both hands to it in an attempt to stop the porch spinning around. "Did you say something about my garden, or was that a nightmare?"

"Dream come true, more like." He grinned. "I'm going to fix your garden."

"You're not."

"No need to thank me," he said. "Mom's asked me to wait until after the wedding to leave town, and Eugene's taken over at work. I have plenty of free time."

"I don't want you in my garden. I can do it myself."

"You're kryptonite to plants. And you're devious as hell when it comes to wrecking my sister's engagement."

She flinched.

"This way we get the best of both worlds," he said smoothly. "I keep tabs on you, you get a great garden— you can tell your parents you did it yourself, if you like."

"No," she said.

"I might have known you'd be difficult." He eyed her chest. "Are you warm enough?"

Sadie folded her arms and resisted the urge to look down. "I'm fine," she lied.

"You're looking seriously haggard," Trey said.

She snapped her teeth together. "I wasn't expecting company."

He took that as another invitation to scan her figure. "I guess that's why your pj's don't match."

Sadie glanced downward and groaned. A chocolate-brown stretch cotton camisole teamed with sky-blue-cotton girl boxers.

"Let's go find coffee," he said. "We'll hit the drive-through, so you don't scare any small children with those red eyes."

Her headache craved caffeine. "I'm not dressed."

"That could pass for workout gear," he said doubtfully.

"Besides, we won't get out of the truck." He pulled keys from his pocket, jangled them at her. "Come on."

Warmth and coffee, or freezing on the porch all too aware of what was going on inside?

"I'm worried that if I agree to coffee, you'll think I'm agreeing to you working on my garden," she said.

"I'm a modern male. I know you're permitted to set as many different boundaries as you like, however illogical they may seem, and change them at any time."

She smiled, and felt marginally better. "I'm also worried I might throw up."

He paled. "If you throw up, I get to do your garden."

"I won't throw up," she vowed, and headed for the truck.

Trey turned the heater up full blast before he reversed out of her driveway. Sadie cupped her hands over the air vent; she hadn't realized how cold she was. She curled her legs on the seat, feeling less exposed that way.

The drive-through line at the Mean Beans on Macon was long enough to suggest that by the time they got home, it should be safe for Sadie to go back into her own house.

"How come you're up so early now that you're not working?" she asked Trey.

He inched forward behind a car packed with a mom and her kids. "A habit I can't shake. When I took over the business I had so much to learn, I needed every hour I could carve out of the day."

She frowned. "You were very young."

"Twenty," he said dismissively, as if that wasn't way

too young to become the main breadwinner for his family. He buzzed down his window so they could order.

"Just a regular coffee," she said in response to his querying glance.

Trey ordered two coffees with cream and sugar. He passed the molded paper tray over to Sadie and they exited the drive-through.

Unable to wait for caffeine relief, she poured two sachets of sugar through the hole in the lid of one cup and poked the stirrer through. Then took a cautious sip of her coffee. *Oh, yeah.*

"Good?" Trey asked, amused, and she realized she'd mewled with enjoyment.

"Not the best I ever had," she said, unwilling to feed his ego by admitting he chose good coffee.

A pause.

"How was the guy you dated last night?"

Not the best I ever had. "Very nice."

"Did you invite him in?"

"I'm not that kind of girl."

He slid a glance at her legs. "Is that right?"

Sadie returned the scrutiny, though she stuck to the above-the-shoulder region. From this aspect, Trey looked more like his brother, or at least the way she remembered Logan, than he did from the front. But Trey's jaw was more defined. Stronger.

He swung a right and pulled into a nearly empty parking lot.

Sadie read the sign on the yellow-and-green building. "Ferg's Flora?"

"Terrible name," Trey said. "Good firm."

"Competitors of yours?"

"Peripherally," he said. "Their landscape-design division is a much bigger chunk of the company than it is for us."

"Is that something you want to expand at Kincaid's?"

He shrugged. "It's not up to me anymore."

"Surely you're still setting strategy, even if you're not involved day to day."

"Landscape design adds value, and that's good," he conceded. "It's hard to differentiate from the competition on plants. With the exception of a few exclusive agreements I've negotiated, we all have access to the same stock."

"And you happen to have an affinity with landscape design," she said.

He grunted. "I'm a businessman—I look at the bottom line." He removed the lid from his coffee and drank. "Logan and my dad were the gardeners."

"Yet you want to create a garden for me," she observed.

"Only because it's a crime to leave it the way it is. How do you feel about liquidambar?"

"I love it," she said. It was one of her favorite trees.

"Forsythia?"

"Beautiful. But if you're thinking about my place, forget it. I want an English-style cottage garden. I'm thinking lavender, roses, daffodils. All of which happen to be hard to kill."

He didn't look impressed.

"I don't care what you think," she said. "I'm doing my

garden, not you." She sipped her coffee, only to have a couple of drops land on her camisole.

Sadie rubbed at them with her finger.

"Do you wander around in those pj's in front of Daniel?" Trey asked. "Luring him?"

Her instinct was to make a smart retort staking her claim to Daniel.

Maybe it was her headache, but she didn't have the energy.

Carefully she set her cup in the cup holder in the center console. She tipped her head back against the seat. "Flattered though I am that you think I could lure him, I don't think it's going to happen."

There was silence while Trey put the lid back on his cup, then slipped it into the holder next to hers.

"So what are you saying?" He stared straight ahead. "You're giving up on Daniel?"

"No. Yes. Maybe." Feeling dizzier than she had since she woke up, she unfolded her legs and planted her feet firmly on the floor of the truck. She took a leaf out of his book and stared through the windshield. "Last night Daniel seemed jealous of my date."

Trey made an inarticulate sound.

"But this morning he and Meg..."

"Right," he said. "Hard to imagine you'd still be interested in Daniel when you've heard him making love to Meg."

Automatically she sprang to Daniel's defense. "I don't expect him to be a virgin. I'm not one myself."

"That's not the point, and you know it."

"I'm not sure I want to keep feeling this way," she said. "Especially if there's no chance I can win."

Trey nodded. "What happened to *I can't let go of something I think is meant to be?*"

He was repeating her words back to her.

Sadie swallowed a pang of regret. "I thought you'd be the first person to encourage me to give up."

"Strange," he agreed. "I guess I've got used to thinking you're a fighter. But knowing when to concede defeat can be just as important as knowing when to fight."

Sadie shivered. She turned up the heat on her side of the cab.

Trey twisted in his seat, and she thought he was going to move across and pull her into his arms. Warmth. Strength. Comfort. Some of her tension yielded.

Trey turned the key in the ignition and the truck engine roared. He hit the gas.

CHAPTER ELEVEN

TREY WAS RIGHT. It was important to know when you were beaten. Flogging a dead horse would inevitably get depressing. Far better to move on. Even if it took a while.

By the time Trey turned the truck into Sadie's driveway, she'd almost convinced herself she'd given up on Daniel, and she felt better for it already. Lighter.

"You think it's safe to go in?" she quipped.

"I'll come with you." He sounded serious.

"No need," she assured him. "I'm fine."

He followed her up the path. Sadie pushed the front door open and stepped inside, Trey right behind her.

Blessed silence.

Sadie's shoulders relaxed. She even smiled. "See what I mean?"

A high-pitched, gasping cry floated down the hallway.

Her smile froze.

"For Pete's sake, they're still at it." Trey winced as the sound came again. "How can you stand to hear this every day?"

"Earplugs," she said cheerily. "Marvelous invention."
Keep it light. Don't admit to him—don't admit to myself—that this is torture.

"This is torture," Trey said, startling her.

"At the very least, it's rude," she said. "This is my house."

His eyes narrowed. "So you're objecting to their manners. Nothing else?"

"Do you know, I didn't kiss my date last night because I didn't want to be unfaithful to Daniel. What a waste!" Her laugh came out brittle.

"I'll go tell them to stop." He took a step away from her, but she grabbed his arm.

"Trey, no."

He turned back, looked down at her hand. Sadie sensed the latent strength beneath the warmth of his skin.

"Trey—" her heart beat faster "—would you mind if I kissed you?"

He jolted, but not so much that he broke free of her.

Sadie took a step closer, looked hard at his face. Made sure she knew what she was doing. That this was Trey, not Daniel.

"Why?" he asked. His voice was casual.

Somehow that made it easier for her to say, "I want to stop thinking. I want to get caught up in the moment." She wanted to let go of love and hurt and futile hope. "And you're a good kisser."

He didn't answer, but she went up on tiptoe anyway, and, eyes open, pressed her lips to Trey's.

A kiss. *Kiss me.*

For one second he didn't move. Then she pressed harder and before she could blink, his arms clamped around her. His mouth was on hers, hot and hungry.

This was exactly what she needed. Sadie met his tongue—seeking, coaxing, tempting—and melded against him. And thought only of this.

His hands slid down the sides of her breasts to her waist, and her body flamed. Then lower to her butt, where his hands curled around her cheeks, cupping them.

Sadie groaned as he tugged her against him. It was immediately clear he wanted her. This kiss wasn't just pity.

She wrapped her arms around his neck like a sex-starved octopus, buried her fingers in his hair. One of his hands moved up, beneath her camisole, and splayed against the bare skin of her back. Branding her.

As she pulled him toward the couch, she stumbled against the side table and knocked a lamp to the floor. Sadie didn't care. She launched herself at Trey, and he went down on the couch with an "Oof."

The couch made a loud scraping sound as it moved several inches across the floorboards.

The noise jolted Sadie into reality. The reality being that she was lying on her couch on top of Trey, and if they didn't stop now, one or both of them would soon be naked.

"Sadie?" His hand threaded through her hair, found the back of her neck.

She shivered into the caress. "I guess that was our kiss."

"I don't think we're done." Trey's eyes were fixed on her cleavage. One finger hooked the front of her camisole, improving his view. He gave a low growl that curled right through her.

"Really, Trey, we should stop." She tried to lever herself off him, but his arm clamped across her back.

"You're talking too much," he breathed against her mouth, and it was as if he'd fanned a flame. Her senses ignited, melting her limbs against him. She sank down, pressed her lips to his again.

He let her explore his torso with her hands for all of one minute. Then he flipped her over...or rather he attempted to. Wanting to stay on top, Sadie resisted. As a result, they both rolled off the couch onto the floor.

Trey cursed. Then he laughed, a rich, deep sound.

Sadie, who'd landed underneath, slapped his shoulder. "I'm the one getting carpet burn in the small of my back." Her cami seemed to have ridden halfway up. "What have you got to curse about?"

"Nothing at all." He nuzzled her neck.

"Get off me." She shoved his shoulders. His *immovable* shoulders.

"I'm enjoying the view," he said. She gathered he was seeing by touch, the way his hands were moving.

Sadie shivered. "Cheap thrill?"

"Sadly, no." He nipped at her bottom lip. "I think I put my back out wrestling your enormous bulk. The physical therapy alone will cost me— Ow!"

She'd slapped him again.

"Sadie!" A voice exclaimed above them.

Meg.

Sadie had forgotten all about Meg and Daniel. Which had been the aim of the exercise. As memory flooded back, she gave Trey another shove, and this time he moved.

"Sadie?" Meg said again. "You and *Trey?*"

"No!" Sadie scrambled to sit up, then realized her pj top was gaping at both ends. She tugged it into place. "Nothing's going on."

"These walls are paper-thin," Meg warned her.

"Yeah," Trey said. "They are, sis."

Meg frowned, then colored. "Ugh, you're my brother and you were *listening?*"

"Sadie and I had to go to some lengths to block out the sound," he said.

Meg eyed the space they'd vacated on the floor. "That's extreme. Next time, just knock on the door."

"Next time, be more considerate of Sadie," Trey told her.

Sadie took advantage of their squabble to finger-comb her hair. She wasn't sure of the protocol in a situation like this. Should she offer everyone breakfast?

Daniel came into the living room. Meg broke off her argument with Trey.

"Daniel, guess what? I just caught these two making out on—" She stopped. "Honey? Are you okay?"

Daniel was holding his cell phone. He looked dazed. More than just too-much-red-wine dazed.

"Daniel?" Sadie prompted.

"My father called," he said. "Mom's had a heart attack."

TREY DROVE THEM ALL to Memphis St. Ignatius Hospital, where Angela Wilson was undergoing cardiac surgery.

"The doctors here are the best," Daniel said as they jogged from the parking lot toward the main entrance.

He sounded as if he was reassuring himself. Not doing a great job of it, going by his pale, set expression.

"She's in good hands," Trey agreed.

"She's fit," Daniel continued. "She has a healthy diet. Maybe she has a little bit of stress, but nothing drastic."

Sadie remembered Angela mentioning at the dress fitting that Daniel's engagement announcement had been a strain on her heart. "It's probably just one of those things," she said.

Meg made a muffled, worried sound.

They reached the entrance, two sets of automatic doors flanking a revolving door.

"I left my purse in the truck," Meg said.

Daniel sent her an uncomprehending look.

"Give me the keys, Trey. I'll be right back." She took the keys from her brother and trotted away.

They were directed to a waiting room on the third floor, where John Wilson, Daniel's father, waited. Daniel embraced his dad.

"No news yet," the senior Dr. Wilson said.

Daniel nodded. "It'll be at least another hour, I guess. You guys don't need to wait," he told Sadie and Trey. "I appreciate the ride."

"I'll stick around till Meg gets back," Sadie said.

"Me, too," Trey said.

Ten minutes later Daniel's phone beeped.

"It's a message from Meg." He pressed to read it. "She's been called to the airport. Emergency fill-in." He stared at his phone, confused.

Trey's glance intercepted Sadie's.

She gave him the tiniest nod—yes, this was about Meg's squeamishness. Annoyance surged through her. Surely Meg could get over her hang-up for her fiancé's sake. Shouldn't she want to be here for Daniel?

"The airline won't let staff refuse to work more than three days a year," Trey said to Daniel. "Meg's already had her three days."

Which was an impressive improvisation—Sadie was certain there was no such rule. She wasn't certain Meg deserved her brother's defense.

Daniel nodded. "Yeah, she'd be here if she could."

"The surgeon said the coronary angiogram showed at least three lesions." John Wilson spoke up suddenly. "It wasn't clear if there were enough target vessels."

"There's every chance it'll look better when he gets into the heart and has a look," Daniel said, to comfort him.

Sadie had done enough human biology in her freshman year at Princeton that she could follow the discussion that ensued between father and son. She asked a couple of questions, and both men seemed to appreciate the distraction offered by explaining things to her.

"I'm going to find coffee," Trey announced abruptly. "Anyone else want one?"

After he'd taken orders and left, the discussion petered out. Daniel's father wandered over to the first-aid poster pinned to the wall. Though he presumably knew all the information it held, he stood there, reading intently.

Daniel moved to a chair at a right angle to Sadie's. "Thanks for sticking around."

"What are friends for?" She touched the back of his hand. "I want to be here for you."

Instinctively he glanced down at his cell phone. There had been no further messages from Meg. He set the phone on the chair next to his and leaned forward, hands clasped between his knees. His right knee brushed her leg, but he didn't pull away. "Sadie, right before I told you guys about Mom's heart attack, Meg said you and Trey were…"

"Making out." Sadie repeated Meg's words.

"Yeah." He met her gaze. "Is that true?"

Sadie nodded.

"I see," Daniel said quietly.

"Is that—is it a problem for you?" Sadie asked, softly enough that his dad wouldn't hear.

Daniel stared down at his clasped fingers. "I like Trey, but you and he don't have much in common."

"Nor do you and Meg."

Daniel pinched the bridge of his nose.

Sadie leaned in. "Would you mind if I was dating Trey?"

He turned troubled eyes to her. "I could hardly object, could I? Not when—" He broke off.

"No," she agreed faintly. Daniel was admitting he was jealous.

"Sadie…" He pulled his chair around so he was facing her, and took her hands in his. "You're a wonderful woman." He swallowed. "You're very special to me. I wish—"

"You wish Trey would hurry up with that coffee?" Trey said roughly from behind him.

Sadie stifled a shriek. "I didn't hear you come in."

"I figured." He didn't look away from Daniel's hands until the other man had released Sadie.

Daniel stood. He ran a hand around the back of his neck. Trey shoved a coffee cup at him.

"Sadie and I are leaving now," Trey said.

She didn't argue. She needed oxygen, needed space to process what had just happened.

"I'll call you when there's some news," Daniel told her. He glanced toward the window that overlooked the parking lot. "I wish Meg was here."

"She would be if she could," Sadie said. It sounded unconvincing, and she wasn't surprised when Trey grabbed her arm and practically dragged her out the door.

He didn't speak until they were outside the building. In the hour they'd been indoors the day had warmed up. The sun beat down on the asphalt and bounced up in waves that made the air shimmer.

"Was making Daniel jealous part of the rationale for kissing me this morning?" Trey asked, without expression. His eyes scanned the parking lot as if her answer didn't matter.

"It never occurred to me," Sadie said.

He looked down at her. Grunted. "Truck's this way."

She followed him between the rows of vehicles. His long legs meant he was soon getting away from her.

"I kissed you because I wanted to kiss *you*," she called after him. Two kids, walking on either side of their mom, giggled. The mom gave Sadie a sympathetic look. Trey strode on.

Her mind traveled backward to that kiss, back to the sensation of his hands on her curves, the intensity in his face… Her stomach fluttered.

Should have had breakfast. Most important meal of the day. All she'd consumed were two and a half cups of coffee—no wonder her veins were buzzing.

Trey pointed his key ring, and up ahead lights flashed on his truck.

Sadie hastened to catch up. "I, uh, really liked kissing you," she said. She didn't know why she felt so guilty. She and Trey had literally gone into the kiss eyes open, intending only a moment of pleasure.

He rolled his eyes. "Sadie, when a beautiful woman asks if she can kiss me, I don't argue. Yeah, it was a hot kiss, but you started it, and it didn't mean any more to me than it did to you. Which was nothing, right?"

"Right," she said uncertainly. So much had happened since they'd kissed, she didn't know which way was up. "Uh…are you sure?"

He held the door of the truck open with exaggerated courtesy. "Certain," he said firmly. "Even if it was the best kiss in the history of the sport, I would never get involved with a woman who's on the rebound."

He closed her door with a decisive click.

A WEEK LATER, Angela Wilson was still in intensive care, her recovery set back by postoperative renal failure. Her condition had been life threatening, but she was slowly improving. Though she'd be in the hospital a while yet, her doctors were optimistic she would be well enough to leave before the wedding.

Which meant the preparations continued. Nancy Kincaid called a Saturday-morning meeting at the Confederacy Inn in Germantown, the hotel reserved for the wedding reception.

Sadie hadn't seen Meg for a couple of nights—her friend had been flying. She'd arrived in late last night, but texted Sadie from the airport to say she would stay at Daniel's. Meg's absence meant Daniel hadn't been around either, though he'd touched base by phone. Daniel's jealousy, or emotional confusion, or whatever it was, had been short-lived. As far as Sadie could tell, he and Meg were as close as ever.

Their meeting was held in Blue Mood, a jazz-themed lounge bar on the hotel's top floor. Meg and Daniel were there, of course, along with Nancy. And Trey.

Sadie hadn't spoken to Trey since he'd dropped her home from the hospital. He'd been distant during the drive...but so had she. She'd had a lot on her mind, not least of which was Trey.

He might be able to kiss her like that and think nothing of it, but she wasn't so sanguine. She felt as if she'd opened a Pandora's box. She'd slammed the lid shut quickly, but not before a few troubles escaped. She shouldn't have kissed him. What was meant to be simple had complicated matters.

Now Trey was talking to his mom and Daniel. He hadn't acknowledged her when she arrived.

Sadie sat down next to Meg on the couch nearest the baby grand.

"How's Daniel's mom?" she asked.

"Doing okay, I think." Meg pulled a lip gloss and compact mirror from her purse. "I haven't seen her."

"Still?" Sadie asked.

"I've been working," Meg said defensively. "And I'm always in a rush to get to the airport or home again." She swiped gloss over her lips. "Besides, it's not as if the old bag likes me."

"Meg!" Sadie said, shocked.

"Honestly, Sade—" Meg glanced over her shoulder to check Daniel was engrossed in his conversation with Nancy "—the woman's totally hung up on education. The moment she learned I didn't have a graduate degree, I swear she started talking more slowly." Meg snapped her mirror closed.

"I'm sure she'll improve over time."

"She's been getting worse rather than better." Meg's mouth tightened with hurt. "I wouldn't mind if she'd gotten to know me and then decided I'm awful, but she judged me from the moment she first saw me." She tipped her head back against the couch. "Once the wedding's over, I'll just avoid her for the next fifty years."

"You live in the same city, and Daniel's close to his parents," Sadie said, worried. "Meg, I know you love Daniel, but people's families are a big part of them. I know what it's like when family can't accept you as you are, because you're different from them. It hurts."

"I know." Meg sounded watery. She pulled a tissue from her purse and blew her nose.

Sadie ached for her.

"Hey, Meg," Trey interrupted. "If you could get over the broken fingernail or whatever your latest drama is and pay attention to this discussion, we might get out of here before midnight."

Sadie glared at him; he spread his palms in a *what did I do?* gesture.

"Girls, I was just saying—" Nancy sat down the other side of Meg from Sadie "—we haven't even talked about what the men are going to wear. I know you'll figure it out eventually, Meg, honey, but not in time for us to actually get things done."

Meg shrugged. Sadie fought a pang of irritation. Probably the same reaction Trey had to his sister ducking out of family responsibilities, she realized. Unlike him, it didn't give her the urge to marry Meg off to a man whose parents didn't like her.

"I'll arrange my own tux," Daniel said from the armchair opposite. "So will the groomsmen."

"Trey, honey, I'm thinking no tuxedo for you," Nancy suggested.

"Great idea," Trey said. "Just a regular suit, then?"

"A *new* suit." His mom's eyes misted. "Remember that suit your dad and I bought Logan for his twenty-first birthday? He looked so handsome...maybe something like that, gray with that fine stripe?"

"Times have changed, Mom," Trey said.

Sadie wondered if anyone else noticed the careful evenness of his tone.

"I guess," Nancy said with regret. "Oh, Meg, I wish your dad and Logan could be here. I always imagined you walking down the aisle on your father's arm. He'd be so proud of you, honey."

Meg hugged her mom, and for a moment the only sound was sniffles and murmured words of comfort.

Trey strode to the picture window. "The terrace down there looks like a good place for photos."

Nancy joined him. "You're right, it's perfect."

The server arrived with their drinks, and Daniel took the opportunity to slip into Nancy's seat on the couch and put an arm around Meg. He dropped a quick kiss on her mouth as he handed her her orange juice.

Maybe I should leave, Sadie thought. *There's no real reason for me to be here.* She would make her excuses and go.

"Some of those roses will need pruning before the wedding," Trey said. "You don't want deadheads messing up your pictures. I'll tell the hotel." He eyed his sister and her fiancé. "Meg," he said, his tone conciliatory, "have you thought about flowers for your bouquet? How about red and white roses with hypericum berries?"

"Or your father liked jonquils," Nancy reminded them. "And Logan's favorites were those Asiatic lilies."

"Whatever," Trey said. "You figure it out and let me know. We'll source them through the garden center."

Nancy made a note on her clipboard. "We need to agree to the layout of the function room, choose a menu for canapés…"

Sadie set down her water glass. "You don't need me for that," she said at exactly the same time as Trey.

He looked at her, spooked.

"Oh, you two," Nancy said indulgently. "I'm not taking full liability for this wedding and then having you all think I should have done it differently."

Trey glanced at his watch. "I have an appointment, Mom, so if you don't mind…"

He was lying. Sadie didn't know how she knew—she just did.

"I guess not," Nancy said, clearly disappointed. "Though I was hoping we could have a nice family lunch in the grill downstairs."

"Don't see how we can do that when half the family's gone," Trey said.

His mother drew in a sharp breath.

"Don't be a jerk, Trey," Meg said. Daniel soothed her, running a hand over her hair.

"What's your appointment?" Nancy asked with forced interest.

Trey hesitated. "Uh…"

Meg planted her hands on her hips, clearly about to accuse him of faking his appointment.

"It's with me," Sadie said.

Nancy's gaze swiveled. So did Trey's.

"I've hired Trey to design my garden," Sadie said.

"Since when do you do landscaping?" Nancy asked.

Trey chugged his Coke.

"Trey has some amazing ideas," Sadie said.

He lowered his glass and looked at her.

That was all she was going to give him. Way more than he deserved. And she'd done that only because today his brusque manner made him seem…vulnerable.

"Well," Nancy said. "Well."

"So Sadie and I need to go—" Trey hesitated "—for our meeting with…"

"That guy," Sadie said. "About…"

"About that thing." Trey grinned, and as she stood to leave, for the first time in days she felt like laughing.

"Is TREY REALLY GOING to design Sadie's garden?" Daniel asked.

Meg wove her fingers through his as they watched Trey and Sadie leave. Trey stood aside to let Sadie precede him into the elevator. Who knew he had manners?

"First I heard," she said. "I guess he's doing it because he has the hots for her."

Daniel made a small, indistinguishable sound.

"What?" she asked.

He shifted to the front of the couch. "I like your brother," he said, "don't get me wrong. But Sadie needs someone a little more…intellectual."

"Maybe she wants a fling," Meg said. Admittedly that didn't sound like Sadie. But then, Meg would have said *she* wasn't the settling-down type. Lots of things were topsy-turvy. "Besides, Trey's smart. If he hadn't got a football scholarship he'd have been a candidate for an academic one."

"I didn't know that." Daniel was still watching the elevator.

Meg nudged him. "If anyone's going to worry about Sadie, it should be me."

"I'm not worried." He smiled down at her. "If she ends up half as happy as I am, I'll be thrilled for her."

Meg wriggled forward and kissed him. She still had to pinch herself that she'd found him, and she'd been uncharacteristically sensible enough to grab him, and somehow he'd been as much a victim of love-at-almost-first-sight as she had.

She wrapped her arms around his neck, buried her face against his collar. "I love it here."

He laughed softly as he patted her back. "Here being…?"

"Right here," she murmured.

"Stay as long as you like," he invited. "Stay forever."

She smiled against his warm skin. "I love you."

His breath fanned her ear. "When we get done here, I'll take you home and show you just how much I love you back."

"If you two could stop canoodling for a moment—" Nancy set down the canapé menu she was perusing "—I'd appreciate your input."

It was another hour before they escaped.

"I thought we might call in at the hospital," Daniel said as he held the door of the Prius open for Meg. "Mom would love an update about the wedding."

"I thought she was mostly asleep." Meg clipped her seat belt.

Daniel came around to his side of the car. "We'll give her a good reason to wake up. Besides, you haven't seen her since the operation. Remember?" Just a hint of tightness in his smile.

"It's all these extra flights to New York—such a pain." She willed him to believe it. "I'm exhausted—how about we head back to your place and you can show me how much you love me."

"Great idea," he said as he reversed out of the parking space.

He was looking as tired as she'd claimed to be, Meg observed as they neared the city. When they got home she would give him a massage. Then, later, order in a romantic dinner for two.

They passed an interchange; she whipped her head around. "You missed your exit."

"We're going to the hospital," he said. "Remember?"

Oh, heck, she hadn't talked him out of it.

Meg slumped in her seat. *Think. Think.* The hospital was about a quarter mile from there. That gave her maybe half a minute.

I could just tell him.

But he would be so disappointed. And she would look shallow and stupid and all those things his family thought she was.

Tears sprang to her eyes. She sniffed.

"Honey? You okay?" Daniel flicked his turn signal as they reached the hospital entrance.

"I— No." Suddenly inspired, she faked a suppressed sneeze. "I have a cold coming on—the cabin temperature was freezing on last night's flight. I've had sore sinuses all day." She faked another near sneeze.

He slowed for a speed bump. "Honey, you can't come into the ICU with a cold."

She widened her eyes. "I didn't think of that. Imagine if I infected your mom...or anyone else." He looked so disappointed that she didn't suggest they get the hell away from this place. "You go visit with your mom. I'll snooze in the car." She would close her eyes and imagine she was somewhere else.

"Thanks, darling." Daniel said. "That's sweet of you when you're not feeling well. I won't be long."

She felt like a heel.

CHAPTER TWELVE

SADIE'S IPOD WAS playing on shuffle as she compared the antioxidant profiles of three different wheat varieties. "Feed the wo-orld," she sang along under her breath. Exactly what she wanted to do.

Although today that ambition took second place behind making Daniel think hard about his priorities—if he was going to marry Meg, he needed to handle his parents better.

The ring of the phone on the wall in Lab Three penetrated the music. She answered.

"There's a Mr. Kincaid to see you," reported Debra, the receptionist. Her bright tone suggested she'd noticed Trey's good looks and was wildly curious about his interest in Sadie.

Why was he here? Sadie glanced at her watch. Damn the man, he must have a sixth sense—she was due to have lunch with Daniel any minute. Maybe she could get rid of him fast.

She didn't take time to freshen her lipstick or tidy her hair, no doubt mussed from her habit of running her fingers through it while she pondered. Trey had seen her at her bleary-eyed worst. Had *kissed* her at her bleary-eyed worst.

She found him in the reception area flicking through

the latest *New Scientist*. With his dark T-shirt stretching across broad shoulders, faded work jeans and solid boots, he was as out of place there as she would be on a catwalk. Yet he looked exactly right.

"I figured you must be due a lunch break," he said. "Can we get a bite?"

Sadie glanced at her watch. "I have plans for lunch. Come back to the lab with me now, and you can talk while I pack up."

In the elevator she pressed for the basement. The doors slid closed.

"I want to thank you for bailing me out with Mom yesterday," he said.

"No problem. I couldn't come up with anything as creative as your Wes Burns story, but it got us out of there."

He grinned at the reminder of Wes, and made a zipping motion across his lips. Oh, yeah, he'd promised never to say that name again.

The elevator reached the second-level basement, and the doors opened. Sadie swiped her card to enter Lab Three.

Trey inspected her work area. "Fancy microscope."

"It's a microspectrometer. Infrared." She began packing up her papers.

"Do you use this for your wheat-protein project?"

She was surprised he remembered that much. "Er, no. This is just something I was doing for my own interest."

"A hobby," he suggested, amused.

"More interesting than collecting stamps," she defended herself.

"Absolutely," he agreed, so smoothly she knew he didn't mean it. He looked at the digital image displayed on the microspectrometer's small screen. "What are you collecting here?"

"Whole wheat kernels," she said reluctantly. She might as well go for the full eye-glaze. Bamboozle him with jargon so he'd be desperate to get out of there. Which would suit her just fine, since she didn't want him getting wind of her lunch plans.

"High-protein wheat is important, but I'm looking at an earlier stage of the life cycle," she said. "Protein content ceases to be relevant if the seed is damaged or is planted in an unfavorable environment and doesn't end up germinating. If we can develop more robust seeds that will survive flood or drought or lack of soil nutrients, then we can grow wheat in conditions previously deemed impossible. And not only grow it, but produce bigger, more vigorous crops."

"How do you do that?" he asked, apparently still with her.

"Antioxidants. All wheat varieties contain them, but some are more powerful than others—the diversity of phytochemicals in wheat bran is extraordinary. It's a matter of identifying the most powerful and finding the trigger that turns them on."

He started to laugh.

She stiffened. "What's so funny?" She unzipped her laptop bag in a short, sharp movement and began gathering papers.

"You can't manage to grow rhododendrons, one of the easiest plants to cultivate, in the finest soil in your own front yard…but here you are planning to help farmers in Africa grow plants in conditions that are literally impossible."

"I never thought of it like that," she said.

"So when will this stop being just a hobby?"

She gave a short laugh. "No idea."

"But it sounds incredible. World-changing."

"Potentially," she agreed. "But there are a hundred different theories as to how to achieve the goal. It's hard to get research funding when the waters are so muddied. I need to convince someone to put money into it. But my boss doesn't like the idea and I kind of overreacted to his negativity."

"What are your options?" he asked.

"Leave SeedTech. Develop my idea further in my own time in the hope I can convince my boss. Apply for a grant. Plenty of options—I just haven't figured out which is the best." She slipped her papers into her bag. "But you didn't come here to talk about that." Though she'd enjoyed telling him about it.

"I'm here about your garden," he said. "You told my mom I'm designing it."

"I was giving you an excuse to leave."

"She's going to want to see the evidence," he said. "I'll design it, and you can plant it if you want. Otherwise I'll supply a couple of laborers from the garden center and you can supervise them doing the work."

It sounded tempting.

The desk phone next to the microspectrometer rang.

Out of habit, Sadie hit the speakerphone button to answer.

"Daniel Wilson is here for your lunch appointment." Debra's voice boomed into the lab.

Trey's face darkened. "I thought you said you were giving up on Daniel."

"We eat together a couple of times a week as friends," Sadie said. "Meg knows all about it."

"Cancel him," he ordered.

"No. There's nothing going on." She stalked out of the lab. They traveled back to reception in silence. As they exited the elevator, Sadie's cell phone rang.

It was Lexie, calling to say she'd confirmed their girls' night out with Meg for tomorrow. Sadie stepped away from Trey to note down the details. When she ended the call, Trey was chatting to Daniel over by the window.

"Daniel said it's okay for me to join you for lunch," Trey said.

Debra looked blatantly envious as Sadie headed to the cafeteria with two gorgeous men. *Too bad one of them's marrying my best friend and the other would like to squish me under the wheels of a rotary hoe.*

At least it should be clear to Trey the cafeteria was no place for an attempted seduction, Sadie thought. The orange plastic trays, cling-wrapped sandwiches and plastic salad tubs weren't exactly the food of love. Though that hadn't stopped her falling for Daniel in this very place.

She closed down those thoughts as she wove between the tables with her tray of lasagna, the hot dish of the day.

"How's your mom doing?" Trey asked Daniel.

"We're hoping she'll move out of ICU next week," he said.

"Great!" Trey said heartily. "That means no delay in the wedding, right?"

"I hope not," Daniel said.

It was the perfect opportunity for Sadie. Of course, Trey wouldn't understand. But it had to be said.

"Maybe it wouldn't be a bad idea to delay awhile," she said. "While you iron out a few issues."

A forkful of lasagna halfway to his mouth, Daniel said, "What issues?"

"She has no idea what she's talking about," Trey said.

She attacked a piece of lasagna with her knife. Trey raised his eyebrows at her vehemence.

"I'm talking about your parents' attitude to Meg," Sadie said.

Daniel looked uncomfortable. "I'll admit it's not the easiest relationship."

"Your mom outright doesn't like Meg," she accused him.

"Is that true?" Trey demanded.

"Mom's adjusting," Daniel said.

Sadie snorted.

"You're right, we need to work on this," he said quickly. He paused. "It would help if Meg would visit Mom in the hospital."

"She's been flying a lot," Sadie said.

"I know," Daniel said.

"I'm sure Meg will visit her soon," Trey said

Daniel didn't look convinced.

LEXIE HAD CHOSEN THE nightclub for girls' night: Urban, tucked in an alleyway off Beale Street. They'd arranged to meet at nine o'clock, which to Sadie seemed late to be going out, but which both Lexie and Meg fretted was too early to be cool.

Over the course of several phone conversations, Sadie had exchanged a lot of information with Lexie. More accurately, Lexie spilled intimate details of her own life, and issued speculation about Sadie's that Sadie didn't feel compelled to confirm or deny. It seemed Lexie didn't know that some people went to bed at ten most nights, accompanied by nothing sexier than a good book.

However, it was so refreshing being considered remotely cool, Sadie felt obliged to dress appropriately. She'd borrowed a couple of items from Meg.

"You don't think this dress is too short?" she asked Meg as she caught a reflection of the hot-pink slip dress in a car window as they crossed the parking lot.

"For the tenth time, no," Meg said. "What will you do if I say yes—take it off?"

Sadie pulled a face at her, then tripped inelegantly as one of Meg's too-big high-heeled shoes caught in a grate.

"Careful, those are my third-favorite shoes," Meg said.

Sadie grabbed her arm to steady herself.

"This is nice," Meg said. "Just the two of us going out."

"Plus Lexie," Sadie said.

Meg laughed. "I can't believe you and Lexie get along so well."

"It's a mystery," Sadie agreed.

Inside, the nightclub was blue and smoky—dry ice, not cigarettes—with silver walls. The volume of the music hurt her ears.

"You'll get used to it," Meg yelled up close, seeing her discomfort. "Then we can talk."

Talk. That was why they were there. Sadie was no longer sure getting Lexie to point out the trouble spots in Meg and Daniel's relationship was the right thing, but Lexie had heard enough complaints from Meg about Daniel's parents that she had no such qualms. Sadie decided she would let the evening flow, and whatever happened, happened.

Lexie had nabbed a table on the edge of the dance floor and bought a round of scary-looking cocktails.

They danced their way through the next music set. A few guys joined them, mostly angling for Lexie's attention, or Meg's. One man in particular seemed taken with Meg, flirting heavily. Sadie couldn't help noticing she was flirting back, though in a much lighter vein.

When the DJ took a break, Lexie started in on her concerns for Meg.

"No relationship is perfect," Meg said. "Everyone has to compromise somewhere." She held her glass up to a passing waiter and indicated they'd have another round.

"So long as it's not you doing all the compromising," Lexie said.

"The important thing," Sadie said, "is to figure this stuff out before the wedding."

The full-on music started again, making talk impossible. Sadie joined Meg and Lexie on the dance floor, not caring that her more conservative dance style set her apart. Meg's number-one admirer was back hanging around her, encouraged by the flirty looks she was darting beneath her lashes.

When the songs turned slower, quieter, they took another break. Before any of them realized what he was doing, Meg's admirer swooped in and kissed her swiftly on the lips before he disappeared to the bar.

"He has a nerve." Meg touched her lips, smiling at his brazenness.

"He's cute," Lexie said as they sat down at their table.

"He's all yours." Meg sounded slightly wistful.

"Actually," Lexie said, "I've given up on casual sex." When both Sadie and Meg choked on their drinks, she tried to look offended, but she couldn't hold it. She laughed. "I don't know if it's you getting married, Meg, or Sadie attracting Trey's attention without having to take her clothes off…"

"I don't have Trey's attention," Sadie protested. Her skin tingled.

"If you don't want him, there are plenty of others who do," Lexie retorted.

Meg shuddered. "Can we not talk about my brother and sex in the same breath?"

"So I've decided," Lexie said, "I'm not going to add one more notch to my bedpost until I meet a guy I really care about. I might even hold out for Mr. Right."

Their new drinks arrived, and they waited while their empty glasses were cleared away.

"That's impressive," Meg said.

Lexie shrugged. "The number of notches is starting to get a little embarrassing."

When the next music set started, Lexie announced she was leaving.

"It's only eleven," Meg protested.

"Trey's giving me a ride home," she said. "He must have heard you talking on the phone to me yesterday, Sadie. He asked if he could come along. I told him it was girls only, but he could take me home." She waggled her eyebrows suggestively.

A wave of primeval emotion swept Sadie. An instinct that made her want to wrestle Lexie to the floor, grab a handful of that blond hair and pull. Hard.

"What about your 'no more notches' policy?" she asked.

"That's the beauty of exes," Lexie crowed. "They don't count as new notches."

After she left, the place felt flat. Meg ordered them another drink, then raised her glass in a toast.

"To freedom." The words were slightly slurred. "To a night with my dear friend Sadie. And Lexie. No men."

Was Meg implying she felt trapped by her engagement? Something unidentified surged through Sadie. She warned herself not to jump to conclusions as she took a sip from her own drink. "You love Daniel, honey," she reminded Meg.

"I do love Daniel," Meg said morosely. "I wish he was here."

Sadie lost her stomach for relationship probing. Who really knew what was going on between Meg and Daniel?

She pulled out her cell phone and thumbed through her recent contacts until she had Daniel's number on the screen. She pressed Call, then held the phone out to Meg.

"Call him. Tell him to come down here."

Meg held the phone to her ear. Then she gasped. "I can't call him! Quick, how do I hang up?" She scanned the keypad and pushed the button to end the call. She dropped the phone onto the table among the empty cocktail glasses as if it was contagious.

"What was that about?" Sadie asked.

"I told Daniel I was flying tonight," she said. "He thinks I'm on my way to Orlando."

"Meg!" Sadie said, shocked.

"He wanted me to spend the evening at the hospital with him and his dad." Her voice pleaded for understanding.

"Sweetheart, you've got to get over this...whatever it is. Daniel needs your support."

"I know," Meg said miserably. "I know."

"What if it was Daniel in the hospital, needing you?"

Meg blanched. She lifted her glass again. "To freedom," she reiterated. It sounded half plea, half defiance.

CHAPTER THIRTEEN

MEG KEPT A CAREFUL EYE out for Daniel as she filtered her way into the arrivals area at Memphis International Airport. Luckily, at 8:00 a.m. the terminal was so busy, if she bumped into him she could say she'd been searching for him in the crowd. A quick check of the arrivals board showed that Flight 2203 from Orlando had landed on time, twenty minutes ago. He was so sweet the way he liked to meet her at the airport whenever he could.

Someone jostled her; she tightened her grip on her roll-on overnight bag as she scanned the crowd. She was just a few feet from the arrival doorway now, so he should be...

There.

To her left. Like her, he was searching the throng with his eyes.

Her heart quickened at the sight of him. His handsome face set him apart from the crowd, but it wasn't just that. He looked open and honest and approachable. That she couldn't approach him in one particular area was her fault, not his. And perhaps a symptom of the brevity of their relationship. Because one look at him and you could see he was a decent guy. A *hot*, decent guy. She smiled to herself at the thought of how she might make amends to him for her deception. Maybe even right now, if he didn't mind being late to the clinic…

"Daniel," she called joyously.

He turned, their eyes met. Meg pushed through the crowd to him. "Sweetheart, it's so good to see you!"

It had been only twenty-four hours since she'd kissed him goodbye, but it felt like weeks. She wrapped her arms around him, kissed him long and hard.

After a second he kissed her back. Hungrily. *Mmm, he tastes so good.*

When he released her, she could barely stand.

"How was Orlando?" he asked.

"Hot." She grimaced. "It hit a hundred ten yesterday afternoon. They had one of those instant thunderstorms. We had to wait on the runway for half an hour before we could unload." She'd asked a colleague who'd worked yesterday's flight for a report.

He let go of her, his fingers springing free as if a coil of tension had snapped. "Liar."

One soft, dangerous word that hardened his face, closed it.

Even though she *was* a liar, it felt like a slap. "Daniel…"

"Sadie called me last night," he said.

Sadie? Meg reeled, clutched tighter at her roller bag.

"I overheard your conversation. You were obviously in some bar."

"Nightclub," she said mechanically. *Sadie* had betrayed her?

"Toasting your freedom," he said.

Oh, hell, now she remembered. Sadie had dialed Daniel, Meg had taken the phone. Then she'd panicked and canceled the call. Or so she thought.

She remembered tossing the phone down on the table. It had sat there, still connected, and Daniel had listened.

"Can we go somewhere to talk about this?" she asked.

"We'll talk here," he said. "Right now I'm so angry I could break something."

Daniel would never hurt her. But she'd hurt him.

Meg closed her eyes. "Darling, I'm sorry. I should have told you right at the start."

"Told me what?" He folded his arms across his chest. She wanted them around her, warm and solid and safe.

"Please, let's go somewhere," she said again.

He shook his head. "Here, Meg. Now."

Meg had the awful sensation that her future depended on her next words. She fingered her name badge. "When Dad and Logan had that boating accident…Dad died out in the water, but Logan was still alive when they found him.

"Logan didn't regain consciousness—we never got to talk to him again." Her throat clogged up; she hated talking about this. "Mom and Trey and I…we sat next to his bed for four days before they decided he would never recover," she said thickly. "They said his brain was ir-reparably damaged. They turned off the life support."

"I'm sorry," he said, and she welcomed the softening in his face. "I really am. But how does that—"

"Since then…" She'd said the hard part, now she

started to rush the words out. "Since then I've had this terror of being in hospitals. Just walking in the door sends me into a panic attack. I haven't visited anyone in a hospital since."

A tour group passed around them, talking at high speed in an indistinguishable language whose syllables sounded harsh to Meg's ears.

"I get that it's difficult," Daniel said. "But this is my *mom*. About to be your mother-in-law. Your family."

"I can't do it. If I could, I would, but I can't." If she said it calmly enough, often enough, he might accept it.

He rubbed the back of his neck. "I don't understand— your mom had a stroke...."

She wasn't proud of any of it, but this was by far the worst part. "Daniel, when Mom had her stroke, I asked for extra shifts at work. I flew more or less constantly." She hung her head. "Trey did everything."

"Your own *mother?*" The rise in his voice drew the attention of an airport security guard, who watched them for a few moments.

She'd shocked him. Disgusted him, even.

"I'm not as noble as you." Her voice shook. Daniel wasn't sanctimonious, but he set a high standard of behavior for himself. He'd chosen to practice medicine in a community clinic rather than an expensive private practice. He consulted on the SeedTech medical panel because he wanted to improve life for those less fortunate. It seemed it hadn't occurred to him his fiancée might not aim so high. "A good day for me is when I make someone's flight better, not when I save a life. But you knew that when we met, and you chose me because I make you happy. That's what I want to spend my life doing."

She risked touching his wrist, her fingers brushing his folded arms, his chest. He inhaled deeply, but didn't move away. *We can work this out.*

"If *I* was in ICU," he said, "would you visit?"

Her pulse jumped at the thought of him being injured. Her stomach roiled. "Of course I would." But the words sounded thin.

"If I was mashed up by a drunk driver, lying in the hospital with my life in the balance, would you sit beside me for hours?"

"Are you conscious or unconscious?" she joked, only it fell flat.

A pause.

Then he said, "Unconscious."

Damn, he wasn't meant to answer that.

Meg swallowed. "Of course I'd sit with you. Though I'd have to go back to work sooner or later. I mean, if you were seriously injured, we'd need me to be earning…" She trailed off. She was babbling, and they both knew it. "This is crazy. It's not going to happen."

"In a few weeks we're planning to stand in front of a minister, in front of the world, and promise to love each other in sickness and in health," he said.

"I know."

"When I say it," Daniel said, "I'll mean it."

"So—so will I," she stuttered.

The stutter was her undoing.

"One of the reasons I fell in love with you is because

you're so lighthearted," he said. "I know I can be too serious—my whole family's that way—but you lift me out of that. With you, I feel brighter, more alive."

She grabbed his wrist. "Then let's get past this."

"But you're *never* serious," Daniel continued. "You don't take responsibility for anything. You think the world will fall into place around you and most of the time it does. But if we're going to spend our lives together—"

"What do you mean, *if?*" she blurted.

"I need someone who can be with me down in the valleys, as well as up on the peaks," he said. "Meg, you can't go through life without traveling in the valleys."

"I know that! I've had my valleys," she said. "I lost my dad and my brother, and that's more than enough. I don't ever want to feel that way again."

"Of course you don't." His eyes filled with compassion, and hope flared inside her. "But what if the worst does happen? If I did get hurt, or worse, one of our kids did? If we had a child with lifelong medical problems? Could you handle that?"

She stared at him, mute. "Everyone handles those things when they happen," she said at last.

He shook his head. "I know from my medical practice that over half of marriages break up when a child dies. Long-term illness or injury of one half of a couple most often leads to divorce."

"Statistics," she said helplessly. "I *love* you."

"We have to at least start off committed to being with each other through everything. For better or for worse, no exceptions."

Her fingers fluttered over the pristine white cuff of his shirt. "Daniel..."

"Meg," he said, "I want a partner. I want to know you've got my back, the same way I'll have yours."

"I do." This was crazy. She was Meg Kincaid, the girl who got any guy she wanted. Who'd broken hearts with her refusal to get serious. And now the man she'd chosen to spend her life with wanted someone better? "I'm with you all the way. For always."

He stared down at her and she poured all her love for him into her eyes. He had to believe her.

"If you're with me," he said, "come with me right now to visit my mom."

The smells and sounds of the hospital, of death, flooded her senses. Dizzying her. Meg gripped the flimsy handle of her roller bag. No security there.

"If I was afraid of snakes, would you make me hold one?" she asked. "If I was afraid of the dark, would you shut me in a closet?"

Daniel's gaze dropped, then met hers again. "Are you with me or not?"

TREY WATCHED SADIE swing her little Lexus into her driveway. Saw her brake suddenly when she registered that his truck was once again in her way.

"Nice evening," he called.

Sitting there, he'd basked in the still-warm beat of the sun, the chirrup of cicadas, the wafting scent of jacaranda from across the street. By anyone's standards, even standards as high as Sadie's, it qualified as a nice evening.

"What do you want?" she asked shortly.

Trey couldn't think why her unpredictability stirred his pulse, but he was getting used to the fact. He stretched his arms behind his head and settled in to enjoy sparring with her. "To run through my proposed design for your garden."

He'd spread out the drawing on the wrought-iron table, anchoring the corners with stones.

"I'm not in the mood." She dumped her briefcase on the porch, giving Trey a nice view of her rear as she bent, then unlocked the door. "Go home and get some sleep, Trey. I'm sure you need it."

Whatever this was about, he had a feeling he was going to enjoy it.

"I'm not tired." He moved the anchor stones and rolled up the garden plan to take it inside.

"Such impressive stamina," she mocked.

"Cupcake," he said, "I have no idea what you're talking about."

"I'm talking about you and Lexie!" she snapped.

Sadie's jealous? The knowledge went straight to Trey's head, then to his mouth—he couldn't stop smiling as he followed her into the living room.

"Ah, Lexie…" he said reminiscently, setting his drawing down on the coffee table. "Lexie and me…"

"You can't start a sentence with *Lexie and me*," she said. "And even if you could, I don't want to know. Plus, you can wipe that smirk off your face—she only chose you because of creative sexual accounting." She began plumping the perfectly plumped, neatly arranged cushions on her red sofa, the one where they'd made out.

Trey almost laughed. But she looked annoyed and upset and vulnerable.

"The thing about me and Lexie," he said deliberately, "is nothing happened."

Sadie paused in her pounding the life out of an innocent cushion. "I couldn't care less."

"I'm just sayin'." He mooched across to the fireplace, propped an elbow on the mantelpiece. "For the record."

She fished in the pocket of her tailored, cream-colored jacket and pulled out her phone. "Then why did Lexie text me this?" She thumbed through her messages, then tossed the phone to him.

A string of emoticons, every single one of them a very satisfied smile.

Trey guffawed. "She's winding you up, cupcake. And doing a damn good job of it."

Sadie sat on the couch, hands folded neatly in her lap, feet crossed at her excellent ankles. "When you say nothing happened..." she said. "Define *nothing*."

Trey wondered how she justified to herself that she was asking this question. In theory, his love life was none of her business. He rubbed his chin. "Hmm, let me see. If I remember rightly..."

She narrowed her eyes.

"I drove Lexie home—she has a town house in Cooper-Young. She invited me in for coffee. I accepted her invitation."

Did he imagine a little indrawn breath?

"We drank our coffee, we talked about football and

TV shows." Trey moved to perch on the rolled arm of the couch, feet planted wide on the floor. "And you."

She started. "You talked about me?"

"Lexie's a big fan of yours. Go figure."

"I don't get it," she admitted. "So then what happened?"

"Then I oiled her squeaky door."

She stiffened, suspecting innuendo. Trey chuckled. "The pantry door. In the kitchen. Then I checked out her CD collection, made love to her, did the dishes…"

"Wait!" she ordered. "What did you say happened after the CD collection?"

"I just dropped that in to see if you were paying attention," he said. "I didn't make love to her. Oof!"

Sadie had grabbed a cushion and thumped him.

"She didn't make love to me, either," he said.

"Huh," she said.

"What's it to you whether I slept with Lexie or not?" he asked. "Daniel's the one you're pining for."

She opened her mouth, closed it again. "I don't know."

"By the way," he said, "I want to apologize for being suspicious of your motives for having lunch with Daniel the other day."

"Could you stop disconcerting me?" she demanded.

He laughed. "You were right to call Daniel on the problem between his mom and Meg. He needs to get that straight before the wedding."

"That's why I said it," she said gruffly. She paused. "Uh, could I please see those garden plans now?"

"I thought you'd never ask." He unrolled the drawing,

spread it on the coffee table "Some of these shrubs are special order, so we'll need to get onto it fast."

She scooted forward on the couch.

"The design centers on a water feature—a rock pool and fountain, right here." Trey touched a point on the paper. "There'll be a bench seat overlooking the pool, which also lines up with a good view of massed plantings below the porch—honeysuckle and Oregon grape holly. The yellow blooms will look great against the house."

Sadie leaned in to see the list of plants he'd written down the side of the page, a mix of Latin and common names. He caught the scent of her hair, lemon and honey. Like Sadie herself, sweet and tart.

He realized he'd lost his train of thought and scanned the diagram to regroup. "Oh, yeah, I put a couple of forsythia over here for summer shade on the sages and salvias. This patch will have a wildflower look, but in reality—"

Sadie sat back. "What happened to my English cottage garden?" she asked. "Where's the lavender? I don't see daffodils, either."

"That look's not right for you."

"But it's what I want." Sadie couldn't believe it. Not one plant she wanted had made it into his plan. "I've told my parents I have an English garden—what happens when they turn up and find this?" Didn't he get where she was coming from?

"Forget your hang-ups for five minutes, could you?" he snapped. "You might be the smartest person in the house, but out in the garden I know more than you do. A garden should reflect its owner. Which is why I've designed something unique, multifaceted, unpredictable."

She caught her breath. "Oh," she managed to say.

"Standout," he added severely.

Excitement fizzed in her veins. She bent over his drawing. "Maybe if you'd mentioned your rationale at the beginning…" Because it was difficult to hold on to her objections when he'd called her unique. Multifaceted.

"Maybe if you'd trusted someone to know better than you," he grumbled.

"I'm sorry." She touched the back of his hand where it rested on the diagram.

Lightning-quick, he flipped his hand over and caught her fingers. The tug went all the way up her arm, into her chest.

"Because this plan," she said, "is actually rather… incredible."

"You're just saying that," he said sulkily. His mouth looked supremely kissable.

She bent her head over his diagram, aware he still had hold of her hand. "You've thought of everything. I can picture it in my head and it's stunning."

He lifted one shoulder as if he didn't care, but one corner of his mouth twitched. His middle finger scraped her palm. Scraped her nerve endings.

She pressed her knees together. "Trey, how can you even think of doing anything else for a job?" she asked. "You're so talented."

Instantly he let go of her hand. "I've been in the garden center my whole life. I've had enough."

"You haven't been doing *this*. I didn't even know you could. Your family doesn't know...."

"Sadie," he said, "I'm going back to football."

CHAPTER FOURTEEN

SADIE GAPED. "You're too old."

Trey stood, walked halfway across the room. "Not playing, idiot. Coaching."

"You already coach a team at your old school, don't you?"

"I'm not talking about Andrew Johnson High, a part-time job with a less than part-time wage. I'm talking college ball."

"Where?" she asked, dazed. She realized now that deep inside she'd always thought he would recognize the strengths of his ties to the family and the business and would change his plans.

"That interview I had the day I came to your place for dinner...the football coach from Berkeley, a guy I played with at Duke, was here scouting out a player. He was also scouting for a new assistant coach."

"Berkeley, *California?*"

"The very same. I've been up there to see him a couple of times. Last week was the final interview. He offered me the job yesterday."

"It's the girls, isn't it?" she said.

"Huh?"

"Your wild oats. You're after the California girls, beach babes, *Baywatch*..."

His mouth curled in a smile that made her want to slap him.

"I hope you realize most of them have implants."

He returned to the sofa. "Is that a fact?"

"Which don't feel nearly as good," she warned.

"To the, uh, wearer or the toucher?" he asked.

"Both," she said firmly.

He laughed, and the deep, appreciative sound made her catch her breath. He noticed, held her gaze. Trey was perhaps the most observant man she'd met, she realized.

"I'll miss you, Sadie." He sounded surprised. "I'll miss talking to you."

"Don't go, then," she said. Where had that come from?

He twisted to face her. "Why not?"

"I—uh—your family…the business…" It wasn't what she wanted to say, but she couldn't frame her thoughts.

"Anything else?" he asked, his gaze intent.

She knotted her fingers in her lap. "I don't know."

He sighed. "You know what else I'll miss?"

She shook her head. She knew what she was hoping for.

"This." He pulled her into his arms.

When his lips touched hers an electrical current jolted her, top to toe. She jerked against him and he took instant advantage, sliding his hands to her butt and pinning her close. She welcomed his tongue, and a low groan vibrated in his chest as he took full advantage.

Protest fled, trounced by need and heat. Trey pulled her closer, if that was possible, fusing his body against hers.

She'd kissed him before. But this was different. This kiss had nothing to do with Daniel. She gave herself up to the exploration of his tongue, the slide of her hands over the firm expanse of his back until she found the hem of his shirt. Her hands slid under and up, until she found warm, bare flesh. He made an exultant sound, then his hands were tugging her shirt from her jeans, hastening to return the favor.

She bucked as his fingers brushed the sensitive skin of her waist, groaned as he slid one leg between hers, the need building inside her to an explosive state. One spark and she would ignite.

"Trey," she gasped, aware there was a decision to be made here, and it wasn't the kind she could make lightly.

"Hmm?" His mouth left hers, but her groan of disappointment turned to a moan of pleasure as his lips trailed down her neck. She tipped her head back, aware of his fingers brushing against her as he worked the bottom buttons of her shirt, then moved upward.

A distant voice penetrated the fog of desire. "Who's that? Sadie?"

It was coming from *down the hall*.

They froze.

"It's Meg," Sadie hissed. "I thought she was flying today."

Already he was rebuttoning her shirt. Sadie traced her lips with her thumb, hoping her lipstick had disappeared entirely, rather than being a smudged mess. Trey ran his hands over her curves, smoothing her shirt, and she squawked.

"It's a bit late for prim outrage, cupcake." He stepped away from her just as Meg walked in.

The whole scene looked incriminating as heck, Sadie thought, kicking ineffectually at the cushion on the floor. There was no way Meg wouldn't guess—

Her friend was walking like a zombie, catatonic.

"Meg?" Sadie took a step forward. "What happened?"

Meg stared at Sadie, her eyes wide with shock.

Oh, hell, she'd seen them.

"It's not what it looks like," Sadie said, at the same time Trey said, "Don't even begin to think there's anything going on, because there's not."

Gee, thanks.

"Daniel…" Meg said slowly.

Sadie's heart lurched. Her friend's tone implied her next words would be *is hurt*. Or *is dead*.

"…broke up with me."

CHAPTER FIFTEEN

"Sweetie, that's awful," Sadie said, even as relief flooded her that Daniel was okay.

Meg sank onto the couch.

"What the hell happened?" Trey loomed over his sister. "What did you do?"

"Quit hassling her." Sadie shoved him, trying not to think that her hands had just been on him, wanting more of him. Wanting all of him. She knelt before Meg, clasped her knees. "What happened, honey?" She shot a look at Trey. *This* was how you asked the question.

He rolled his eyes.

Meg pushed her hair off her face; she'd been asleep, Sadie realized. "He—he said I don't take responsibility, and I expect the world to fall into place around me."

"That's not true," Sadie said crossly, if not honestly. Because even if it was true, Daniel had no right to dump Meg so close to the wedding.

Daniel dumped Meg.

It was as if Sadie hadn't fully comprehended that the first time. Now, realization burst over her like Fourth of July fireworks.

Daniel is free.

Sadie sank back onto her heels. *He's free.*

No no no no no. Not while Meg was sitting right in front of her, brokenhearted.

Then Trey's hands were on her shoulders, not at all tenderly, as he manhandled her aside. He plunked himself down next to Meg, slung an arm across her shoulders. "It's a tiff," he said. "You're both under pressure with the wedding coming up. It'll blow over."

Meg shook her head. "It won't."

Sadie cleared her throat. "I'll bet right now Daniel's regretting what he said."

"You keep out of this," Trey ordered, his voice harsh.

"I behaved stupidly." Meg buried her face in her hands. "Badly. I lied to Daniel and he caught me." She emerged to look at Sadie. "That call we made to him last night, on your cell? The phone didn't switch off properly and he heard you and me talking."

"What?" No mistaking the menace in Trey's voice.

"I thought you turned it off," Sadie said faintly.

"I apologized, but there's more than that," Meg said. "Stuff I can't see how we're going to fix. He despises me." She clutched Trey's hand.

"Meggie, he probably doesn't *despise* you," Trey said uncomfortably.

"He doesn't," Sadie assured her. "He said idiotic things in the heat of the moment. All guys do that." She was drawn to Trey's gaze, read the message there loud and clear: when he'd said he would miss her...the heat of the moment.

Got it, she transmitted back, then ignored him in favor of Meg. "I'll bet Daniel will turn up in the morning with masses of flowers and a world-beating apology for being such an idiot."

"He won't."

The conversation went around in circles, with nothing seeming to improve Meg's perspective.

Sadie's sympathetic words were punctuated by awful thoughts. Such as—it would be safe to date Daniel as soon as Meg found someone else, which probably wouldn't take long. And to save any awkwardness, it would be best if Meg moved out—a move that was probably overdue anyway.

"Sweetie, go to bed. I'll bring you some cocoa," Sadie said at last.

Meg hugged her, then wandered from the room, looking lost.

"Cocoa?" Trey asked.

"That's what my mother serves for comfort." Sadie glanced around the kitchen. "I hope we have some."

WHICH WAS HOW TREY ended up at the Save-A-Lot buying cocoa at ten o'clock at night.

By the time he returned, he'd figured out how to deal with Sadie. First up, he wasn't even going to think about kissing her again. Or doing anything else with her. This thing he had for her, this inexplicable desire, was just a symptom of his burning need to get out of town. It wasn't as if he was *hurt* by her obvious continued interest in Daniel.

Which she hadn't been able to hide when she realized Meg and Daniel were over.

He watched as she made the cocoa, squinting to read

the instructions on the pack, then measuring scoops of the brown powder with scientific precision. She even measured the milk before pouring it into the mug.

She stuck it in the microwave, setting the time to one minute, thirty seconds.

"Meg likes her drinks hot," Trey said gruffly. "Better give it another thirty."

"It says one-thirty on the pack." She waited until the microwave binged, then tested the cocoa. Then she put it back in the microwave for another half minute.

"That accident with my cell phone," she said, "when Daniel overheard Meg and me. It *was* an accident."

"Right." Actually, he believed her. He'd coaxed more details out of his sister, and it seemed Meg had meant to turn off the phone, but failed. Probably due to the cocktails Sadie had plied her with, but that case wouldn't stand up in court.

Through the semi-opaque microwave door Trey watched the mug revolve slowly.

"Maybe the fact they broke up means they weren't meant to be together," Sadie said.

"Whatever lets you sleep at night."

She pressed her lips together.

"I guess you'll be going after Daniel now," he said, needling her. Jabbing himself.

"I'm not a vulture." But she didn't meet his eyes.

"No one died—it's just a breakup. And you want him."

She didn't deny it. Trey shouldn't be surprised—he knew how she felt about the guy. But coming right on the heels of that kiss they'd shared…a kiss that had spun his head around and left him wondering which way was up…even thinking about the possibility of not leaving town just yet…

He was furious.

AFTER A HALF DOZEN BEERS, Trey's ex-brother-in-law-to-be—something about that sounded wrong, but Trey's brain was too fuzzy to figure it out—was no longer so buttoned-down perfect.

In fact, that last song Daniel had sung—with only minimal input from Trey, but quite a bit of help from the fat guy sitting at the far end of the bar—had been positively bawdy.

Sadie wouldn't find her precious Daniel so perfect right now, Trey thought. And was slightly amazed that even the quantity of alcohol he'd consumed tonight hadn't dulled his anger.

She'd kissed the hell out of him, then lit up like a Christmas tree at the thought of Daniel being a free man.

But he needed to put that resentment aside—what did it even matter who Sadie kissed?—if he was to accomplish his goal. Which was to inspire Daniel to get Meg back.

His sister was miserable, his mom was panicking. How was Trey supposed to leave town with them in such a state? If Daniel would just forgive Meg for her transgressions—the biggest of which was her not visiting Daniel's mom in the hospital, for Pete's sake; how hard could it be?—they could get this engagement back on track.

Right now it looked impossible, but Trey would do it. Sadie had underestimated him if she thought she had a clear road ahead. Ditto if she thought that kiss meant anything to him.

"You're sounding paranoid," Daniel slurred.

Damn, he'd said some of that out loud. "Ignore me, buddy—it's the beer talking." Trey held up a finger to tell the bartender they wanted another round.

A minute later the bartender came over with the drinks. He took Trey's proffered twenty. "You've had a request," he said to Daniel. He pointed at a group of old-timers in a booth the other side of the room. "For 'Danny Boy.'"

Daniel blinked. "That's m'name."

"Really?" The bartender looked at Trey for confirmation. "Shouldn't be too much of a challenge, then."

Daniel took a slug of his beer. "D'you know how that song starts?" he asked Trey.

"Badly," Trey said. "I hate that song."

"It's beautiful," Daniel protested. Except it came out *beaufitul*.

"Am I in as bad shape as you?" Trey puzzled aloud.

"Pretty close," the bartender said.

Trey groaned. He really needed to wrap this thing up, and he couldn't do that until Daniel agreed to go after Meg. An agreement Daniel needed to remember in the morning.

Daniel was humming experimentally, making sure he could nail "Danny Boy."

Trey took a controlled swig of his drink. "The trouble with Meg," he said, "is she's spoiled." He planned to lay the blame for that on his parents, then appeal to Daniel as the man to help Meg overcome her flaw.

"Not spoiled," Daniel said. "Irresponsible."

Irresponsible sounded a lot harder to get past than spoiled. "Yet sweet and generous," Trey said quickly. "And kind."

"'S true," Daniel agreed. "So why can't she come see my mother in the hospital?" he asked the bartender.

"Beats me." The guy sounded as if he might have heard this question a few times tonight already. Trey vaguely remembered the subject coming up.

"She said it's 'cause her brother died in the hospital," Daniel said.

Trey jolted on his bar stool. "She said that?" Meg gave the impression nothing worried her, especially not decade-old memories. He felt vaguely disturbed at the thought of his sister still having that much of a reaction to Dad's and Logan's deaths.

"She can't go into a hospital," Daniel said. "Any hospital."

"Seriously?" Those memories probably flitted through Trey's mind every day, but they didn't stop him functioning.

"When your mom had a stroke…" Daniel prompted him.

Now that he thought about it, Meg had told Trey she couldn't rearrange her work schedule. Maybe it was more that she *wouldn't*.

Sympathy mingled with irritation. Obviously she had a problem, but why shouldn't she snap out of it the way everyone else had to?

Daniel's humming had grown louder, and now he swiveled his bar stool around and broke out into the opening lines of "Danny Boy."

Ugh, that song was maudlin.

Two verses later, the fat guy at the end of the bar was blowing his nose, looking emotional at Daniel's rendition.

"The thing with women—" Trey had used the time to process his thoughts "—is sometimes they act crazy."

Daniel nodded as he sang about flowers dying and warm dreams.

Didn't Sadie act crazy ninety percent of the time? Trey never knew what she was going to do next. Which was weird, when she was so sedate.

Not, obviously, when she was kissing him. That wasn't sedate at all.

"A guy's gotta get past a bit of crazy," Trey said. He could imagine Sadie's reaction to the idea that women were nuts, so guys had to tolerate them. If he'd still been on speaking terms with her, he'd have been tempted to call her and run that line by her. Just for fun.

"Meg said she wouldn't come to the hospital if I got smashed in a road accident." Daniel took a break between verses to air his grievance.

"Ouch." That sounded bad, even for his irresponsible sister. Sadie wouldn't let a guy down like that.

"Sadie would come to the hospital," Daniel said.

For a second Trey thought he'd spoken his thoughts aloud again. But no, it seemed Daniel's mind was headed the same direction by sheer coincidence. "Uh, yeah," Trey said, disconcerted.

"Sadie is very caring." Daniel swung his stool back around to the bar, his musical turn forgotten.

Yeah, she cared too much for her best friend's fiancé. Trey grunted.

"I wish I loved Sadie," Daniel said.

"Well, you don't." Trey rammed his fist into his jacket pocket before it accidentally punched Daniel in his self-absorbed head.

"Hard to believe she and Meg are the same age," Daniel said. "Sadie's a lot more mature. And she's smart. I like that in a woman."

"Meg's smart, too," Trey said. "More street-smart than book smart, but that's important."

Daniel nodded. "My parents don't like her," he said with beer-fueled honesty. "They're intellectual—" *intellekshul* "—snobs. The air-stewardess thing…"

"Do you know how hard it is to get into that job?" Trey asked. "They probably get more applicants than medical school."

"Prob'ly," Daniel agreed. "Tell my mom that."

"So you don't share your parents' views?"

"Of course not." Daniel drained his beer. "Hell, I only went to medical school because I couldn't live with the icy disapproval at home if I didn't. My folks set high standards pretty much across the board."

"Sounds tough," Trey said.

Daniel shook his head. "Turns out I love being a doctor. And I like being organized. I like to get things right. But I know I can take it too far. That's why Meg's good for me. *Was* good for me." He belched, which Trey figured in the Wilson family was probably a disinheritable offence. "Sadie's too similar to me."

"Are you going to go after her?" Trey asked.

"Sadie?"

"Meg," Trey said through gritted teeth.

"In the end, you're going to have good and bad times," Daniel rambled. "What matters is choosing the right person to weather them with."

"And Meg's right for you," Trey suggested heartily.

Daniel looked confused. "Sadie…"

"Is mine," Trey said. Where the hell had that come from?

Daniel's eyes widened. "Uh…" Then he turned bug-eyed. "Here she is now."

Trey turned very slowly on his stool. Sure enough, Sadie stood in the doorway of the bar, exasperation in every line of her body.

She saw them, and her blue eyes sparked. "I can't believe this," she said, hands on hips. Her stance thrust her curves out enticingly, and damned if Daniel didn't notice, going by the way his gaze dropped. "I've been looking everywhere for you. And what do I find? While Meg is at home devastated, you—" she jabbed a finger at Daniel, which made a nice change from Trey "—are out having a good time."

Trey thought about the songs he'd had to listen to and concluded no one was having a good time.

"This is your fault." Sadie rounded on him. "Don't you care that your sister is brokenhearted?"

"Sure I do. I'm here to help Danny boy woo his bride

back," he said grandly. Unfortunately the words came out slurred.

She rolled her eyes. "Meg's flying out to Buenos Aires tomorrow afternoon," she told Daniel. "She'll be gone three days. If you want to fix this fast, tomorrow morning—" she glanced at her watch "—*this* morning is the time. And the good news is, she's agreed to talk to you."

Daniel blinked. "*She's* agreed?"

"You hurt her," Sadie said. "She doesn't owe you anything."

That concept proved too difficult for him to grasp.

"Okay," he mumbled. He rested his forehead on the bar.

"What's wrong with him?" Sadie asked, alarmed.

"He's drunk, cupcake." Trey put an arm around her waist, pulled her to him. Mmm, she felt so good. Lucky he was drunk, because sober he was too mad at her to do this.

"So are you," she said. He noticed she wasn't pulling away. "We need to get him sobered up in time to see Meg."

"Why do you want him to talk to Meg? This could be your big opportunity, cupcake." He decided not to tell her Daniel had been singing her praises. Yeah, he was a jerk.

"Meg's my best friend," she said. "I can't bear to see her so unhappy."

"So you'll give her another shot at your man? Kinda masochistic."

"I always told you I would only go after him if things didn't work out between them," she said.

"You're a good woman, Sadie Beecham," he drawled.

"You make me sound like an ancient spinster who cooks up her secret apple-pie recipe for the church bake sale."

"I can see that in your future, now that you mention it."

She thumped his shoulder. Not lightly.

"Ouch. I'm glad you're not in better shape," he said. Then he eyed her *shape* with blatant appreciation.

She grimaced. "Not only are you drunk, you're drooling. You need to polish up your act."

"Yeah," he said. "I should be more like Daniel."

They both stared at Daniel, lying with his left cheek mashed into the bar, which pushed his mouth into goldfish lips. While they watched, he emitted a damp snore.

Sadie gave a snort of laughter. "You definitely need to be more like him." She shifted against Trey, a delightful friction down his right side.

"You're sexy when I'm drunk," he said.

"Jerk," she said pleasantly.

"You don't have to be over Daniel to sleep with me, do you?" he asked. "Because if it's just sex, I don't have a problem with the rebound thing."

"There's one little standard I insist upon," she said sweetly. "I have to like the guy."

"You like me." He chuckled. "You hate how much you like me."

Daniel jerked awake for a moment, said, "Sadie?" then subsided again.

"We'd better get him out of here," Sadie said. "Can you walk?"

"Of course I can walk." Trey climbed off his stool gingerly and was relieved to find himself steady. "Where are we taking him?"

"His place… I assume he has his keys." Sadie began to pat Daniel's pockets.

Trey batted her hands out of the way. "No cheap thrills. I'll do that."

As it turned out, Daniel didn't have his keys. He probably had one hidden somewhere, but Sadie didn't fancy poking around outside his house in the small hours of the morning.

"We need someone who won't mind being disturbed this late, and who knows how to revive a drunk," Trey said.

Sadie raised her eyebrows. "Are you thinking who I'm thinking?"

CHAPTER SIXTEEN

THEY GOT LEXIE out of bed, but instead of her looking a wreck, as Sadie would have, her blond hair cascaded fetchingly around her shoulders, which were covered only by the thin, silky straps of her nightgown.

Within two minutes she had coffee on the go and was mixing up what she called her Patent Hangover Prevention Tonic. An impressive multitasker, Lexie flirted like mad with Trey as she blended the drink, but it seemed he was too under the weather to respond.

When she went into the dining room to find a glass, Sadie followed.

"We should try to get some water down Daniel, too," Lexie said, opening a cupboard in the sideboard. "And if he can swallow some ibuprofen, so much the better."

"Did you sleep with Trey the other night?" Sadie asked.

Lexie pulled out a highball glass. "Wow. Total non— What's that thing called when something doesn't follow what went before?"

"Non sequitur," Sadie said.

"Yeah, that's it." Lexie grinned. "You got my text, right?"

"I suspected exaggeration." At least she did after Trey told her to.

Lexie chortled. "You got me. Nothing doing."

Who knew relief could feel like the sun coming out after a hurricane?

"That's got to be good for your new, sexually restrained lifestyle," Sadie encouraged Lexie as they returned to the kitchen.

"I'm thrilled," the other woman deadpanned as she shook a couple of ibuprofen tablets from a bottle. "Let's see if we can get these down him."

By 4:00 a.m. Daniel had swallowed coffee, water and pills in two back-to-back cycles—Lexie's medication strategy bore no resemblance to the label on the bottle—and was restlessly asleep on Lexie's couch.

Lexie "generously" offered to let Trey stay, too, since he wasn't in any shape to drive back to Cordova.

Sadie refused. "I'll take him to my place, then drop him at his truck in the morning so he can collect Daniel."

Lexie's wink said she wasn't buying Sadie's pragmatic approach.

DON'T BLOW IT, Meg told herself as she slicked gloss on her lips before checking her reflection in the mirror above the mantelpiece. She knew what she had to do, and she would do it. Even if it killed her. *Don't be stupid—it's not going to kill you.*

"He'll be here in five," Sadie said.

Meg shot her a grateful glance. "Thanks for taking the morning off to stay with me."

"No problem. Work's no fun at the moment, anyway." Sadie had her laptop set up on the dining table and was

working on something incomprehensible "for relaxation."
"When Daniel arrives I'll stay out on the porch. You
can call if you need me." She glanced around the room,
whose high ceiling gave an illusion of space that was
destroyed as soon as you put half a dozen people in there.
"Maybe I need a bigger house."

Meg felt guilty—her stuff took up much more space
than Sadie's. She felt even worse when she thought about
how non-soundproof those walls were. "I should move
out, give you some space. Even if Daniel and I don't get
back together…" A sob took her by surprise, and she
clamped a hand over her mouth.

She expected Sadie to say *Of course you won't move
out. I love having you here!*

Instead, Sadie pushed her chair back and moved restlessly to the window, coffee in hand.

Sadie wants me gone, Meg thought, appalled. *She's
sick of my irresponsible behavior, too.* She glanced
around the room, looking for something to straighten.
But the bungalow was immaculate. Even the pile of laun-
dry Meg had folded last night had been cleared away.

Meg swallowed. Surely Sadie didn't want to get rid of
her. Meg loved her other friends, Lexie and that crowd,
but she didn't need them, trust them, the way she trusted
Sadie to be in her life through thick and thin.

"I'll make coffee," she offered.

Sadie looked up in surprise. "There's a pot on the
counter."

"I'll pour you another cup," Meg said.

"I'm overwired as it is." Sadie set her empty mug
down on the dining table.

Meg darted forward and grabbed it. "I'll take this to the kitchen."

Sadie smiled. "Someone has ants in her pants."

It was an old expression of Mary-Beth Beecham's. Meg smiled. "Maybe I need a dose of cod-liver oil."

Sadie smacked her forehead. "I knew I forgot something."

For a moment the bond between them was so tight, closer than any sisters could have been. Meg hadn't felt this close to Sadie in weeks. Maybe that was the problem.

"If Daniel and I get back together, I promise we won't shut you out," she said.

Sadie turned distant again. "You haven't shut me out at all. Don't be silly."

Meg didn't think so, either. In the past, she'd been as bad as every other girl she knew about temporarily abandoning her friends during the intense start-up phase of a new romance. But with Daniel, whom she owed to Sadie, she'd really tried.

"How's your—" Meg racked her brain but couldn't remember a single detail of Sadie's work "—research thingy going?"

"My research thingy's going okay, thank you."

They never talked much about Sadie's work because Meg didn't get the scientific jargon and Sadie wasn't big on layman's terms. Maybe Meg should have tried harder.

I've been a really bad friend to Sadie, and she's just figured it out. That's why she wants me to leave. Meg chewed her lower lip, getting rid of the gloss she'd applied to look perfectly dewy.

She paced the room, thinking.

"Meg, could you keep still?" Sadie demanded.

Meg froze. She'd never heard Sadie impatient with her before. She eyed her friend, who looked tense, worried. Was something going on that she didn't know about? That she hadn't bothered to ask about?

She and Sadie had fallen into clearly defined roles early in their friendship. Meg had the glamorous life, the one that required endless gossip and dissection and speculation. Sadie just got on with her job, whether it was the job of being the smartest girl in school or a super biologist. She listened to Meg's woes, admired her outfits and her boyfriends, and on the rare occasions she wandered into those areas herself, asked for Meg's input.

"Sadie, I know you and Trey made out, but are you seriously seeing each other?" Meg asked. She was still hurt Sadie hadn't told her about Wes Burns, that she'd been forced to hear it from Trey, of all people. But if Sadie didn't think Meg was much of a friend, maybe she'd stopped telling her the important stuff.

"No!" But Sadie had turned pink. Something was going on. And she didn't want to tell Meg. She'd probably told Lexie, with whom she'd forged a bizarre alliance.

Meg blinked hard...then jumped at the unmistakable sound of Trey's truck pulling up. She touched her dry lips—did she have time to regloss? Doors slammed and a moment later heavy footfalls thudded on the porch.

She wasn't ready. She'd been thinking about Sadie so

much, she hadn't rehearsed what to say to Daniel. Now, thankfully, it came to her in a flash, a solution that would fix things with Daniel, and get her away from this awful tension with Sadie.

He walked in the door; she was vaguely aware of Trey behind him. She drank in every inch of Daniel's beloved face. Sadie had mentioned he might be under the weather, but he looked as immaculate as ever in a perfectly ironed striped shirt and chinos.

"Hi," he said quietly.

"Let's go see your mother," Meg said. "Right now."

"Meg," Sadie said, worried. "Are you sure?"

Daniel hesitated. "Don't you think we should talk? Figure things out?"

"We'll talk on the way. I want to see your mom. Please, Daniel." *Before I chicken out.*

He turned back to the door, then stopped.

"Take my truck." Trey tossed his keys.

Daniel caught them.

SADIE COULDN'T CONCENTRATE on her email for wondering how Meg was doing. She was afraid her friend had been hasty, rushing to the hospital. Daniel might have let her take it more slowly if he'd believed she was making a good-faith effort.

Sadie sat back from her keyboard, unsure how she felt.

If Meg and Daniel got back together now...well, that would be it. Sadie would have to choke the life out of any lingering hope, and throw herself wholeheartedly into her role as maid of honor.

She sat very still, waiting for the impact to hit her. There it was...regret...impatience...envy that her friend would have found a lasting love.

Not total devastation. How odd.

"I'm thinking this is a good opportunity to sow grass seed," Trey said, sticking his head around the front door.

"What the—?" Sadie whirled around. "Don't sneak up on me!"

"Where did you think I was?" he asked, bemused. "Daniel took my truck."

She pressed a hand to her frantically beating heart. Trey's gaze followed. "I forgot."

"What were you thinking about with such utter concentration?" he asked. "The starving people of Africa?"

"Uh, not exactly." She clicked out of her email. "What were you saying when you snuck up on me?"

He rolled his eyes. "Grass seed. I don't have anything else to do until Meg gets back. I might as well sow some."

"Sure," she said.

Twenty minutes later Trey's truck pulled up outside. As Sadie watched through the window, Meg emerged. Which left the truck empty.

She hurried outside and down the porch steps. "What happened?"

Meg started to explain, but at that moment Trey came around the side of the house. He'd taken his shirt off. Whatever Meg said was lost, though Sadie was vaguely aware her friend was still talking.

Sadie hadn't seen him bare chested since…forever. Even though she'd had her hands inside his shirt the other day, she was totally unprepared for this perfect storm of broad shoulders, defined chest, flat abs tapering to lean hips. A light sheen of sweat made him look like a poster model for a soft drink, and damned if those advertisements didn't work, because Sadie's throat was suddenly dry as a dust bowl and she needed…quenching.

"Sounds like you really screwed up," Trey told his sister.

Sadie snapped out of her trance. "Don't talk to her like that!" What had she missed? Bad news, going by the shrunken look on Meg's face. Sadie put an arm around her friend. "Ignore him, sweetie. Tell me all about it."

"There's not much more to tell," Meg said.

Great, she'd revealed some fiasco and Sadie had been so busy ogling Trey, she'd missed it.

"Well…" Sadie said.

Meg closed her eyes. "You think Daniel's right, don't you? You think I'm selfish."

"Okay, so maybe this didn't go so well," Sadie began tentatively.

"I threw up all over the hospital lobby!"

"Uh…"

"That's way worse than *didn't go well*."

"I'm sorry," Sadie said.

"Like I said, I ran out. I couldn't stay." Meg scrubbed at her cheeks with her palms.

"Surely Daniel can understand you have a genuine fear," Sadie said.

"The last thing he said was, 'If you walk out of here

now, that's the end for us.'" Meg rubbed her hands over her face. "I'm going to my room."

"You seemed distracted," Trey said to Sadie after Meg left.

Damn his powers of observation. "I had a late night, thanks to you dragging Daniel to a bar. So shoot me."

"That's not why you were distracted," he said.

She blushed. He must have seen her eyeballing his naked torso.

"This is your big chance," he said.

What, to jump him while he had his shirt off?

The idea had merit.

"You said you wanted to be sure they weren't going to get back together," he said. "This is about as certain as things get."

"You mean...Daniel?"

Trey shook out his fingers at his sides. "Looks like he's all yours."

And Trey clearly didn't feel the slightest jealousy. Infuriating, after Sadie's violent feelings toward Lexie. Did he really think she could participate in that incredible kiss with him, then move right on to Daniel? Okay, so she'd entertained the thought herself. But she'd quickly realized it wasn't that simple.

Apparently, for Trey, it was that simple. She spun on her heel and walked away.

"Where are you going?" Trey called.

"To get my hair colored and my nails done," she snapped.

"There's nothing wrong with your hair," he said.

Nothing wrong. Jerk!

"And to buy new lingerie," she said.

That shut him up.

CHAPTER SEVENTEEN

AFTER SADIE REVERSED her car out of the driveway, Trey worked like a demon under the broiling sun. Hoeing, sowing, watering. Sweat poured off him as if he was in the seventh circle of hell.

His own personal hell.

He'd lost his mind. He'd been around Sadie so much that her craziness had finally infected him and now he was acting like a lunatic.

How else to explain the consuming turmoil of his thoughts? He couldn't stop thinking about her buying new lingerie and prettying herself up—which she damn well didn't need to do, and if Dr. Daniel thought she did, then that just showed what a fool he was.

Trey had never even seen her *old* lingerie. And he wanted to. Hell, he wanted to see her oldest, rattiest lingerie, just long enough to get it off her.

No point wasting money on new lingerie that would be needed only fifteen milliseconds.

Except…he wasn't going to get to see it, new or old.

Dammit. He dug a spade into the soil, narrowly missing his booted toes. He swore loud and long.

"Trey? You okay?" Meg had heard his cussing from inside. It wasn't like him to swear extensively.

"I'm great," he snarled.

She blinked against the sunlight—she'd been face-down in a pillow the past two hours, and now the day dazzled her. "How's the garden going?" She shook her head. "Don't tell me—I can't concentrate."

"Heaven forbid you should have to listen to anything you don't want to," he muttered.

"You're such a jerk," she said. "My whole future just fell apart, so excuse me for not wanting to hear about some stupid plants."

"Even if those plants and others like them put you through college?"

"Don't guilt-trip me," she said.

"You're not the only one whose life isn't going exactly as planned," he said, "so if you want me to join your pity party, forget it."

"No, *you* forget it," she said. "I'll call Mom, someone who cares about me."

"You mean someone who won't tell you to your face what a selfish, childish pain in the butt you are."

Her face turned hot. "Why don't you hurry up and leave town?"

"I would love to leave town," he roared. "But Mom asked me to stick around for your wedding and now I've been hand-holding your boyfriend back into liking you, all because you're so pathetic you can't go and see a dying woman in the hospital."

Meg froze. "She's not dying! What have you heard?" Poor Daniel, she had to get to him right now. She had to—

"I don't know if she's dying," Trey admitted. "But neither do you."

"Believe me, I want to visit Angela. I can't explain

this thing to you, this problem I have, because I don't get it myself. All I know is I have an extreme, involuntary reaction to hospitals."

"I knew this would happen," Trey said bitterly. "I knew you'd screw up this engagement, because you're such a child, and I'd be the one mopping up the mess. Sadie never had to worry."

Meg had no idea what he meant about Sadie. "I don't need you mopping up my mess."

"Because you're so good at doing it yourself," he jeered. "You haven't dealt with your own problems since you asked me to beat up Jem Garner in sixth grade."

He'd done it for her, too. Logan had dismissed the hurt she'd felt when Jem called her ugly, but Trey had obligingly thumped the twerp. Then taken the punishment from Dad later. It was only now that Meg saw the irony of Trey getting a whack on the backside for hitting another kid. Her own role in that event hadn't been heroic. She'd felt bad for getting Trey into trouble, hadn't been able to face him. So she'd hung around Logan for the afternoon. Leaving Trey isolated.

"You know, Meg," Trey said, "you've always had it easy. I know, you lost Dad and Logan…" He held up his hands. The gesture had bugged her for as long as she could remember—it said she was unreasonable and he wasn't. "But so did I. Unlike you, I had to take responsibility for a business and for my mother and my sister, when I was nowhere near ready. All I'm asking is that you take responsibility for yourself, instead of expecting everyone else to bail you out or make allowances."

Why did she even try to explain? "Forget it," she said.

Halfway back to the house, she turned around. "You know, Trey, you used to be kind of a cool brother. You were always bossy and a pain, but whenever I needed someone to tackle a bully, or to tell it like it was, or to stand in my corner...I always called on you, right from when we were little kids."

He let his spade drop to the ground. "That's because I was closest in age to you."

She shook her head. "Logan was quieter, more considered. Strong in his way, the kind of oldest brother a girl wants. But not as much use in a fight."

She stared at him, chin in the air.

Trey stared back. Then he picked up his spade. "Didn't you have a phone call to make?"

So much for that.

Back in the house, Meg felt a distinct lack of enthusiasm as she picked up the cordless phone from the kitchen counter and dialed her mother. Nancy knew nothing about her breakup with Daniel.

"Mom, it's me. I have bad news." Nancy's instant concern brought on a new wave of self-pity. "The wedding's off." Meg told the story, pausing to blow her nose at regular intervals.

"So—" she hiccuped "—I thought I'd come stay with you for a while. And if you could make some calls, cancel the wedding...maybe we can get our down payments back." She knew that was highly unlikely.

Silence down the phone.

"Mom? You still there?"

"I'm here," Nancy said quietly. "This is your home, Meg. Of course you can come."

Relief rushed through her. It would be a longer commute to the airport, but that was fine. She pictured herself living with her mom for years to come, until Mom died—peacefully in her sleep, without going near a hospital—after which Meg would grow old alone in the family home, cultivating a fondness for cross-stitch and multiple cats.

"But the calls to cancel the wedding," Nancy continued, "you'll need to do those."

Meg felt a small shock of panic. "Mom, no! People will get mad. It's too upsetting. Besides, I'll be flying."

"You have a cell phone," her mom said. "Meg, from what you just told me, you've been using flying as an excuse. I can't let you get away with that."

"It's my job!"

"I'm wondering now if you really did have to work so much right after I had my stroke," Nancy said. "We all thought the airline was so hard-hearted, not giving you time off. But you didn't ask for any, did you?"

Meg swallowed. "Mom, that was years ago."

"Margaret Alexandra Kincaid, I'm ashamed of you." No mistaking the hurt in her mom's voice.

Meg opened her mouth to protest, but Nancy continued to sear her with her words. "What's worse, your father would be ashamed of you."

Then Meg's mother hung up on her.

DANIEL'S INVITATION TO dinner three days later took Sadie by surprise.

She accepted—of course she did. Daniel picked her up from her place—with Meg gone to stay with her mom there was no potential for awkwardness—and took her to La Maison Jaune, sited as its name suggested in an old yellow house on the banks of the Mississippi River.

Sadie had no idea if it was a date or not. It certainly wasn't the ideal date. Daniel looked dapper, as always, in a striped shirt and dark pants. He even wore a tie, which Sadie felt flirted with date territory. But his eyes were heavy, his mouth tense above his smooth-shaven chin.

He was perfect company—polite, interested in her work, full of respect for her achievements. Yet Sadie found herself wishing for Trey's irreverent presence.

"This wheat-protein project has so much potential," Daniel said as they started on their entrées. "You must find it very rewarding."

Sadie sliced into her duck breast. "I guess." On impulse, she said, "But there's something I want to do more." She told Daniel about the antioxidant project, amazed she hadn't done so earlier, back when she'd first fallen in love with him.

"Wow." He savored her idea, along with a mouthful of blackened mahimahi. "Sadie, if you're right…"

"I know," she said.

"But if you're wrong…"

"I know," she said.

"Maybe you should run it by a peer review panel," he said.

"Maybe," she said restlessly. She'd thought of that. It made sense. But she didn't want a recommendation by committee. She wanted someone who knew her to believe in her, a hundred percent.

Sadie couldn't help remembering that Trey hadn't

questioned her ability to succeed. *Trey doesn't fully understand the science.*

But he did understand Sadie and what motivated her. Perhaps better than anyone.

"Have you spoken to Meg recently?" Sadie asked.

Daniel shook his head. "That's over."

"But you loved her." Should a man give up on love that easily?

"Of course I did. Do. Did." Daniel's dithering got on Sadie's nerves. "At least, I loved the person I thought she was—fun and sweet and caring."

"She's all those things. So I can't imagine you're over her yet," Sadie said.

"She can't commit to the wedding vows," Daniel said. "In sickness and in health. That's more than a minor detail."

He had a point. As did Trey, saying his sister needed to grow up. Meg wasn't perfect. But neither was Daniel, contrary to what she'd first thought.

"Meg's never been in love before," Sadie said. "I think, for you, she could have been something she wasn't for other people."

"You can't be sure of that," he said.

"You know, Daniel, Meg might have struggled with the *in sickness and in health* part of the wedding vows, but maybe you would have found the *for better or for worse* a challenge."

He set down his wineglass. "Meaning what?"

"You set high standards for yourself and others," she said. "It's one of the things I like about you. But it seems to me you dumped Meg the first time she didn't measure up to your expectations."

His face turned white. A buzzing sound came from his jacket pocket.

"Is that your phone?" Sadie asked, when he appeared too dazed to move.

He reached for the phone, read the display. "It's Trey."

"Uh, maybe you shouldn't mention that you're—"

"Hi, Trey. I'm in the middle of dinner with Sadie," Daniel said.

Sadie sighed.

He listened; his eyebrows rose. "Er, okay." He hung up. "Trey will be here in five minutes. He has something to tell me."

Probably along the lines of *Sadie will stop at nothing to get her hands on you.*

WHEN HE ARRIVED, Trey somehow managed to look better than Sadie remembered. At the same time, in his dark shirt and pants, he looked like the bad guy next to angelic Daniel. She shouldn't find him so tempting.

"You never give up, do you?" he asked Sadie as he sat down next to her in the booth.

"Nope." She thought about grabbing Daniel's hand across the table, but she couldn't be bothered. "Nor do you."

His eyes glimmered appreciation.

Daniel was glancing around for their waiter. "Will you order some food, Trey?"

"I only came to pass on some information," Trey

said. He eyed Sadie's midnight-blue dress. "If I'm not too late."

"You're not too late," Sadie said, and meant it. Meant she wasn't pursuing Daniel.

He didn't seem to get the significance. "One word," he said. "Nosocomephobia."

"Noso— What's that one? Staircases?" Daniel scratched his head.

"I get it," Sadie said, excited.

Trey rolled his eyes. "No way do you know what it means." But his mouth tugged in a resigned smile.

"I have enough rudimentary Greek to figure it out."

"Geek," he said appreciatively.

"Well done," she said. "What made you think of it?"

"Is it elevators?" Daniel asked.

"Meg reminded me how I used to be the best brother a girl could have—the kind you want on your side in a fight," Trey said. "*Used to be* being the operative words. Thought I'd better rise to the challenge. I enlisted the help of the internet."

"So you've told Meg about noso-whatsit?" Sadie asked.

He nodded. "I'm leaving it up to her now. Because she really does need to handle this herself."

"You did a good thing." She patted his hand on the table.

Trey's gaze snapped to her. Then he slid his hand out from beneath hers and stood. "I'll leave you guys to it." He strode out of the restaurant.

Sadie watched him go, watched how he commanded the attention of every woman in the place.

"Farm animals?" Daniel suggested, his brow furrowed.

"For goodness sake, Daniel," Sadie snapped. "You need to decide how you feel about Meg, then get off your butt and do something."

CHAPTER EIGHTEEN

MEG PAID HER bill, took her receipt from the receptionist and walked outside. There were no cabs around, but
over the past three days she'd discovered that this close
to the airport it wouldn't take long. She pulled out her
cell phone.

She gave the dispatcher details of where she was right
now. And her destination. Then she waited.

The world didn't look any different than it had when
she'd arrived here for the first time three days ago. Could
the treatment really have worked? So fast? She'd been
told determination to succeed was a big factor, and
maybe she'd come here desperate enough to do whatever
it took…but the thought that she could have achieved this
earlier made her feel stupid. And ashamed.

The cab arrived after ten minutes. Meg didn't talk
during the ride—normally, she'd have started talking to
the driver about the weather and moved on from there.
But her adviser had suggested she was ready to put what
she'd learned into practice and Meg was too nervous to
make small talk.

She concentrated on her breathing, on a rational
inner dialogue. On ignoring the buildup of sweat in her
armpits, on her palms, down her back. On the warm
feeling she got when she remembered the text message

Trey had sent, which she hoped had literally changed her life. One word—*nosocomephobia*—had told her he was still on her side, even if she had to do some of her own fighting.

It was past noon when they reached Memphis St. Ignatius Hospital.

So far, so good. She was hot, but not dizzy. Her mind was relaxed. Relatively. Her breathing was almost regular.

She paid the driver and walked up to the main doors. Where she came to a total stop, causing someone behind her to nudge her, then veer around her with a muttered curse.

No stopping now.

She put one foot in front of the other, did the same thing again, then again, and suddenly she was inside the automatic doors.

The smell. Ugh, the smell. Disinfectant and sick people and floor wax and latex. Meg breathed through her mouth, minimizing the odors.

Ahead of her, a receptionist looked up and smiled, and Meg followed that smile.

"Mrs. Angela Wilson," she said. "I'm here to visit."

She made it to the elevator and all the way to the fifteenth floor. Then she ran to the bathroom and threw up.

She'd been neglecting her script, she realized.

Hospitals are filled with doctors and nurses who care, who help sick people get better. People come to a hospital so they can be made well.

It was actually working. Meg's nausea receded and she left the bathroom.

What if Daniel was here? He might be mad at her for visiting his mom now they were unengaged.

She reminded herself she'd chosen this time because he and his dad would be at work. This visit wasn't about impressing Daniel. She'd realized she could never measure up on the Wilson scale.

Outside the ICU was the small office she remembered from nearly twelve years ago. Visitors needed to be buzzed in individually. Meg approached the desk.

"I'm here to visit Logan Kincaid." She cringed. "Angela Wilson," she amended quickly. "Here to visit Angela Wilson."

What an idiot. She was going crazy.

The nurse gave her an odd look. "Are you family?"

"I'm her daughter-in-law." Meg kept her ringless left hand in the pocket of her jacket. She'd returned her engagement ring at the same time as she canceled the hotel, the flowers, the church. Her beautiful dress.

"Room four, on the left." The nurse buzzed her in.

Meg evened her breathing as she entered, trailing one hand lightly against the wall. Though it turned out she didn't need it. She felt quite steady.

With any luck, Mrs. Wilson would be asleep. A picture of Logan, deep in a sleep from which he would never wake, flashed through her mind. Instead of pushing it away, she looked, lingered, as she'd done earlier in the hypnotic trance. His young man's face, soft in the cheeks still, but with the clearly defined nose and chin. Poor, dear Logan.

Room four, here she was.

Meg slipped through the door, which was ajar.

Daniel's mother lay on her back, the top half of the bed levered up. Weren't people supposed to look smaller, less intimidating when they were ill? Angela Wilson looked every bit as ferocious as she did in the full bloom of health. Thankfully, she was asleep.

Meg sank silently onto the visitor chair. She froze, then after a moment of no movement from Angela, risked putting her purse on the floor.

Angela's eyes snapped open.

"Ah," she said, and her voice at least was smaller, "the waitress in the sky."

Meg had figured from the start that Daniel's parents didn't respect any job that didn't require at least an honors degree.

"Hello, Angela," she said, pleased her voice was steady. "How are you feeling?" She wondered how up-to-date Angela was, if Meg would have to pretend she was still engaged.

"Don't tell me the engagement's back on," Angela said, a little breathless.

Apparently not.

"I'm going to assume it's the medication making you rude," Meg said. She had nothing to lose with this woman. "Don't worry, the engagement's still off and it'll stay that way."

"Then why...?" Angela lifted her hand off the blanket to convey the rest of her question.

"Not for you," Meg said. "For *my* mother. And my brother."

Angela's forehead creased. "They're in the hospital?"

"No, thank God." Meg pulled her chair closer to the bed. "I guess Daniel told you I'm squeamish. That I don't like hospitals?"

A snort from the woman.

"Turns out it's a bit more than that," Meg said. "When my mom had a stroke a few years back, I didn't visit. I left everything to my brother." She shivered with the shame. How could she have thought she could absolve herself of responsibility to that extent? "Trey, my brother, just figured out I have nosocomephobia—I'm not even sure if I'm saying that right."

"You are," Angela said, surprising Meg.

"You've heard of it?"

"I *am* a psychologist," Angela reminded her. "So now you have something to blame for your immature behavior."

"I'm glad I'm not one of your patients," Meg said.

Angela's eyes widened. "You managed to overcome your problem enough to come here today," she said skeptically.

"I spent the past three mornings at the Phobic Disorder Center."

"Those quacks."

"I figured you'd turn your nose up," Meg said. "But I'm here now, with my symptoms under control."

Angela pressed down on the blanket with both hands and attempted to move herself up the bed. Instinctively Meg went to help. It took half a minute of careful maneuvering, but eventually the woman was propped higher.

"Thank you," she grunted. "So what were these purported symptoms of yours?"

"They were real," Meg said. "Nausea, dizziness, tunnel vision, heart palpitations…"

"And these phobic-center people, what, hypnotized you?"

Meg nodded. "They back it up with cognitive behavior therapy. I'll be going back every morning the next few days—I'm on short-haul afternoon and evening flights this week—then visiting the hospital after each session to put what I've learned into practice. I want to be sure that if my mom ever gets sick again, I can be the daughter she needs."

"How noble," Angela said drily.

"Better late than never." Meg glanced at her watch. "The nurse told me fifteen minutes maximum. I'd better leave." She picked up her purse.

Angela's fingers pleated the pale blue hospital blanket. "You can come again tomorrow, for your practice visit."

"Oh." Meg wasn't sure she wanted to. Visiting Daniel's mom had been a symbolic milestone, but the woman was nothing to her now. She'd thought she might visit a pediatric ward next, provide company for a lonely child.

"It's very dull here." Angela fixed her gaze over Meg's shoulder.

"Okay," Meg said. "I'll see you tomorrow."

"Assuming the heart palpitations don't overcome you first."

SADIE WAS IN THE MIDDLE of the complex task of getting her coffee just right when her cell phone rang. It was Meg's mom.

"Sorry to interrupt your work." Nancy had been conditioned by Mary-Beth to think of Sadie's job as second only in importance to running the United States of America.

"No problem. I'm just having a coffee."

"That daughter of mine hasn't answered her phone to me in three days." Nancy sounded exasperated. "I figured you can tell me—is she genuinely upset, or just having a temper tantrum?"

Sadie stopped stirring her coffee. "I don't understand. Isn't Meg staying with you?"

Silence.

"She said she might come, but we argued on the phone," Nancy said slowly. "When I didn't hear from her, I thought she'd changed her mind."

Tension clogged the line. Sadie struggled to breathe. "Her stuff is gone from her room." Uh-oh, dumb thing to say to Meg's mother. "At least, some of it is." She thought fast. "Maybe she flew somewhere nice and decided to take a vacation." *Without telling anyone.* "Her roster is on the fridge at home. I'll go now to check. I'm sure she's on a beach somewhere, working on a tan."

"You're probably right," Nancy said with false cheer. "Sadie, dear, you will call me right back, won't you?"

THE FIRST PERSON SADIE called after she got home was in fact Trey.

"According to the roster, she's been working late

flights to and from Miami," she told Trey. "But I'm pretty sure she hasn't been home in between. We don't even know for sure if she showed up for work."

"If she hadn't, the airline would have called her registered home address, which would be your place, or maybe Mom's."

"The roster on my fridge ends today, which is her day off." Sadie straightened Meg's collection of Las Vegas fridge magnets. "I called the airline, but they won't tell me where she's rostered from tomorrow."

"I'll phone Lexie, see if she's heard from her," Trey offered. Sadie tried to mean it when she thanked him.

"I guess I should try Daniel, too," she said.

"Yeah." He paused. "How are things going between you and the doctor?"

It took her a moment to figure out what he meant. "Trey, I'm not seeing Daniel."

"Why not?" he demanded, so sharply that she knocked a couple of fridge magnets to the floor.

"It's complicated." She felt guilty about Meg, angry with Daniel for hurting her friend…and thoroughly befuddled, as well as turned on, when she thought about Trey.

That seemed to kill the conversation. A moment later Trey ended the call. Sadie tried Meg's cell phone just in case. Voice mail. She left a message, then called Daniel. "Have you heard from Meg lately?"

"No," he said, trying and failing to sound distant. "Should I have?"

"I guess not. She, uh, moved out of my place and I'm not sure where she's gone."

"She *what?*" A crash came down the line, as if Daniel had just upended his chair.

"She said she was going to stay with her mom, but Nancy said she never showed up."

"You mean…she's missing?" Daniel's voice was a high-pitched croak, like a teenager whose voice was breaking.

"Not in the police sense, no. We just don't know where she's staying. Trey's calling Lexie… Hello?"

He'd hung up on her.

She called Trey back on his cell phone. He reported that Lexie hadn't seen or heard from Meg, but she'd phoned another stewardess, who confirmed that Meg had definitely been flying the Miami run. She wasn't missing.

"She's avoiding the people who care about her," Sadie said. "Nancy said they got into an argument, and I know I was distracted when she wanted to confide in me about the breakup with Daniel."

They both knew why Sadie had given less than her full sympathy to Meg's troubles, but Trey had the decency not to mention it.

"I yelled at her last time we talked," he admitted.

"It's our fault she's run off," Sadie said. "We knew she was hurting."

"It's not our fault." But he lacked his usual arrogant certainty.

Sadie slipped into a chair at the kitchen table. "Where are you?"

"Out on the lake."

"Your sister's missing and you're fishing!"

"I was already out here the first time you called," he said patiently. "Which was all of ten minutes ago."

"Have you caught anything?" she asked.

"I'm doing more thinking than fishing," he said.

"What are you thinking about?"

"Nothing as important as what you think about."

"Shut up," she said companionably.

He did, and they shared silence for a minute.

Trey broke it. "Come home, Sadie. We'll set up search-party central here in Cordova."

CHAPTER NINETEEN

BY HER FOURTH day at St. Ignatius, Meg had made progress with Angela. She'd been promoted from "waitress in the sky" to air stewardess.

"One day soon," Meg told her as she plumped her pillows on Friday, "you're going to call me a flight attendant."

"Ridiculous, politically-correct term." Angela leaned forward for Meg's ministrations. "Couldn't you have been a pilot?"

"Why would I want to do that? Pilots are shut away in the cockpit with only a copilot to talk to." Satisfied with the pillow arrangement, Meg returned to her chair. "Wait, I know, to impress my future mother-in-law."

"You have no ambition." Angela eased her shoulders back into the pillows. "That's what I don't like."

"You don't like me because of my job?" She'd suspected as much, but the woman's admission still startled her.

"I didn't say I don't like *you*," Angela said testily. "But Daniel's always dated women with brains."

"Don't start with the postgraduate degrees," Meg muttered.

"Intelligence is important, and a postgraduate degree implies its presence." Angela touched the dressing on her chest, as if she was in discomfort. "I liked that Sadie—you could see she's smart. My husband liked her, too."

Meg frowned. "Did Dr. Wilson go to the dress fitting?"

"He met Sadie when Daniel called in at home with her one weekend," Angela said. "Before you were on the scene. I really thought something might come of that."

"They're just friends," Meg said, still processing the news that Sadie had met Daniel's parents before Meg and hadn't said anything.

"Not back then. She was mad about him, and Daniel was definitely interested."

No! Meg stood and walked swiftly to the window. Far below, cars moved in and out of parking spaces, like remote-controlled toys.

Angela eyed her with interest. "Didn't you know?"

Meg licked her lips. "I was away. In Paris."

"That's the other problem with a job like yours," Angela said. "You don't see what's going on under your nose."

Meg wasn't listening. Sadie and Daniel? Sadie had liked Daniel, in *that* way? It must have been a rebound thing, after she broke up with that vet. Because Sadie wasn't interested in Daniel. Was she?

"Sadie is much more Daniel's type than you are." Angela didn't sound vindictive. More…sympathetic.

The nausea Meg had managed to avoid during her hospital visits roiled in her stomach. Her vision grew hazy, narrowing to pinpoints.

"Sit!" Angela barked, and somehow Meg lurched to the chair.

"Head between your knees, breathe slowly," Angela ordered. "Don't you dare make me get out of this bed."

Meg smiled through a shallow breath. Her vision cleared, and she could see the linoleum through the gap between her knees. After a few more seconds, she sat up.

"Well, that was silly," Angela said, surprisingly kind.

Meg nodded, not trusting herself to talk yet. She pictured Logan, lingered on the image, then sent it away.

"Once he met you, Daniel didn't have eyes or thoughts for anyone else," Angela said matter-of-factly.

"But you're right—Sadie is his type." Oh, no, what if Sadie and Daniel got together, and Meg had to watch them—

"Is she as brave as you?"

"What do you mean?"

"These visits…" Angela waved a hand around the room. "It took guts for you to come here. I'll bet your heart's shaking like jelly on a train right now."

"Thanks for the reminder," Meg said.

Angela actually laughed. "When you're good at something, it's easy to be brave," she said. "Your friend Sadie strikes me as someone who wouldn't be troubled by phobias. Very rational."

"She's amazing," Meg agreed. "She can cope with anything. I haven't appreciated her enough."

"I daresay amazing goes both ways," Angela said briskly. "My point is, Sadie is living in her comfort zone, just as you have been in yours. Stepping out of that to come here, overcoming your fear…that's something special."

She was right. Tranquillity seeped through Meg, laying to rest her memories of those awful days waiting for Logan to die.

"Thank you, Angela." This would be the last visit she would make, she realized.

"What will you do now?" Angela asked, as if she sensed Meg's decision. "Do you think you'll see Daniel?"

Was Angela saying she wouldn't mind?

"I love Daniel," Meg told her. "I let him down, and I'm sorry for that. But he let me down, too."

Angela bristled in defense of her son.

"I can't be with someone who's going to write me off at the first mistake," Meg said. "I'm way too flawed for that. I need someone who'll accept me as I am, and take it from there."

"Very New Age." Angela sniffed, but there was no condescension in it.

"I know I still need to make some changes," Meg said. "Grow some independence. I won't go back to Sadie's." They both needed some space, Meg thought. Especially if there was a chance Sadie and Daniel... "Anyway—" she perched on the edge of the bed "—I'll figure it out. But this is goodbye."

Then she did what might be the bravest thing she'd ever done—she opened her arms.

Angela hugged her.

"YOU REALIZE THIS is the Millennial Centennial all over again," Sadie said on Saturday afternoon.

Trey kicked back in his mom's dining chair, stretched

his arms behind his head. "I wasn't aware the aim of this exercise was to find you a date."

The yearbook from Meg's senior year at Andrew Johnson High School lay open on the table in front of them. In the kitchen, Nancy was working her way through the Daughters of the American Revolution (DAR) telephone list and selected highlights of the bridge-club member list. Next door, Mary-Beth Beecham was calling a bunch of garden-club members, and Sadie's dad had reluctantly agreed to phone his golf buddies.

"But if you want me to ask if you can date their son right after I say, 'Have you seen Meg?' it could be arranged," he continued.

"I'm just saying I don't think Meg will thank us next time she's back home, when she gets stopped in the street by every second person wanting to know if she solved her 'little problem.'"

"She shouldn't go disappearing, then," Trey said. "And she shouldn't know so many people—it's unnatural." Unlike Sadie's teen fiasco, they were calling only people who qualified as friends of Meg's—thousands of them, it seemed. If they didn't have the friend's current number they would go via the parents. Meg had a phenomenal capacity for keeping in touch with people.

Trey started dialing. "Next on the list is the Morgans—you remember Skip Morgan. Want me to find out if he's available?"

"Sure," Sadie said.

Trey shut down the call. "That better be a joke."

"You're the one who seems to think I'm still desperate."

His eyes wandered over her olive-colored tank and short black shorts. Since she'd arrived in Cordova last night his manner had been casual and friendly. Nothing in his words or actions suggested he'd ever wanted her.

His eyes told another story. She'd caught him looking at her like this—hot, speculative glances—several times. But when she challenged his glance with one of her own, his face shuttered. It was driving her nuts.

She picked up a copy of *American Landscape* magazine and fanned her face. She thought she heard a snicker from Trey, but his expression was blandly innocent as he dialed the Morgans.

They hadn't seen Meg, Sadie gathered from the one-sided conversation. Predictable. This was a waste of time. Meg had texted all of them—her mom, Sadie and Trey—simultaneously first thing this morning to say she was okay and would be in touch soon. But she'd switched the phone off right afterward, and Nancy didn't consider one text message to be proof her daughter was stable and safe. The airline had confirmed Meg was working, but wouldn't release more information than that. Sadie figured she was probably staying a few days in a motel near the airport for some private grieving over her breakup with Daniel.

Sadie flicked through the magazine and quickly became engrossed in the photos of stunning landscapes. Her dad had asked this morning when he and Mary-Beth could see her English country garden. She'd been tempted to give him a date twenty-five years out. Instead, she'd turned the conversation to her job.

So much for Trey's commitment to creating a fabulous

garden for her. He hadn't done a thing since the day Meg left. Since Sadie had implied that she was going out to buy new lingerie to impress Daniel.

She froze. Was that why Trey wasn't acting on the undeniable spark between them? Because he thought she was seeing Daniel? She'd told him yesterday she wasn't, but one thing she knew about Trey, he had a suspicious mind where Daniel was concerned.

She needed to clear up any misunderstanding. She flicked unseeing through the magazine as her mind worked on the problem. There must be some subtle way to convey what he needed to hear, without exposing herself to humiliation if in fact he had no interest in her….

"Good magazine?" Trey asked. "Because, you know, we're trying to find my sister here."

"This is fascinating." Sadie focused on the page in front of her. "A historic botanical garden near Boston runs a residential course that's producing the country's best landscape designers."

"Fascinating," he said. "Now start calling."

"I didn't buy lingerie," she blurted out.

Oh, yeah, supersmooth segue. This was why she worked with a bunch of other nerds in a science lab— she wasn't fit to be out in society.

"Excuse me?" Trey said with deceptive politeness.

"I told you I was—" she lowered her voice in the unlikely event Nancy could hear her from the kitchen "—going to buy lingerie."

"You meant for Daniel," he said, his voice expressionless.

She winced. "I was joking. Obviously I wouldn't do something so insensitive when he and Meg had just broken up."

"And since then?" he asked.

"Why do I have to answer all the embarrassing questions?" she demanded. "When was the last time you slept with Lexie?"

The phone rang in the kitchen.

"Three years ago," Trey said. "It was a one-off."

Sadie wished she hadn't asked.

"Did you buy lingerie later?" he said.

And now she owed him an answer.

"No."

Their gazes met, meshed.

"That was Lexie Peterson on the phone," Nancy announced, walking into the dining room. "She said she wants to help find Meg—she's coming tomorrow."

Sadie blinked, breaking contact with Trey.

Nancy collected their empty cups. "Would you like another coffee, or is it time for something stronger?"

"Something stronger," Sadie and Trey said simultaneously.

FOR THE FIRST TIME ever, Meg couldn't get enthusiastic about putting on her uniform and heading to the airport. Usually the urge to fly was a compulsion, an itch she couldn't ignore.

The destination wasn't the problem—she loved Vegas.

She locked the door of the studio apartment she'd borrowed from another flight attendant, who was living with her boyfriend—a trial arrangement—and didn't want to give up her apartment until she was sure it would work out. Either way, Meg had a month before she needed to find a place of her own.

One month.

In one month she would have been marrying Daniel if she hadn't been such an idiot. And if he hadn't been so unforgiving.

The airline-staff shuttle arrived at the curb at the same time she did. The airport was only fifteen minutes away, on a route that passed right by St. Ignatius Hospital. Angela had been transferred out of ICU this morning, according to the operator who answered Meg's inquiry earlier. Daniel would be so relieved.

At the airport Meg attended the preflight briefing, then headed to the gate lounge area. The loudspeaker departure announcements, a shopping list of destinations, failed to work their usual magic of building her anticipation. By the time she'd trundled her overnight bag all the way to gate twenty-five she was wishing she'd picked up a coffee on the way. The feeling intensified when she saw the crowded gate area. The flight was overbooked—she didn't envy the ground crew the inevitable shouting matches when some passengers were told they couldn't fly.

Busy exchanging a sympathetic glance with the poor guy working the desk, she almost fell over the out-stretched legs of a dozing passenger.

"Sorry, sir, I didn't— *Daniel?*"

It was him. Her Daniel. He'd shot awake when she

stumbled over him, and now he jumped to his feet. "You came," he said.

"I *work* here." Her eyes ran over his stubbled jaw, his rumpled shirt, unlaced shoes. He looked as if he'd been caught up in a Calvin Klein store explosion. "Are you flying to Vegas?"

He shook his head. "I'm in here on a medical clearance." He waved a temporary pass in her face.

"You only get those if the authorities call you in. To see a patient. In an emergency." She examined the pass. "This is a three-hour pass, dated yesterday."

"Which is why I haven't been able to leave." He ran his hands through his hair. "Do you know how hard it is to sleep in an airport? I spent half the night dozing in the men's bathroom, trying to avoid security staff."

She couldn't think of anyone less likely to sleep in the bathroom than Daniel. His mom would be horrified. She almost giggled at the thought, but confusion won out.

"So who's your patient?" she asked.

"You are. How do you feel?" He put a hand to her forehead and she went stupidly weak at the knees.

"I'm a little dizzy," she said.

"Thought so." He grinned. "Let's get you away from this crowd." One hand on her elbow, the other balancing a medical bag on her wheelie case, he steered her to the adjoining gate, serving the much smaller flight to Denver. They sat in an empty bank of seats.

"When Sadie told me yesterday that you'd disappeared, I phoned Astrid—" he'd met her colleague at a party they'd attended, Meg recalled "—and told her I needed to see you. She arranged a pass for me, through a friend in security. Good thing she's a romantic," he added.

"A very good thing," Meg agreed. Astrid could have been fired.

"We found out you were working this flight, but Astrid's friend was working yesterday, not today. So I had to come in last night."

"I guess that makes sense," she said. "In a totally crazy way."

His face crumpled. "Meg, you disappeared." His voice cracked; his lack of self-possession shocked her.

"I didn't disappear," she said unconvincingly. "I'm staying at a friend's place."

He exhaled sharply through his nose. "You've been visiting my mother."

She caught her breath. "You know?"

He took her hands in his. "Okay, I didn't tell you the full story… It makes me look pathetic."

"This I'd like to hear," she said.

He grinned that lopsided grin she'd fallen in love with, but this time it had a sheepish tinge. "When Sadie said you'd gone, I went crazy. I called the police, but they wouldn't investigate because I made the mistake of telling them I was your *ex*-fiancé. And since you'd been turning up to work, they said they wouldn't investigate even if I was your actual fiancé—a status I'm keen to restore, by the way," he added casually.

A swarm of celebrating butterflies danced in her stomach. *Don't get your hopes up.* "Hmm," she said, aiming for enigmatic.

He laughed and dropped a kiss on her mouth, suggesting she hadn't nailed enigmatic.

"I raced out to the airport to find you and, uh, ended up being forcibly removed by security."

"Daniel!" she said, delighted.

"Then it occurred to me to ask my mother."

"You guessed I would visit her?"

"Hardly. I thought as a psychologist she might have some insight that would tell me where you'd gone. I wasn't going to let her rest until she'd given me every possible idea."

"The poor woman was in ICU," she said.

"*I* was dying." His ferocity silenced them both.

Daniel swallowed, then continued more quietly. "I told her I love you, that I'd made a big mistake letting you go, and that if I could convince you to give me another chance I was going to have to have a different attitude. One my parents undoubtedly wouldn't like, but they'd have to get used to it."

She gaped. "What did Angela say?"

"She gave me a lecture about nosocomephobia—Trey had already mentioned it, but the word went right out of my head. Mom told me what you'd done, going to the phobia center, then turning up at the hospital every day." He lifted her hand to his mouth, kissed her knuckles. "It's the bravest thing I ever heard."

She laughed shakily. "Daniel, there are cops pulling people from burning cars and soldiers defusing bombs every day."

"You have courage," he insisted. "My mom agrees—

not that I asked her opinion. She's on her way to becoming a fan of yours."

"On her *way?*" Meg said, indignant.

"She's slow to change, but she'll get there." He pulled her into his arms. "Meg, I came after you because I love you. I was an insensitive jerk." He gazed into her eyes.

"Keep going," she encouraged him.

Daniel swatted her backside, drawing the attention of a couple of passengers. "I'm sorry. If I promise to do better, will you come back to me?"

She tilted her head to one side. "Kiss me."

His mouth came down on hers before she'd finished talking. And all the anticipation that should have shown up earlier about her flight was right here, right now. Where it would always be. With Daniel.

After a very satisfying minute or two, he lifted his mouth from hers...to the applause of a planeload of passengers to Denver. Meg waved to the crowd.

"Stay with me," he said.

"I'm working." The thought of spending so much as a night without him made her want to weep. Which she could see didn't bode well for her continued flying.

"You're too sick to work." He opened his medical bag and pulled out a stethoscope. "Now, Miss Kincaid, if you could just breathe normally for me..." Pushing her jacket aside, he slipped the stethoscope between the two middle buttons of her blouse, making sure to cop a feel on the way through.

"Daniel!" She jolted as the cold metal landed on the upper slope of her left breast.

"Hmm," he said, distracted, doctorly. Then copped another feel on his way out. Meg started to giggle.

Next he whipped a thermometer out of his bag, which he waved in the general direction of her ear.

"Oh, dear," he said.

"What?" Meg asked suspiciously. She was pretty sure that thermometer hadn't even beeped.

"Elevated temperature." He stowed the thermometer back in its case. "What's the threshold where they won't let you fly?"

"A hundred and two."

"Yours is 102.2."

She started to laugh. "I can't skip work!"

"I'll issue a medical note," he said. "But maybe, if you're due to fly tomorrow, you could take a couple of days' vacation." His voice sank. "It's only fair to warn you, you may not be allowed out of bed in the morning."

Meg was in serious danger of melting right there in the terminal. She kissed Daniel long enough to seriously cloud his judgment. Then she said, "I have a better idea."

CHAPTER TWENTY

A RED MUSTANG pulled up in front of the Kincaids' house at noon on Sunday.

"It's Lexie," Sadie said, looking out the living-room window.

"Not that Lexie who was so awful to you when you were younger?" Mary-Beth bustled over to look. "I never liked that girl, so full of herself and—"

"Actually, Mom, she's not that bad," Sadie said. "She's nice, in fact. Slutty," she added, thinking about that "one-off" Lexie and Trey had shared a few years back, "but nice."

Her brother Kyle, here for his weekly golf game with Dad, came to the window, drawn by the "slutty."

"She might need help with that suitcase," he said, and disappeared out the door at the speed of light.

"Suitcase?" Sadie echoed. Indeed, Lexie was pulling a case from the trunk. The moment she saw Kyle, she stepped back and waited for assistance. On the sidewalk she dithered outside the two houses. Then headed for Sadie's.

Sadie felt absurdly touched. Although there was every chance Lexie had picked her so she could flirt with Kyle. But if Sadie had had the choice between Kyle and Trey she'd definitely have gone for Trey. Even if Kyle wasn't her brother. Okay, this was getting weird.

She went out on the porch to greet Lexie.

"I have news," Lexie announced portentously.

Ten minutes later they were all sitting around Nancy's kitchen table, including Kyle, who until now had expressed zero interest in Meg's whereabouts. Sadie had ended up opposite Trey.

They hadn't said a lot to each other since he'd admitted doing the dirty with Lexie and she'd admitted *not* doing it with Daniel. Trey was obviously unaffected by her news. Sadie hated that she even cared he'd been intimate with Lexie. She willed herself not to watch the two of them obsessively for signs of lingering lust.

But she felt Trey's eyes on her. Knowing him, he was enjoying that she was jealous. Yes, she might as well admit it. She wasn't sophisticated enough to kiss a guy the way she'd kissed Trey, then not care who he slept with.

"I left a message a couple of days ago with Carrie, a flight attendant who works with Meg," Lexie said. "Turns out she was in Japan and her cell phone doesn't work there. She arrived in early this morning, got my message and called me." She paused dramatically.

Sadie slapped her wrist. "Tell!"

Trey's foot touched hers under the table; she moved away.

"Ouch." Lexie rubbed her wrist, feigning hurt. "Carrie said she and Meg were going to meet in Vegas this weekend, but Meg left a message to say she couldn't make it, she was going on vacation."

"Where to?" Trey asked.

Lexie widened her baby-blue eyes. "I don't know *everything,* Trey."

"That's next to useless," he said, disgusted.

"If she's on vacation," Sadie said, "maybe we should respect that. I really think she's fine."

"No!" Nancy said. "It's out of character for her to go off like this. I'm worried."

"So, vacation places she might go when she's upset," Trey said.

"Reelfoot Lake," Nancy said. "We rented that cottage the summer after Brian and Logan died. If she wanted to remember..."

"Or Hot Springs," Trey suggested.

"That'll be it," Sadie said. The Kincaids had vacationed several years running in the Victorian spa town in the Ouachita Mountains in Arkansas. "Meg loves Hot Springs."

"We should go look for her." Lexie's suggestion won agreement all around.

"Sadie and I will head to Hot Springs," Trey said.

"I'll come with you," Lexie offered.

They really should accept, Sadie thought, since Lexie had come all this way and had produced the only solid-ish information they had about Meg's plans.

"Better if you go to Reelfoot Lake," Trey said. "Kyle, are you good to go up there?"

"You bet." Kyle wedged his hands in his pockets, as if to stop himself doing an inadvertent high five.

Mary-Beth Beecham looked dismayed.

Lexie heaved a sigh of resignation. And winked at Sadie.

TREY FLOORED THE GAS and the truck obediently passed a convoy of RVs heading west on I-30. They'd been driving three hours, which meant they'd reach Hot Springs in around thirty minutes. Kyle and Lexie's drive to Reelfoot Lake was only a hundred miles—they'd called over an hour ago to say they'd arrived and were asking around for Meg.

"Do you really think Meg's okay?" he asked Sadie. "Or were you just saying that?"

Sadie rolled her eyes. "I'm sure she's fine. Why don't you ever believe a word I say?"

"Maybe your motives are so convoluted, I never know what Machiavellian plot you'll hatch next."

"I'm unpredictable, like you said." She grinned. "That's an attractive quality, don't you think?"

"Men like uncomplicated women who know how to show them a good time."

"And I was so trying to impress you," she said with phony regret.

Having Sadie beside him, all cute and snarky, was a bonus on this wild-goose chase. The news that she wasn't sleeping with Daniel—and, it seemed, had never slept with Daniel—went beyond bonus and into jackpot.

Now he just had to decide what to do about it.

He wanted to sleep with her, that was a given. More than once, another given.

What did *she* want?

He was pretty sure she wanted to sleep with him. So far, so good.

Beyond that? She knew he was leaving town soon, so

she couldn't be expecting anything long-term. It wasn't as if there was any room for misunderstanding.

There was a lot of benefit to spending time with someone before you started dating them, he realized. You got to say what you meant, with none of that second-guessing that happened when you were already involved.

Under his breath he whistled along to the radio. Yep, this was shaping up pretty well.

Just so long as he didn't think about the elephant in the room.

Because the downside to having all those full and frank discussions before he dated Sadie was that he knew she was in love with Daniel.

At least, she thought she was in love. So far as Trey could see— *Forget it.* As far as she was concerned, she loved the guy.

Trey had given the issue some consideration. If he wanted a relationship…obviously a guy would be nuts to date a woman who wanted another man. But sleeping with her? That was different. Sadie's attachment to Daniel meant she wasn't looking for a relationship with Trey, either. *Perfect.*

"Thirty miles," Sadie said, and he realized they'd just passed a sign.

Trey glanced at the dashboard clock. Four o'clock. "How about we spend a couple of hours looking around, then assuming we don't find Meg, we'll stop for dinner and figure out what's next?"

Sadie scrubbed a hand over her face. It made her look about fifteen. "Sounds good."

Trey parked on Central, the main street in the historic

area. "We used to stay at Freeman's Hotel, about a block from here."

They checked out bars, restaurants, hotels, and found no sign of his sister. Trey didn't believe she was here. Which meant they were free to move on to other things.

"Let's eat," he said when they reached The Tavern, a restored Victorian hotel and restaurant that claimed a top New York chef as a consultant to the menu.

Since it was Sunday night, most of the visitors had left town. The locals had eaten early—just a couple of tables lingered over dessert.

The menu featured classic, slightly old-fashioned fare. Sadie chose the brie-stuffed chicken breast; Trey opted for a steak with béarnaise sauce. With sides of fries and mac & cheese.

Sadie wrinkled her nose.

"Energy food," he said.

The waiter arrived at their booth with Trey's beer and Sadie's red wine. They clinked glasses.

"To our first date," Trey said.

Her eyes widened. Then she leaned back against the padded booth seating. "I don't recall you asking me on a date."

"And yet here you are." He grinned. "I'm that good."

"Amazing," she said drily.

He reached across the table for her hand. "For a neurotic scientist, you have a way of grabbing a guy's attention, Sadie."

She let out a shuddery breath. "You've been on my

mind, too. Though speaking objectively, calling me a neurotic scientist wasn't your best move."

He ran his thumb over her palm, and her fingers curled around it. "What if I tell you neurotic scientists are my weakness?"

"That...helps," she admitted.

"And if I throw in cute and pretty and funny and determined?" Just thinking about her made him smile.

"You left out know-it-all."

"Not your best feature...though endearing in its own way," he added, laughing as she pinched his wrist. "Was there anything nice you wanted to say about me, since we're building a romantic atmosphere here?"

She untangled their hands to take a sip of wine. "You're well aware of your good points—" her eyes sparkled as they roamed his face and shoulders "—so I won't bore you with them. I could cover your bad points, though."

"I think you already mentioned most of them over the past few weeks, cupcake."

"There may be more," she warned.

"Tell me later. Right now we need to stop talking. I'm getting mighty frustrated with the amount of clothes you have on."

She burst out laughing. "You're outrageous."

"It's not like you haven't thought about it," he said. "A simple yes is all I need."

"Trey..." His name was barely more than a breath. "Do you really want to do this?"

His whole body went on alert. "More than you can imagine," he said, his voice strained.

She laughed, a husky sound that wound him even tighter. "Me, too," she said. "So where to from here?"

Excellent question. "We passed a couple of bed-and-breakfasts just off Central," he said.

She hesitated—the suspense almost killed him—then she nodded.

"I just lost my appetite for food," he said. "Let's go. I'll cancel the food, pay the check, on the way out."

"Can you imagine," she said as she gathered up her purse and her sweater, "what our moms will say when they hear about this?"

Trey stopped. Yes, he could imagine, and it was scary. "I wasn't thinking we'd tell them," he said carefully. Maybe sharing sordid details was a girl thing. But since her mom and his were best friends, that couldn't happen this time.

"I think they might notice—" she slipped out of the booth "—when I start flying up to Berkeley for weekends, or if you're coming back to see me, or whatever. And spending the holidays together will be a dead give-away."

Trey felt as if he was caught up in a hurricane. Sadie's words—Berkeley, weekends, holidays—flew past him, several bumping against him like debris.

What the hell had just happened? He'd asked Sadie to go to bed with him, and she thought they were *together?* She knew he was leaving!

The bed-and-breakfast she'd agreed to, which a minute ago had been the promise of long-anticipated delight, now loomed like a trap. And he was the stupid dumb animal about to walk into it.

"I need to go to the bathroom," he said. He *needed* to figure out where this had gone wrong. And how the hell he was going to reset her expectations. Fast.

"I'll wait out on the deck," she suggested. "It's a gorgeous evening."

He hadn't noticed the doors at the back of the restaurant open to the outside, a willow tree beyond the railing. "Great," he croaked.

He forced himself not to run.

IT WAS BAKING HOT out on the terrace, which probably explained why no one else was out there, but the faint hint of a breeze riffed across Sadie's senses.

She wandered over to the rail, by the willow tree, and found herself looking down on a narrow, shallow creek. Any smaller and you might call it a drain, but as it was, it had pebbles on the bottom and clear water running over the top and Sadie considered it a creek.

She wanted to take a snapshot of this moment—of the willow, the creek, the railing, Trey, her—and hold it next to her heart. Something had happened tonight, something strange and wonderful and it felt like… *It feels like falling in love.*

Could it be?

Could she have fallen for a man who teased her, who called her on her fears and her pride, who wasn't the least bit awed by her brain, who had crazy ideas for his future because he'd been hurt in the past?

Could she have fallen for a man who came through for his family time after time, who understood her neuroses and wanted her anyway, who had no respect for the creativity he couldn't stifle, who had a compelling interest in her 34Cs, who made her feel eminently desirable, who tested her wits and made her laugh?

I love him.

Her cell phone beeped in her purse; she ignored it.

But...I love Daniel. Don't I?

Not for a while she hadn't, she realized. And her feelings for Daniel had been like a cozy fire she warmed herself in front of. Loving Trey was like being *in* the fire.

So what now?

This likely wasn't going to be easy. Falling in love with a guy who planned to hightail it out of town was almost as dumb as falling in love with a guy who then fell for her best friend. But she was used to working for what she wanted. So was Trey.

They would make it happen.

She heard a footfall on the decking behind her and knew it was him.

"Sadie." His voice was gruff, rougher than she'd heard before.

She turned, and in the moonlight saw deep emotion etched in his face. He wrapped his arms around her, molding her to him from head to toe, as if every inch of him needed to touch her.

"Trey," she said huskily.

"Shh." It was a warm breath against her temple. "It's okay, sweetheart."

His mouth brushed hers. Then came back, clamped over hers, and he kissed her with earthshaking ferocity.

She parted her lips on a startled cry, and he moved in,

seeking, finding, then demanding more. Heat rose within her, and she matched his ardor. One large hand cupped her head, his fingers kneading her scalp and sending shivers right down to her calves.

This wasn't like any other kiss they'd shared. No humor, no teasing, no spirit of competition. Just a raw intensity that made bone melt into flesh, nerves fuse into one charged mass. It was a kiss that said they could get through anything.

"You're beautiful, Sadie," Trey said when he tore his mouth from hers. "Amazing."

He gave her the confidence she needed.

As he trailed his lips and his tongue down her neck, she said, close to his ear, almost inaudibly, because maybe her courage wasn't right up there yet, "I love you."

CHAPTER TWENTY-ONE

Trey tensed.

His hands dropped away, leaving her exposed, unprotected.

He frowned down at her. "*What* did you say?"

She'd jumped the gun. In probably the worst possible way. "I know it's too soon for you," she said nervously. "But it's true. I love you. I shouldn't have said it, but it just hit me right now and I was so excited…"

"How convenient," he said grimly.

Convenient? She loved him and he found it *convenient?*

"Er, Trey? Are we in the same conversation?" She rubbed her arms, cool where the breeze found them. "Because I'm not up for another of those days where I ask you to the dance and you make me feel like an idiot."

He barked a laugh. "Then don't *act* like an idiot." He raked a hand through his hair. "How could you think I would believe you?"

"Hey," she said, annoyed now. "I didn't go laying my heart out on a platter for you to pick over and discard. And I'm not in the habit of lying."

"You're still in the habit of self-delusion," he said. "Hell, Sadie, I expected you to be upset—that's why I rushed out here as soon as I got Meg's text. But I thought you had more self-respect than *this*."

"What text?" Sadie rummaged in her purse for her phone. The little envelope symbol for a new message showed on the screen. She pressed to read it.

Daniel and I just got married! Honeymooning in Vegas. Back Thurs. Much love, Mrs. Wilson.

Married? Meg and Daniel?

Sadie stared down at the phone, unable to identify the emotions that rolled through her in successive waves. "I...hadn't seen this," she said.

Trey snorted.

"I hadn't," she said, more loudly as she realized whatever she was feeling, it wasn't grief. As for jealousy... maybe envy that her friend had married the man she loved, but nothing related to her own former feelings for Daniel. She grabbed Trey's arms, her fingers closing around firm flesh. "Trey, I'm telling you I love you!"

"And I told you long ago I would never settle for being second choice," he said, disgusted. "Forget it, Sadie."

Something wasn't adding up here, and Sadie's scientific brain couldn't find the logic. "You mean your rebound thing?"

"I mean second choice," he said. "As in my whole life to date. But not anymore."

She processed the words, found a chord of memory. "You told Meg you were the last choice to run the business after your dad and Logan died."

"That's right. Dad never asked me to join the firm. It was always going to be him and Logan."

"Because you wanted to play football!"

He shrugged.

"That's what your I-hate-the-garden-center thing is about," she said slowly.

"I don't hate the—"

"That's why you get so edgy when your mom talks about Logan. You think she's comparing you."

His jaw tightened. "I don't get edgy."

She let go of him and backed up against the railing. "And now you're giving up a business you've built, leaving your connection to your dad, leaving a family who loves you, just because the garden center wasn't always intended for you."

"Not only did the business not choose me, I didn't choose it. I had things I wanted to do, things I never got to do because I've been standing in for Dad and Logan."

"And now you're turning me down," she said, outraged, "because you think you'd be second choice after Daniel."

"I know I would! And if you think I'll ever be Daniel Wilson's stand-in…"

"That's just dumb," Sadie said. She took a deep breath, tried to calm herself. "Trey, I don't understand what's changed between now and five minutes ago, when you said you wanted to date me. You didn't seem to care about Daniel then."

"I wasn't asking you to *date* me," he said. "I wanted to have sex."

"You were only asking me to go to bed with you?"

"That's right." He bit out the words.

"You said it was a date."

"It's a euphemism."

"*Date* is not a euphemism for *sex*."

"It can be," he said, less aggressively.

"So when you say to a woman, would you like to go out on a date, you're asking would you like to have sex?"

"Pretty much."

"That's disgusting," she said.

"So is deciding you love me when you hear Daniel's got married."

"I don't love Daniel," she said desperately. "Trey, please, believe me. You're the one."

"I don't think you'd outright lie about loving me," he said. "I think you're attracted to me physically, and now you've deluded yourself into believing you love me, in place of Daniel."

Red fury hazed Sadie's vision. "You're right," she said. "I can't possibly love you. Why would I want a guy who goes through life with a chip on his shoulder and can't see a good thing when it's right in front of him?"

"If by a good thing you mean *you*..."

"I mean a family who adore you, your amazing landscaping talent, which by the way you love but won't admit it, and—and your whole life. Which includes me, you jerk."

Trey's mouth set in a hard, narrow line. "Fascinating though your thoughts are, it's time we headed back to Memphis."

"I'll make my own way home," Sadie said.

AN INQUIRY TO A friendly-faced barista in a coffee cart on the square revealed that Hot Springs did not possess a rental-car office. Or a train station or a bus station.

Maybe Sadie had been premature in vowing to make her own way home.

She could think of only one other option.

Standing on the sidewalk on the east side of the square, she stuck out her thumb.

Twenty seconds later a truck pulled up.

"Get in," Trey growled through the open window.

"No." She hitched her purse strap up her shoulder. "You don't want my love, you don't get my company, either."

"I don't want your company. I just don't want to turn up at your parents' place without you." He paused. "And what you were offering wasn't real love."

"You don't know that. You don't want to know." She stepped forward, past the truck, and stuck out her thumb again.

"You're not damn well getting a ride with some psycho killer." He was beside her again.

"You can't think I'm that stupid," she said. "I'll only accept a ride from a woman."

"Don't make me drag you in here," he snarled.

A car pulled up behind the truck. The driver honked

the horn. A moment later a man stuck his head out the window. "Are you okay, miss?"

"She's not a miss," Trey muttered. "She's a lunatic."

"Falling in love with you sure makes me a lunatic," Sadie retorted. "I'm looking for a ride," she called to the other driver. "I'm going to Memphis, but you can let me out at the interstate."

TURNED OUT THE OTHER guy was going to Memphis, or so he claimed.

So much for *I'll only accept a ride from a woman.*

Trey was powerless to stop Sadie climbing into the white Dodge sedan. He wrote down the license plate—not trusting himself to remember when he was so damn mad at her—so when the cops found her mangled body, he could give them the information along with an excellent description of the abductor.

But even storing those details didn't make him comfortable about Sadie choosing to ride home with a complete stranger, even if he did look harmless. Trey tailed the Dodge to the I-70 on-ramp to verify the guy was at least heading east in the direction of Memphis. Then, since he was going that way anyway, he followed the car onto the nearly empty interstate. The plan was to put his foot down, blast past Sadie in a burst of righteously indignant acceleration.

But the Dodge stuck at precisely seventy miles per hour, which he found suspiciously serial killer-ish behavior, so he hung around behind it. Of course, driving at seventy was the kind of thing Daniel would do, too.

The kind of behavior a woman like Sadie found attractive.

He shook off a sudden pang of jealousy. Sadie wasn't about to fall for the guy who'd offered her a ride, just because he stuck to the speed limit. She didn't give her affections that lightly.

She'd said she loved him.

Trey turned over in his mind the memory of that whispered *I love you*. Not faltering—there'd been no hesitation—but a sense of surprise had lurked in the words. A wondrous secret, unexpectedly shared.

His body had reacted in the most extraordinary way. The hairs at his nape had risen, his heart had thundered like a train. The urge to whoop and dance her around that terrace had possessed him.

Then he'd come crashing down. It was Daniel she loved—she'd made that clear from the beginning. To declare suddenly that she'd switched her affection to Trey...what man would accept that?

Even if a part of him was desperate to.

No way, he wasn't desperate. Not for Sadie Beecham, the girl next door.

He needed to get back on track, get out of Memphis and start his new life.

He fumbled for his phone. With his thumb he typed a text message to Sadie. Rest area 2m ahead get out there I'll drive u home.

Through the back window of the Dodge he saw Sadie suspend her animated conversation with Serial Killer and glance down, presumably at her phone.

A couple of seconds later his phone beeped with her message. No.

He thumped the steering wheel, then propped his phone against it so he could type a reply and watch the road. Don't be stupid hitchhiking dangerous.

So is txting while u drive came the reply. Trey cursed.

He didn't get to type another message before his phone beeped again. Go home; leave town; do whatever; just stay away from me.

Who put semicolons in a text, for Pete's sake? How geeky could you get?

Not leaving u to get strangled by a psycho, he typed.

Dammit, Sadie was laughing! He could see her in profile, head tilted back as she shared his words with her driver buddy.

Not joking. He stabbed the keys furiously. Sticking right with u until home.

There was a long pause, and he thought he'd shut her up. He should have known better.

I don't need u. I might love u, but I don't need u. U don't seem to know the difference, which means u can't be the man for me.

Trey gripped the wheel tighter, and his phone slid out, landing on the floor. He fumbled carefully for it, keeping his gaze on the Dodge. He felt that if he turned away for just one moment, the jerk would hurt Sadie.

He wouldn't let anyone hurt her.

He thought about the look in her eyes when she'd realized all he wanted from her was sex. Then when he'd thrown her love back at her.

In the car up ahead, Sadie seemed to be laughing again. He wiped his palm against his jeans, then began to type. U got over me fast what a surprise is your buddy there the next Mr Right-for-Sadie?

As he hit Send, he felt a twinge of remorse. He brushed it off, just as he'd brushed off that sweat from his palm. He was only telling the truth, showing her what she was like.

He waited for her reply.

It never came.

CHAPTER TWENTY-TWO

SADIE ROLLED HER chair back from her desk and swiveled to see her whiteboard. The wheat-protein mind map she'd drawn was doing nothing to inspire her. But at least they were about to sign off the current phase of the project. The next phase would be...

Boring.

She glanced guiltily around, as if her colleagues could read her thoughts. This was her job—she loved it. This was where she excelled, commanded the respect of several widely acknowledged geniuses. Was geniuses the plural of genius? Or should it be genii?

She still hadn't figured out the solution for getting to do her new project. Trey's face popped into her mind, but she dismissed him. Another problem that wasn't about to go away.

She should be able to handle heartbroken by now, after the Daniel fiasco. But losing Trey—*I never had him*—wasn't like losing Daniel. Whom of course she'd also never had.

Losing Trey was like excavating a garden ready to become landscaped perfection...no, Daniel was more landscaped perfection, and she'd discovered it bored her. Losing Trey was like throwing herself into a jungle adventure, only to have the jungle spit her out.

Garden. Jungle. Another thing that was going wrong. Or rather, going nowhere.

Trey had left her the design for her garden and the list of plants. He'd emailed the offer of one of Kincaid Nurseries' staff to do the work, no charge. In a moment of excessive pride she'd turned him down and said she would do it herself.

Trey had told her from the beginning she couldn't do it, and deep down she knew he was right. She'd been so determined not to let her parents see what a failure she was at growing things, she'd ended up with nothing.

She was a coward.

She didn't want to be.

Sadie closed her office door, then picked up the phone and dialed.

Her mom answered.

"Mom, I need to talk to you and dad about my garden."

"Sadie, is that you?" Mary-Beth asked anxiously.

In her panic, she'd plunged straight in without the usual courtesies.

"Yeah, it's me. Mom, can you get Dad on the other phone, so we can talk?"

When her father picked up the extension, she said, "Mom, Dad, as you know, I've been planning my new garden for a while."

"Is it ready at last?" her dad said. "When can we come?"

"It's not ready," Sadie said, "because I've killed every plant I ever bought. I can't grow things like you guys. I want to be able to, but I can't…." Ugh, she was sniveling.

"And now my garden is a bomb site and Trey's not working on it, and it's never going to be okay again."

She was crying, talking nonsense, but somehow her parents made sense of it.

"Snap out of it now, Sadie, love," her dad said. "Your mother and I will come see this garden, and we'll figure out how to fix it."

"But I can't—"

"*We'll* fix it," Mary-Beth said. "It sounds best if you don't touch it again, dear."

Sadie gave a half sniff, half laugh. "But it's such a long way for you to come."

"Half an hour," her father scoffed. The same father who'd commented frequently about the fact she lived so far away she'd be forgetting her upbringing and becoming a stranger to her nearest and dearest.

"There's a ton of work," she warned them. "Maybe I should hire someone."

"Don't you dare," Mary-Beth snapped. More calmly, she said, "Sadie, sweetheart, do you realize how long it's been since your father and I have been able to do anything for you?"

"Last time was when we found you a date for that dance," her father mused.

Sadie shuddered. "Let's not talk about that."

"The fact is, Sadie Beecham, you have a habit of making other people feel useless," her mother said.

"I don't—"

"You're so blasted good at everything, the rest of us can only sit on our hands. Occasionally I get to dish out the cod-liver oil, but I know you only take it to be polite."

"Mom…" Sadie closed her eyes. How did Trey have more insight into her parents than she herself? "I only let you see the things I'm 'blasted good' at. Everything else, I hide away from everyone…but believe me, I have a closetful of failures."

"What closet?" her father asked, confused.

"Uh, it's a metaphorical closet, Dad. It— Never mind." She drew a breath. "It all comes down to this—I'm a hopeless gardener, and I would really love your help."

"Well, then, you've got it, dear," her mother said, as if Sadie was a simpleton.

MEG AND DANIEL FLEW home on Thursday evening and the first thing they did was open a bottle of champagne with Sadie.

Sadie had heard of radiant brides, and Meg was one of those, but a radiant groom was something new. Daniel was lighthearted, blissfully happy.

Sadie couldn't believe it when Meg told her how he'd camped at the airport waiting for her. Her friend seemed calmer—or maybe that was just because there wasn't such a big contrast between her and Daniel anymore.

Having been honest with her parents about her failings, Sadie had thought long and hard about coming clean to Meg about her past feelings for Daniel, and that when she'd thought she was acting in Meg's best interest, her judgment might have been clouded.

Though she would have felt better for the confession, in the end she decided not to burden her best friends with it. They shouldn't have to worry about her emotional state, and they certainly shouldn't feel a need to be careful of her in the future. Sadie knew she was a hundred percent over Daniel, but she suspected Meg might consider that impossible.

Meg raised her glass for the fifth toast so far. "Here's to Mom and me patching things up. I think she's forgiven me for running away. And in about ten years she'll forgive us for not inviting her to the wedding."

She'd explained earlier that they'd decided not to get in contact with anyone until after the wedding—they were certain of what they wanted and, as Meg put it, "We'd had enough of people trying to talk us out of it."

"Quite right," Sadie mumbled.

"And here's to Lexie." Meg proposed toast number six. "Lexie and Kyle." She caught Sadie's eye and they both burst out laughing. Kyle was relentlessly pursuing Lexie, much to Mary-Beth's horror, and so far Lexie was holding fast to her no-more-notches policy.

"Lastly…" Meg said.

"You said *lastly* three toasts ago," her devoted husband pointed out.

"Lastly again," Meg said, "to you, Sadie. You're the sister I never and always had."

"You're drunk, darling," Daniel said indulgently.

But Sadie knew what she meant. She blinked away tears as she raised her glass.

"I'M SORRY, BOB." Trey put down the landscape magazine he was flicking through. This conversation deserved his full concentration. "I've thought it through, in and out and upside down. I've realized this isn't the job for me."

By the time Bob Cotton hung up a few minutes later, he'd accepted Trey's decision. Which Trey wasn't a hundred percent sure of himself. Assistant coach for the Berkeley football team. He wouldn't get a better start in coaching than this.

But after wanting for so long to get out of the garden center and back onto the football field, at the last moment he'd proved incapable of grabbing the opportunity with both hands and running for the touchdown.

He'd realized he would miss so much about his current life. Not the sense of responsibility for his family and the business, that's for sure. But the plants...the dirt.

He had no idea what he was going to do now.

Football fields have dirt. Regret pricked him. Then he reminded himself that football fields were pristine grass that got rollered and watered after every game. Nothing unpredictable or messy or...sumptuous about it.

Sumptuous. What the hell was that?

If he wanted dirt and plants, he could get a garden of his own.

One like Sadie's. Only without the know-it-all, know-nothing, fickle woman attached.

He missed her. He hadn't seen her since the jerk in the Dodge had deposited her outside her home on Sunday night. Trey had waited until the guy cleared off, then he'd left. He'd noticed the rude gesture Sadie made, but declined to respond. For a nerdy scientist she sure was unladylike.

But now...he missed talking to her. He wanted to

hear her make jealous jibes about Sexy Lexie. Wanted to know if she'd worked out how she was going to do that new project.

Meg and Daniel had returned from their honeymoon cooing like the proverbial lovebirds, and that had made him miss Sadie, too.

Restless, he headed to the packing room, where his mom was putting in her one day a week, packing mail orders. The room had an internal window that allowed him to survey the store. Trey could hear the muffled announcement of today's specials over the PA system.

"Did you hear Meg is giving a talk to a medical convention about that hospital phobia of hers?" Nancy asked.

"I heard." His sister wasn't so grown-up that she wouldn't turn her entire life into a drama production with herself as the star. He found himself smiling at the thought.

"You seem mellow," his mom observed. "You looking forward to Sunday?"

Three more days, and Trey was officially leaving town. He planned to take a vacation first, mainly in New York.

"Can't wait," he said.

Nancy's smile was bittersweet. "I'll miss you."

"Eugene will do a great job," Trey assured her. "If anything comes up he can't handle, I'm only a phone call away."

His mother made an exasperated sound. She clamped her lips together as she shook her head.

"What?" Trey asked.

"Sometimes you're a first-class jerk," she said.

"Mom!" He got enough of that from Sadie. He missed that, too, which was truly pathetic.

"Why can't you just be gracious and accept a compliment?" she asked. "You can't really think I'm talking about the business when I say I'll miss you."

"Uh…" That was exactly what he'd thought. "Of course not. But you've got Mary-Beth right next door. And Fred Thomas down the road has had his eye on you for years—you might consider dating."

His mother bent over the carton of plant food she was splitting. Something about the way her shoulders moved…

"Mom? Did I upset you?"

When she lifted her head, her cheeks were red but thankfully dry. "I'm trying to tell you I'll miss you, Trey. *You*. My son." Her voice rose.

"Okay," he said quickly. "I get it. You'll miss me. I'll miss you, too." When had his mom turned neurotic?

Instead of looking pleased, she scowled. "Sometimes I wonder if you even see me, or if all you see is a millstone around your neck."

"You're not a millstone," he said, shocked.

"You've made it fairly obvious you think it's my fault you haven't had the life you wanted," she said. "That insistence you had on filling in for your brother and your father."

"My insistence? Mom, you asked me to come home from college and help out!"

"For a *couple of years*," she said. "I asked you to put

your studies, your football, on hold, not to be a damned martyr."

He'd given up his aspirations and now she was throwing it back at him?

"All I ever heard from you was how much you missed Dad and Logan," he shot back.

"Of course I missed them!"

"How things would be so much better if they were here, how different I was from either of them."

She stilled. "You *were* different, you *are* different. I never said it would be better if they were here."

"Only every five minutes," he said. "Try, 'If your dad was here we'd have won that contract.' Or, 'Logan would have had those trellises fixed in a jiffy.'"

"Oh, Trey." She clapped a hand to her mouth. "I'm sorry. I was just honoring their memory. Trying to make them a part of our present, not only our past. I never meant to make you feel you weren't good enough."

"It doesn't matter," he said. "I know I did a good job with the business. It's just not where I want to be now."

"You did a great job!" she said fiercely. "And I told you so, often. So don't be unfair."

"Let's just leave it, Mom."

"I will not leave it," she snapped. "I've had years of telling you how different you are, how unique, and now you're saying that was an insult?"

"More…a comparison," he said carefully.

"How does 'you have a genius for numbers' become an insult?"

"You said that right after you mentioned Logan's incredible capacity for hard work outdoors. Like you were offering me a crumb."

She looked stricken. And now that he'd said it, Trey felt like a scumbag. He sounded like a five-year-old, needing constant reassurance from his mommy. But if you looked at that exchange she'd just mentioned, there was no indication she'd been throwing him a bone.

As Sadie would say, he was being pathetic. His mom's compliment had likely been heartfelt. About him, not about how he compared with his brother.

Maybe Trey had been a first-class jerk.

"Mom, I'm sorry," he said.

"No, I'm sorry." Forgiving as she'd always been, she rushed at him and wrapped him in a hug. "It never occurred to me you were comparing yourself with your brother...or that you thought I might be."

"Maybe I was a little paranoid," he said sheepishly.

"I love you, Trey. Because you're you, *because* you're different from your father and your brother, not *despite* the fact." She kissed his forehead, three times.

"I think I get where you're coming from." It was weird—nothing had changed about what she'd said in the past, but now he saw it in a different light.

Her laugh was shaky. "At last he gets it, right before he leaves town."

"Have I been a total pain in the butt?" he asked.

His mom returned to her worktable and picked up the next order form. "No more than your sister, but for different reasons. It's going to be quite nice not having either of you need me."

"I didn't—" He was going to say he hadn't needed

her all those years, but in that moment he realized it wasn't true. He'd lost his dad and Logan, just the way she and Meg had. He'd never let himself acknowledge the hole their deaths had left in his life, but he'd needed the family connection—and, yes, the business—to fill the hole. To make him feel as complete as he could with half the family gone.

His mom scanned the order she held in her hand. "All I want now is for you to find a nice girl and settle down."

"Don't hold your breath," he said drily, even as his brain chanted *Sadie, Sadie*.

"Oh, look." Nancy waved the order at him. "Sadie's buying some plants for her new garden."

Trey rolled his eyes. "Subtle, Mom."

She grinned, unrepentant. "Oh, my, will you look at this?" She read down the list. "How's that girl going to keep a garden like this alive? It'll be carnage." Meg must have let slip to their mom that Sadie's thumbs were more black than green.

"Actually..." Meg had told him the answer to this question and he'd been storing it up until he had time to think about what it meant. "Her parents are going to do it. They reckon it'll take about two months to get it all planted—they'll pretty much be living at Sadie's now Meg has moved out. After that, they'll come into town once a week or so to do some maintenance."

He was so proud of Sadie for having admitted she couldn't do it, for having asked her parents for help.

"The perfect solution," Nancy said.

"I was thinking…" He stopped. "I'd been thinking I could help her out, but she won't need me now."

"Not for her garden, anyway," Nancy said. She paused in her taping up of a boxed order. "I thought you'd had enough of being needed."

"I— You're right." What was he thinking? Sadie had told him she didn't want him to do her garden. She'd told him she loved him. Which meant all she needed from him was love.

Which he'd chosen not to give because he didn't want to be second best. Because she'd been in love with Daniel.

But she'd said she loved him—Trey. What if it was true? What if, regardless of what she'd felt for Daniel, her love for him was real and true?

He'd thrown it back at her. Called it shabby and second-rate when in his heart he'd wanted to cherish that love. He'd resisted because, what, he didn't think she could look at him without seeing Daniel? Without making a comparison where he would always fall short?

Right now, that seemed like breathtaking stupidity.

He could readily believe that a client would, without regret, reject their existing garden designer in favor of Kincaid's, because Kincaid's was better.

But he couldn't accept that Sadie would consider him a better man than Daniel? Or at least, better for her.

There was a difference between being second and being second choice.

He never wanted to be second choice…but he could be second.

Because he loved Sadie.

Kapow.

"Trey? Did you hear me? I said I'll get these plants out to Sadie on the noon truck," his mom said hopefully.

He shook his head, his mind still blown by the realization that he loved Sadie no matter what. He had to have her.

"I'll take them myself," he said.

His mom turned away with a smile that was way too satisfied.

CHAPTER TWENTY-THREE

SADIE WAITED ON her porch for the delivery from Kincaid Nurseries. She'd said 1:00 p.m. sharp, having taken a half day off work, and now they were late. Mom and Dad were arriving tomorrow morning—they'd need something to plant.

A white truck painted with the Kincaid logo rounded the corner in her peripheral vision. About time.

She stood, brushed the front of her shorts, tucked her hair behind her ears. The truck pulled into her yard. She recognized the driver by the set of his shoulders, long before she could discern his face.

Her eyes pricked. "What are you doing here?" she called through the open window.

Trey turned off the engine. "Delivery for you." He climbed out of the truck and stood before her, rugged and masculine in his jeans and light plaid shirt. "*Special* delivery," he amended.

"Special, how?" she asked suspiciously.

He tossed her a careless grin that took her breath away. "I'll get to that. First I need to say I've been an ass."

She blinked. "Really?"

"Don't sound so surprised."

"You've always been an ass. It's the admission I'm surprised at."

He laughed. Then he sobered and took her hands in his.

"Sadie, I'm sorry I hurt you when you told me how you felt back in Hot Springs. I was so hung up on not wanting to be your second choice."

Sadie tensed. This sounded like the start of something amazing.

Which didn't mean she should let Trey off the hook.

"Idiot." She smacked his shoulder. "You knew from the start Daniel wasn't right for me. So how could you be second choice?"

"I'm an idiot," he agreed humbly, but with a glint in his eye that promised the imminent resumption of his former arrogance. "It might seem obvious to an exalted brain like yours, but I finally figured out that second doesn't mean second best." He told her about the conversation he'd had with his mom, where they'd ironed out a lot of their grievances.

"That's fantastic." Somehow she'd ended up in his arms, sitting on the porch steps.

"It is fantastic," he agreed, "because it frees me up to say this to you." He put a couple of feet of space between them, so he could turn and face her.

"I love you, Sadie. I love the way you make me laugh and how you kiss. I love that you think you're right all the time and you have the most outrageous schemes. I love that you kill gardens."

"You can't love that," she protested, right before she planted a chain of kisses along his jawline.

"I adore it," he said firmly. "I love your confidence

and your insecurity." His voice turned a little ragged. "I love that you're a hot geek."

"I *love* listening to this," she said. "Keep talking."

He chuckled. "Which brings me to the *special delivery* part."

She pulled away reluctantly, to listen.

"Sadie Beecham, your Kincaid garden special comes with the husband option thrown in completely free."

She gaped.

"I want to marry you," he clarified.

Joy bubbled through her, but she narrowed her eyes. "Is that another euphemism for sex?"

He had the grace to look ashamed of his earlier behavior. "Pretty much," he admitted. "And for some other stuff, too."

"Such as?"

"Be mine always, the mother of my kids, holder of my heart."

"Did you just say *holder of my heart?*"

"It seemed a good idea when I thought of it."

"I'm not so sure," she said. "But the rest of it was wonderful."

He caressed her bottom. "The thing is, I figure marriage to you is going to be some crazy adventure, and I'm up for it. Soon as you like. The sooner the better. But there's also the matter of my wild oats—I'm reluctant to abandon their sowing."

"Understandable," Sadie said.

"So I figured you could sow them with me?"

Her heart flipped. "Doesn't having a woman tag along defeat the purpose of the whole wild-oats thing?"

"Not if the woman is the hottest, funniest, cutest gal I know."

"Good logic," she said.

He kissed her deeply.

"You're aware I have a job that means everything to me, right?" she said when he let her go.

"I'm hoping it doesn't mean *everything*," he said.

"It means a lot. I can't give it up."

"I wouldn't ask you to—now who's the idiot?" He ducked her swat. "Daniel mentioned that you scientists get sabbaticals."

"I've never taken one."

"Would you consider taking one now?" he asked.

"I'd have to think about it," she said slowly. "Yes!"

"I love a woman who thinks fast." He kissed her.

"You love fast women," she retorted.

"I love you."

The next kiss was so hot, Sadie felt she needed dousing with a bucket of cold water. "Okay, I think the wild-sex part of your plan is going to work out just fine," she panted. "But where do you see us sowing these oats?"

"That nine-month landscape-design course run out of the historic botanical garden in Massachusetts," he said. "The one you found in the magazine."

Sadie gaped. "I was thinking Vegas, the south of France, Paris...and you want to run wild in Massachusetts?"

His grin was sheepish. "Turns out it's who you're with that matters when it comes to wild. I realized you're right about me and gardens. I don't much like the retail side, but I really want to be a landscape designer."

"So you're saying I was right and you were wrong," she crowed.

He muttered something that might have been "Know-it-all."

"But you want to coach football," Sadie said. "You could still do that."

"I was having trouble letting go of the football career I supposedly sacrificed," he said. "Who knows, maybe I would have made it to the NFL. But life didn't turn out that way, so there's no point trying to make it happen."

"A botanical garden," she mused. "That might be just the inspiration I need to start my antioxidant research. And if it doesn't work out…you don't mind if I commit professional suicide, do you?"

"I'll be with you all the way, cupcake."

His kiss was sweet and long and giving and taking.

"I may have lost track," he said, "but by my reckoning you haven't told me you love me yet."

"I told you back in Hot Springs. I'm way ahead of you, buster."

"True." He rubbed his chin. "I was hoping to hear it again, at least a million times."

"I love you, Trey," she said. "I always will."

He grinned. "How embarrassing is it that I was hung up on getting away to run wild, and it turns out the hottest woman I know is the geek next door."

"Pretty embarrassing," Sadie said smugly, and turned her mouth up to his.

* * * * *

COMING NEXT MONTH

Available July 12, 2011

#1716 THE HUSBAND LESSON
Together Again
Jeanie London

#1717 BEYOND ORDINARY
Going Back
Mary Sullivan

#1718 HER SON'S HERO
Hometown U.S.A.
Vicki Essex

#1719 THE PURSUIT OF JESSE
An Island to Remember
Helen Brenna

#1720 RECONCILABLE DIFFERENCES
You, Me & the Kids
Elizabeth Ashtree

#1721 INVITATION TO ITALIAN
Make Me a Match
Tracy Kelleher

USA TODAY *bestselling author B.J. Daniels takes you on a trip to Whitehorse, Montana, and the Chisholm Cattle Company.*

RUSTLED

Available July 2011 from Harlequin Intrigue.

As the dust settled, Dawson got his first good look at the rustler. A pair of big Montana sky-blue eyes glared up at him from a face framed by blond curls.

A woman rustler?

"You have to let me go," she hollered as the roar of the stampeding cattle died off in the distance.

"So you can finish stealing my cattle? I don't think so." Dawson jerked the woman to her feet.

She reached for the gun strapped to her hip hidden under her long barn jacket.

He grabbed the weapon before she could, his eyes narrowing as he assessed her. "How many others are there?" he demanded, grabbing a fistful of her jacket. "I think you'd better start talking before I tear into you."

She tried to fight him off, but he was on to her tricks and pinned her to the ground. He was suddenly aware of the soft curves beneath the jean jacket she wore under her coat.

"You have to listen to me." She ground out the words from between her gritted teeth. "You have to let me go. If you don't they will come back for me and they will kill you. There are too many of them for you to fight off alone. You won't stand a chance and I don't want your blood on my hands."

"I'm touched by your concern for me. Especially after you just tried to pull a gun on me."

"I wasn't going to shoot you."

Dawson hauled her to her feet and walked her the rest of the way to his horse. Reaching into his saddlebag, he pulled out a length of rope.

"You can't tie me up."

He pulled her hands behind her back and began to tie her wrists together.

"If you let me go, I can keep them from coming back," she said. "You have my word." She let out an unladylike curse. "I'm just trying to save your sorry neck."

"And I'm just going after my cattle."

"Don't you mean your boss's cattle?"

"Those cattle are mine."

"*You're* a Chisholm?"

"Dawson Chisholm. And you are…?"

"Everyone calls me Jinx."

He chuckled. "I can see why."

*Bronco busting, falling in love…it's all in a day's work.
Look for the rest of their story in*

RUSTLED

*Available July 2011 from Harlequin Intrigue
wherever books are sold.*